AWAITING ORDERS

a novel by

Farrell O'Gorman

Idylls Press
2006

First paperback edition October 2006

Idylls Press
P.O. Box 3566
Salem, OR 97302
www.idyllspress.com

ISBN-10: 1-59597-008-8
ISBN-13: 978-1-59597-008-4

Lyrics to Grateful Dead songs *Truckin'* and *Friend of the Devil*, by Robert Hunter, copyright Ice Nine Publishing Company. Used with permission.

Excerpt from *One Day in the Life of Ivan Denisovich* by Alexander Solzhenitsyn, translated by Ralph Parker, copyright © 1963 by E.P. Dutton and Victor Gollancz, Ltd. Copyright renewed © 1991 by Penguin USA and Victor Gollancz, Ltd. Used by permission of Dutton, a division of Penguin Group (USA) Inc.

Excerpt from *The Last Gentleman* by Walker Percy. Copyright © 1966 by Walker Percy. Reprinted by permission of Farrar, Straus and Giroux, LLC.

The author would like to thank Alex Vernon, author of *The Eyes of Orion: Five Tank Lieutenants in the Persian Gulf War*, for his thorough reconstruction of the chronology of the war and the experience of the ground troops who fought it.

Library of Congress Cataloging-in-Publication Data

O'Gorman, Farrell.
  Awaiting orders : a novel / by Farrell O'Gorman. -- 1st ed.
      p. cm.
  ISBN-13: 978-1-59597-004-6 (alk. paper)
  ISBN-10: 1-59597-004-5 (alk. paper)
  ISBN-13: 978-1-59597-008-4 (pbk. : alk. paper)
  ISBN-10: 1-59597-008-8 (pbk. : alk. paper)   1. United States Navy--Officers--Fiction.
  2. California--Fiction. 3. Persian Gulf War, 1991--Fiction. I. Title.
  PS3615.G67A96 2006
  813.6--dc22
                              2006024163

For Tasha

If a man lives in the sphere of the possible and waits for something to happen, what he is waiting for is war.... In war the possible becomes actual through no doing of one's own.

Walker Percy, *The Last Gentleman*

"Why do you want freedom?.... You should rejoice that you're in prison. Here you have time to think about your soul."

Alexander Solzhenitsyn, *One Day in the Life of Ivan Denisovich*

Part One

May - July, 1990

◁ 1 ▷

In March the chaplain had pointed to the word *Commencement* at the end of the Corps Calendar and said *Read it, boys, it's just the beginning.* Even so it had seemed the end, seemed it all through the lingering weeks of drill and exams and ceremony. But today they woke and remembered. They woke and knew it was another day of celebration but also of expectancy and an uncommon gravity. The very air of the piedmont morning was heavy with pollen, with the scent of honeysuckle and the steady thrumming of bees, and all the walk to the parade grounds Wes worried that the grainy yellow powder blanketing the campus would foul his dress uniform. In fact he generally cared no more about his appearance than regulations absolutely demanded—excessive preoccupation with such superficial concerns could, he told his classmates only half-mockingly, distract the future officer from the truly important aspects of a martial education. But today was different. He found himself, almost unexpectedly, approaching the grounds like a groom approaches the altar.

Spring had come on slow that year and the breeze running down the westward mountains was still cool in the late morning when the speaker finished his remarks. The retired general was no rhetorician, Wes thought—his own father might have done better—but the man's presence belied any need for words. He was of medium height but broad and his sagging flesh did little to soften a figure that looked as if it had been made of concrete blocks. The face was no exception. As Wes mounted the platform to receive his commission he saw its skin tighten in a pasty white whorl at the back of the old man's left jaw, just over the spot where the bone had been wired back together in Korea. He saluted, stood taut as the old man took one hand and thrust a piece of paper into the other. "Make us proud, son," he said. Wes gave a grim half-smile and pumped the hand twice, eyes wandering from the scar to the bright array of medals below. It was noon now and the rich golden sunlight seemed almost palpable as he began to move through it toward the stairs and back down into the crowd below.

His family was waiting, and after his class broke ranks in the warmth of the afternoon they gathered with friends for idle talk, photographs, introductions and goodbyes. The crowd began to thin after a few hours but the Hammonds lingered on as the sun began to approach the top of the circle of pines that surrounded the Institute grounds. By the onset of evening Wes found himself standing alone with the two other men in his family, talking, and all their talk was of war.

His father, a tall man whose face looked naked without glasses, had the most to say. Drew Hammond had missed Vietnam because of law school and his only child's birth but spent a lifetime compensating for it. Military history was his passion, and though it cost his legal practice dearly it had brought him recognition beyond the normal scope of the amateur. Earlier that year his study of a local cavalry unit's action in the Mexican War had won an award from a national historical association. Such recognition had, Wes noticed with some annoyance, increased his father's sense of authoritative knowledge on a variety of questions not necessarily limited to the military. His mother's father had landed at Normandy but never said much about the war he actually fought and had less to say as he grew older. Throughout the day the old man had stood near Wes, silent, as his eyes against the sun's declining seemed to sink deeper and deeper into his weathered red face.

The three of them stood clustered together beneath a broad open tent at the edge of the grounds. Over the shoulders of the older men

Wes saw women, girls in sundresses whirling about them, cups in hand and laughing together as they moved toward crystal bowls that glinted in the long dying afternoon light. He watched them hoist silver ladles, the bright drink cascading back into rich scarlet below, and for a moment he wished he were with them.

Drew Hammond put a hand on his son's back and cocked his head toward the grandfather. "Well, this young man is headed west."

The voice that answered was almost a whisper. "Going to fight the Indians, it sounds like."

This was the older man's retort to the commencement address. The speech had been filled with predictable phrases, with the expected exhortations to strong character amongst the new officers, but had ended with what Wes thought was an ill-thought out analogy of "the new American moment" to those which followed the defining wars of the two previous centuries—for the most crucial struggle of the twentieth century, the general claimed with a tottering fury, had been not the fight against the Nazis but the now completed Cold War that grew out of it. In its wake, he said, Americans would have to learn to fight a new kind of war, or keep a new kind of peace; the struggles of the decade to come would be not prolonged conflicts but instead short, fast-paced battles, like the Indian wars of the last century but on the international scene that this great country now dominated. It was a new kind of challenge, a challenge to preserve and extend what had been tenuously won over the previous five decades—*freedom* (he had enunciated the word fiercely, shaking his huge head at the crowd like a lion). It was a challenge for which, he believed, the men assembled before him were entirely fit.

Wes liked the sound of this but was not yet quite so sure what he was fit for, and the orders he had received led him to believe that he would not find out anytime soon. "Sounds to me," he answered his grandfather hesitantly, "like I won't be fighting much of anybody."

"That's a blessing, son." His mother, tall, elegant in high heels, still serenely coiffed as she had been this morning. "And we're just proud that you've done so well." Leaning into the circle she smiled and gave him an imploring look that made him wish he were alone with the men again. "We just wish you weren't going so far away."

"But the West, the West!" his father said, shifting his drink, freeing up a hand to gesture. "All the great ones started there—Scott, Grant, Johnston. Lee. The general may just have his chronology reversed, you know," he said significantly over the top of his glass. It was a rare weekend off for him and he had spent much of it in the company of bourbon. Through the raised glass Wes saw his face above the slanting amber pool, bulbous eye and arched brow glaring back at him like a grotesque reflection of his own.

His mother ignored her husband and looked at Wes in her own preferred manner, as if he were a framed photo on her shelf. Her eyes lingered on his new shoulderboards. "He'll be fine. I just know it."

"Of course he will," said the grandfather, leaning toward Wes but keeping his face toward the treetops where the sun now burnt deep orange behind the black latticework of pines. Dark figures behind them were beginning to pull stakes out of the earth ("Strike the tent!" his father cried). The spring day had yielded to a thick humming twilight into which his brightly garbed classmates had already disappeared; now the women, too, were gone. Wes took a final look at the campus, stark stone lecture halls dwarfed beneath the brooding central barracks whose own looming face was lost in the shadow now creeping down the lawn toward them. *Have colors been observed? Why didn't I hear?* As he watched his mother begin to tug at his father's arm, the slow flood of memory swept over him and he knew that he would never again hear the low sound of taps wafting through the pines. It was time to leave.

Wes had been commissioned an ensign and was slated to become a navy helicopter pilot (an assignment that had made his father exclaim, "Air cavalry!" despite the fact that the navy, of course, had never had cavalry of any kind). Five years ago, no one would have been more surprised by such career plans than Wes himself.

Upon finishing high school he had perfunctorily enrolled at the state university and been assigned to a drab dormitory alongside a pleasant, leafy quad. He had a number of friends from home there, and together they exulted in their newfound liberty—stayed up late watching MTV and playing video games, found ways to procure beer and liquor, drank too much on the weekends and often during the week. Not that his grades were bad. He had been a competent if bored student in high school and remained so here, trudging through a succession of mandatory first-year courses taught in crowded classrooms by distracted graduate students. When he studied he did so with one of the succession of dates he found at hand, girls who like himself were astonished to find out how low, suddenly, was the price of a night of passion—an annoyed roommate at worst. Reflecting over Christmas break, he decided that this was not too bad a life. Maybe something was missing. Maybe next year he would rush a fraternity.

Midway through the spring semester things changed. Two boys on the fringes of his circle began having serious academic difficulties; one had started smoking marijuana with breakfast, and when the campus suddenly began enforcing its drug policy he was discovered in his room with a small stash of cocaine (the photo in the school paper showed him with a wide, nervous smile, alongside one of the German Shepherds that had barged into his room, hand stretched toward the animal as if to pet it). A week later a girl that Wes and several of his acquaintances had briefly dated the previous semester suddenly disenrolled after slowly putting on weight for several months.

This succession of events unsettled him. To distract himself he stayed up all one Tuesday night drinking with some boys on his hall, only to lapse into a brooding funk and skip all his classes for the rest of the week. In a confessional moment he called Tom Blanton, another high school friend at the university and one of the steadiest people he knew. They had gone to see a few movies the previous semester. When Tom announced that he had recently accepted Jesus Christ as his personal Lord and Savior and invited him to a fellowship meeting that night, Wes stammered a few words of congratulation, hung up the phone, and wandered outside for a long run in the dark drizzle of the early March evening. When he saw Tom across the quad a week later, he detoured around the chemistry building and kept walking.

Over spring break he went home, spent a lot of time in his room, and talked to his parents as little as possible. He determined that he was going to go back to school, settle on a major, and get his life together. No more wasted time. He would commit himself to something.

He selected a new friend to be his aid in this endeavor, a long-faced boy from Nashville who was on his flag football team and on the fast track as a finance major. The next week Mike Rawlings shepherded Wes into the business school and convinced him that he was a natural salesman. "Now, Wes—" Mike put a hand on his shoulder—"there's one thing you've got to understand." He looked him straight in the eye: "Your first job is to sell *yourself*"—he paused significantly— *"to* yourself."

By the end of the day Wes had signed up as a marketing major.

He immediately began investigating summer internships and within a few weeks had landed one with a medical supply company out of Atlanta. His new business school acquaintances congratulated him: it was a prestigious firm, and Wes had done well to establish an association with them so quickly. They all piled into Mike's used BMW and went out to eat at one of the tonier sandwich shops on the strip bordering campus. Still wearing their interview suits, they swaggered in brazenly; no one checked their IDs. Mike bought a round of Heinekens on his dad's credit card. Wes would always remember holding the cool, green glass and watching Mike tuck his paisley tie inside his shirt as he speculated on the possibility of lining up dates with some sorority girls they had met at the career fair: "Boys," he said, munching thoughtfully on a long, cheese-covered fry, "it's going to be a great summer." A trickle of grease ran down his thumb, meandering its way toward his stiff, white cuff.

The next week Wes received his assignment. He would be helping his new company establish the marketing strategy for a new line of adult diapers.

Two weeks later he applied for admission to the Institute.

He had not done so at the urging of his parents. Wes would later realize that his father had been too distracted to push his only son toward military school, for every moment he could wrench free from his job and family was spent in the previous century. Drew Hammond had displayed no particular interest in either Wes's enrollment at the state university or his tentative exploration of a business career. In fact, he seemed to have no strong interest in his son's future at all. Wes eventually realized that his father was not guilty of any hostility toward or even particular neglect of him; he simply seemed incapable of believing that anything of much significance could occur in the late twentieth century, which, unfortunately, included any decision his son might make.

But when Wes took it upon himself to apply to the Institute, his father gave notice. Wes remembered sitting in the study—a rare occasion—and announcing his plans. His father was ensconced at his desk amidst a jumble of documents and maps, peering out at his son's world through the dim circle of light cast by his lamp. Wes was trying to explain himself.

"It'll have to be a full four years. A few of the credits will transfer, but I have to go through plebe year."

His father's eyes widened over his wire glasses. "And you'll actually get a commission?"

"Not everybody does, but I want to. Through ROTC."

His father sat back and looked straight at him. A smile was creeping over his face, and he began twirling his pen in his fingers the way Wes had seen him do when he read alone in the study late at night. "Have you thought about West Point?"

He had, but ruled it out. It would take too long, another year before he could even get the paperwork together to apply.

"But, the Academy! The Academy! Wouldn't it be worth it?" His father was becoming animated, rumpling maps with his elbows as he leaned toward him. "What's a year?"

A year too long, Wes knew. He submitted his application and started plebe year that August.

His father seemed to adjust well. The college had, after all, produced a small but significant group of leaders who had their own place in the nation's history. The most famous of these were Confederate and thereby appealed to his father's chronological prejudices, if not necessarily his regional ones. Drew Hammond had spent the last twenty years near the southern town where his wife had grown up, but his own father had been from an itinerant Army family and his mother from Pennsylvania. In rare moments he would begin to talk to Wes about the cool, pristine landscape of central *Pee-Ay* as though it had just occurred to him how strange it was to find himself in this climate, in a town become an exurb where the descendants of sharecroppers still mingled with those of the landowners they had labored for and both now were being swallowed up amongst the newcomers who arrived daily along the web of highways and housing developments that seeped steadily out from the great city nearby. Drew Hammond often seemed to see the latter as reminders of his own chronological misfortune, and visits to his son's campus provided him some easy respite from them.

Wes's own first attraction to life at the Institute had less to do with any sense of its storied past than with an image from his own childhood. When he was twelve, his parents had driven him up into the long blue foothills for the wedding of some third cousin. It was the first wedding he had been to and the only thing he remembered about it was the groom's brother, lean and hard in a grey cadet uniform. At the reception Wes had stood with his mouth drooping open, holding a plate of cake in one hand and staring while his mother and father chatted with this figure. He seemed somehow much older but not, like Wes's parents, a creature of another world altogether. He could hardly believe that they were successfully communicating with one another. The cadet stood straight, his taut white dress cap curled against the grey blouse by a firm gloved hand, as if his body were a single flexed muscle. The young men around him, even the ones in tuxedos, looked slovenly by comparison. He had just finished his first year at the Institute and while most of his conversation seemed rehearsed his eyes brightened when he announced, "It was the hardest thing I've ever done. Right now it almost feels like I've never done anything, really, except this."

All the dark drive home Wes tried to convince himself that the cadet had been looking at him when he said this. Stretching out in the back seat with his face turned toward the opposite window, he wondered: What would it be like to have to go through something like that? He had started football practice that year, and two hours a day of that was hard enough. As the family station wagon sped through the early summer night, the boy inside looked at the stars and imagined himself grey and white in a cadet uniform.

When Wes applied to the Institute six years later he could not have said what role that faint recollection played in his decision. A

few years more and he would outright laugh at it. Eventually he recognized that what drove him there was not the uniform, but rather
the promise of doing something difficult and therefore significant. For
Wes slowly realized at the Institute that what had appalled him about
his first year of college life had been not its apparent immorality but
rather its self-evident mediocrity. In part he had wondered if, left to
his own devices, he would simply stop going to class, self-destruct as
some of those around him had. But more deeply he feared he might
in fact meet the standards of success that had been presented to him,
might find himself easing into some lucrative but obscure corporate
job. That spring he had looked at his new business school friends and
a voice within him began whispering *if you do not act now you will
become one of them.*

During his first year at the Institute it sometimes seemed to
him that he had in fact become an altogether new person. He found
himself immersed in another, starker world, and though there were
hours—whole weeks—when he was exhausted and frightened, he kept
burning brightly in the back of his mind a vision of the day when he
would reemerge into the mundane world he had known before, his
familiar self become something sleek, hard, almost unrecognizable.
That vision brought him through the sleepless nights of hazing, that
and some satisfaction in the very concreteness of the tasks set before
him: to push his blazing chest off the soggy ground again and again,
gulping in blades of grass along with the damp air and the sweat that
rolled off his cheeks already as the sun began to crawl above the rolling
blue horizon—forty-seven more and he would be done. It was a world
with rules, a world of prescribed goals that were not easily achieved
but were comforting in their very unmalleability.

Having met them, Wes finally found his return to the mundane
not so much triumphant as disorienting. On the early summer afternoon that he first walked out the campus gates no longer wearing a
plebe's stripe, he felt so light-headed that for a moment he wondered
whether he could drive his car back down the mountain.

Though he did not often admit it even to himself, the three years
following had been somehow disappointing. Once he settled into the
routine of Institute life, he found it lacked the grandeur of the struggle that was plebe year. Increasingly he found himself immersed in a

round of books and studies that seemed typically collegiate, albeit in an uncommonly rigorous atmosphere where every free moment was occupied with duties—polishing brass, ironing shirts, organizing activities for the new plebe class. Over time Wes came to resent these tasks, their inherent triviality, and to sink himself more and more into his books. He had chosen a physics major because it was, for him, the least difficult of the sciences and would stand him in good stead in any branch of the service. But the subject he grew to love—though he refrained from revealing this to his father—was history. To the steady *thok* of his heavy brass clock he immersed himself deep into the boundless night studying Patton's North Africa campaign and Churchill's speeches, fascinated by the relentless decisiveness of the one and the swelling call to glory of the other. In time he began to sense the living history of the Institute itself as he marched about the grounds. A few men who rivaled Patton and Churchill themselves had walked here, he knew, and he preferred recalling their spirits to worrying about keeping in step.

But even as he found new depths to life at the Institute, he began to recognize that there remained within him hungers that could not be satisfied on its grounds. Granted liberty on Saturdays and eventually for entire weekends, Wes's classmates got into their cars and headed straight to the state university he had already left. And he joined them, at first hesitantly, but finally welcoming the respite from the daily round of his existence, inwardly rejoicing as the car banked down the last undulating hill and began to accelerate on the long straight asphalt through pine barren and swamp ever faster until the last miles through the avenue of moss-draped oaks felt like riding a bullet down the end of a rifle barrel that reached all the way back to the mountain where they had begun. They came for two things and Wes having been there before knew which he wanted more, not the drink but the woman, for the one was mere means or prelude to or placebo for the other, and time was short. And in the pungent clamorous bars he sought her as night fell, sought not only the night of amorous abandon all the cadets spoke of but also the one he might explain himself to, the one who might come to know him. And once or twice he thought he might have found her but after a few months of phone calls and letters and weekends she had met some frat boy in her econ class and he was back to at best a night with a girl who did not know him or at worst a night with cadets on the floor of some friend's cousin's apartment and maybe, two or three times, a fight with the cousin's roommates. On Sundays he felt soiled and all the drive back swore he would never do this again, and maybe for a few weeks he would not. Back at the Institute he would shower and nap, then go for a run and open his books to immerse himself again in the discipline he had chosen. For this was his life, and the weekend trips mere dream or nightmare.

In this manner he passed his last three years. His grades in history as well as his painstaking diligence in physics—he approached new formulae like rounds of plebe year pushups—assured that he would graduate near the top of his class academically. In military bearing and leadership he was near the middle, weighed down by occasional uniform demerits and his steadfast refusal to volunteer for leadership duties that he considered trivial. He had not entered the Institute to organize a platoon of plebes for trash pickup after football games.

It was in part his revulsion for such tasks that led him, when his final year came round, to apply for naval flight school. Perhaps out of a hidden desire to spite his father, whose sympathies were all army, perhaps because of some half-conceived desire for boundless travel, he had chosen the navy long ago, and the relative isolation of the aviator seemed to promise a kind of lonely glory that was not to be found leading a division of motley sailors shipboard. His grades and physical aptitude ensured that he would be accepted, but the competition landed him a spot flying helicopters rather than jets. And there was, his temporary orders said, to be some delay in the beginning of his training. He was to be stationed at a temporary personnel unit in California while awaiting further orders.

Such qualifications did little to dim the essential luster of his last weeks at the college, weeks when he spent the twilight hours on long runs around the campus and flights of nostalgia. His own history had become fused with that of the Institute, and he allowed himself to imagine that he might carry it on with honor. On the morning of commencement while he waited for his parents, leaning on the cool marble of the main gate and surveying the bright world outside, he looked up to see a hawk sweeping low out of the naked sky and felt better than he had since he finished plebe year.

Then things began to change.

After graduation Wes had two weeks of leave and he spent the first of them at home, sleeping late, calling old friends, unpacking and packing again. His mother would wander in and out of his room to run her fingers across the top of his bags. "We know you'll do well, son. We just wish you weren't going so far away."

But he would only murmur a word or a phrase and turn to avoid her eyes.

Later his father would pass in the hall outside and, sometimes, lean in to say hello. After dark he roamed the halls like a ghost. On the two nights Wes stayed out late with friends he pulled back into the drive and saw the light on in the study and a relentless sadness swept over him as he thought of his father in there, alone, head bent low into the dim sphere of yellow light that hovered over some forlorn document.

He had expected the time at home would be good but he found himself distracted and restless, so he loaded the car early and turned it westward.

He savored the next three days alone, days spent gazing carelessly over the steaming concrete and out into the countryside, ear cocked and hand searching blindly for radio stations, pulling into hot roadside diners and back out on the road with his window open and the thick evening air beginning to rush in. Every mile of the drive reminded him of the newness of his life. As he watched the country transform itself around him, heavy pine forest giving way to plains and arid highlands and vast inviting sky, a paradoxical sense of freedom began to mingle with the secret and thoroughly un-American pleasure that he took in having someone else tell him what to do. Yes, he was free from home and love and all the usual boring encumbrances. But most importantly, he had not chosen to shed them of his own will—he had been ordered to do so. Most importantly, he was free from decision.

He had not fully realized the advantages of his position until he talked to those few people he had kept in touch with at the university, those who had stayed. As graduation approached, so many had dissolved in anguish in the face of the uncharted mystery looming suddenly before them. One boy he knew, in his last semester, had dropped out and gone back to work for his father's gasoline distributorship; one of his own cousins suddenly married a boy she had ignored for years and was pregnant within two months. They knew not which way to turn, were paralyzed by potentiality. Had he stayed, he realized, he would have been among the worst of them, for he was cynical by nature and had trouble convincing himself what was worthwhile and what was not.

No, he was incredibly fortunate. A summer of idleness, then stern discipline and direction. He would be told what to do.

So he had believed. But when, months later, the idleness continued, he and John would spend whole mornings around the officer's conference table mocking the etymologies of their young manhood, of *commencement* and *commissioning*. After reading the paper Wes would push his coffee cup aside, drive his elbows into the wood, and stare quizzically at his friend: "What, in fact, have you commenced, ensign?"

And John would pull his gaze in from the window, cock an eyebrow, and lean back in his chair: "And you, ensign? On what mission have you been sent?" Then he would lay his own fingers smoothly on the surface of the table, as if he were about to say a prayer or serve a meal.

◁ 2 ▷

What Wes would remember most vividly about his first week in California was neither the strange new landscape nor the lieutenant's dry welcome and explanations. What he would remember was the hour the warrant officer spent talking to them, slowly and sensuously, about chasing whores in the Philippines and Thailand.

That was the day Wes first met most of the other young officers with whom he would spend the coming months, and later, together, they realized that they had all circulated through the warrant's office at some point during the day. No two ever described it in exactly the same way. The room's darkness made it seem a world separate from the building in which it was situated, as did its decidedly unmilitary décor. Walls and shelves laden with absurd relics from the far reaches of the globe—statuettes, paintings, blurry photographs, tapestries. Every ensign who had been in the room noticed a different one.

When Wes entered this chamber his eyes had been drawn immediately to the man himself, who leaned back in a heavy chair behind his desk, breathing powerfully through a blazing cigar. From his own chair Wes could only dimly make out the coarse black hair on the back of the older man's hands, the broad yellow smile, and a twisted and pockmarked face that amidst the smoke and shadow looked almost noble. And then at some moment he could not identify, a thick voice began to fill the room, offering no formal greeting but instead suddenly issuing forth in stories, rising and falling in a steady rhythm until with a relish that offset its essential languor it conveyed little more than a slow succession of images: "—anchor off Phattaya Beach on a muggy April morning, swing down the ladder to the liberty boat, then cast off from that big steel bitch and bob toward shore, dammit, over the cool blue water to the hot sand, even the goddam breeze is hot, so hot it stings, but you get under the trees, buy a fat steak and a sweaty whore and spend a night with her and her kid sister on those stinking sheets, go jump in the fucking ocean, head back up to the bamboo and start over again. Yessir. That was good duty." Then he spat somewhere behind the desk.

In the pause that followed Wes glanced around at the others in the room, some of the ensigns he had just met—who was in here with him?—but before he could make out their faces the voice resumed, now in a tone weighty with the authority of experience:

"Let me tell you men something."

The cigar brightened like a coal amidst the thickening smoke, and then a pair of arms slid forward on the desk and the great, craggy head emerged from the cloud: "This is it for you. No responsibilities, no worries. Nothing. You get a good paycheck, all the free time you could ask for—to do with what you will. What you *will*. You got a damn free ticket to life!" he roared, and the yellow smile beamed at them, as if its wearer were suddenly astonished at his own good fortune. Then it was swallowed up again. "It could last a year, it could end tomorrow. Enjoy it, men. Soon you'll be trudging through flight school or working your ass off on a ship, or maybe you'll be a loser and get sent back. A few more years and you'll be married to some bitch raising kids—then you're dead. Life ain't ever gonna be this good again, so make the most of it." He scanned each of the faces in the room. "You won't be here much longer."

He settled back in his chair and showed his teeth as the burning orange point played in the darkness around his eyes. "You men won't let me down, will you?"

When Wes emerged into a sunlit white hall with what turned out to be four other ensigns, the one closest to him—blond, trim, with a wide, swinging gait—kept his head turned down toward the glossy tile floor until they turned a corner into a small lounge. Then he looked up to reveal a red, straining face that suddenly burst into bright laughter. "What the hell was *that?*" His broad expression reflected the late morning light that surrounded them, and when Wes thought of Cullen that was always the image that first came to his mind.

Cullen's smile spread to them all, all but the one short officer whose nametag said DONKERS and whose mouth was working as though it were chewing on something sour. "*I* can't believe it. How did someone like that become associated with our chain of command, with *any* chain of command? I'm going to talk to the lieutenant *right now.*" With an awkward sideways step he bustled away, the thick key chain on his belt loop jangling down the hall after him.

The pale, lanky ensign on Wes's right glared after him. "Dork!" he exploded, then grinned in self-satisfaction and began gnawing on a piece of gum. This was Stick, whom Wes had noticed most clearly in the warrant's office because of the expression on his face, rapt or absent he could not tell—eyes wide, wet, and unfocused, locked slightly to the left of straight ahead, features utterly immobile. But now his black eyes sparkled beneath his blacker brow as he thrust his hands into his pockets and raised himself up on the flats of his feet. "The warrant's awesome, the warrant's my *man,*" he said, leaning forward for emphasis. "Hey"—he gave a long look at Wes and the other two—"what are you guys up to tonight? I'm trying to put a little party together."

Stick leaned into Cullen and kept talking, their figures merging and voices fading as Wes turned to the fourth member of their party. John was half a head shorter than he and Cullen, a full head shorter than Stick, lightly freckled, hair brown and tending to red and as long on top as he could get away with. Sunk into a couch now by a vending machine he listened and looked on with a wry smile, chin in hand, feet propped on a coffee table as though he were stuck in a waiting room but had nothing better to do anyway. "Sure," he would say to Stick's invitation. "Why not?" But there was something odd about the way he said it and then kept looking at them, patiently, as if he actually expected an answer.

That was two days after Wes had reported for duty at a plain building on the small naval weapons base that took up a mile of the long brown coast just south of Los Angeles.

The morning he arrived, only a day after he had awoken alone in the middle of the New Mexico desert, he had sat up with a start at five a.m. in a nearly empty hotel off a crowded freeway. He felt a sudden need to get his bearings and, sleepless now, wandered out onto the balcony to look at the stream of cars already rushing by, isolated beacons whose brightness might have borne witness to the souls inside them but whose headlong flight and sheer number somehow depressed him. A few hours ago, he had been one of them. But still he looked on until he felt a sudden immense loneliness welling up inside of him and could bear it no more. Then he went back into the room and turned on CNN. Market numbers scrolling across the bottom of the screen; the president, playing golf; peace and capitalism in Europe. Soon he slipped on some civilian clothes and walked over to buy breakfast at a garishly lit diner next door. The food was bad, and his stomach swelled with tepid coffee and grease as he showered and methodically assembled his uniform. The red numbers on the bedside clock advanced in silence. Time.

Self-conscious and wary in his dress whites, he drove out into the morning and navigated a long horizon of palm trees and power lines until he arrived at the gate that marked his destination. A guard saluted, scanned his orders, gave directions.

He parked in a small lot where he could just glimpse a thin, flat line of gray over a last slight rise in the land. The Pacific. He turned his back to it and walked toward a door where, beneath the sign that said BLDG 54, he saw a freshly painted line: TEMPORARY PERSONNEL UNIT. With a quick pang of anxiety—his snarling stomach felt as if it were turning in upon itself—he checked his shoes for dirt, removed his cover, and walked through the door.

At the end of the long white hall he found only a drowsy yeoman with a cup of coffee. There was no one else in the building today, the sailor explained. Most of the staff was on leave and the Officer in Charge was in San Diego for the day. He would return tomorrow to talk to new arrivals. The yeoman yawned, shuffled through Wes's orders twice, told him to leave. "Just go get yourself settled somewhere, sir, and come back at the same time tomorrow." He stamped the orders and then reached behind his desk and pulled out an auto magazine.

And that was all.

As Wes walked out his steps were easy. He noticed for the first time, with a kind of wonder, how thin and light the air was here. The sky had brightened considerably during the brief time he had been in the building, and the flat blue sea was beginning to glitter now, stretched long and promising across the furthest line of his vision. He was standing in the parking lot looking out over it when another car pulled in. He slid into his own car quickly, as if he had been caught idling, only to see another ensign in whites emerge and proceed toward the building holding a brown folder like his own.

He thought that he should somehow feel guilty for his extended liberty but driving to the hotel finally admitted to himself that he was secretly pleased to have the day off. He changed into shorts and a tee-shirt and checked out. Then he drove down into San Agustin and found a beachside cafe where he ate a good brunch out on the deck. He sat with a glass of iced tea, filling it with sugar that only sat on the bottom no matter how long he stirred, and read the paper. Then he went back to his car, changed into his bathing suit, and walked down to the ocean.

He was surprised at how cold the water was, at that and how when he swam out the town rose so quickly above the beach—houses and streets nestled up amidst the hills, how clear they were. At the farthest edge of the swimming area he clung to a buoy and looked back at the coast, to his left the town and the base and the further crowded shore curving up toward Long Beach and Palos Verdes, to his right the land falling away and more open along the edge of Camp Pendleton. Two islands jutted up clearly from the sea down that way; more loomed behind him, aligned one behind another so he could not tell how many. The land rose stark and dusty out of the ocean here and made the landscape more full, as much a part of the world as the sea and sky that engulfed the thin green earth where it trickled to an end back along the marshy Atlantic seaboard he knew. But it was not only elevation that made the difference. All at once he realized that there were no trees here, at least not enough to impede his eye as it roamed free from hill to hill all along the dry rolling coast.

He floated alongside the buoy. Gulls circled overhead, lighting at his post as he swam back in.

Later he ran along the beach, dodging the clumps of rubbery seaweed that littered the shore, before rinsing and walking up to his car. He found a new hotel in town, checked in, and began to look through apartment guides.

In the evening he went to a little Mexican restaurant next door where a blonde woman in a sombrero sold him a fish taco while a little dark man wiped the tables down. Surf music played faintly overhead. He took a seat in a booth three rows down from the only other customers, an Asian girl and a boy with a ponytail who smiled at one another beneath a pinata. There were others hovering just below the ceiling—a tiger, a golden bear, a droopy lobster—but this one was a bright blue donkey, and as it twisted slowly over the room its eyes seemed to stare at him.

He sat and ate in silence and began to sense the strangeness of his own presence in this place. The pangs of wonder that swept over him made him feel somehow uncomfortable and alone, and so he paid the bill and left. On the street, where it was dark and he could hear the long rumbling rush of the sea, he felt even worse. He ducked into the hotel and went straight up to his room.

That night he watched the news and read a paperback, a novel about submarine warfare that had been a bestseller just a few years ago. The hero spent a lot of time trying to crack Soviet codes and worrying about his nine-year old daughter growing up in a world threatened by nuclear armageddon. Wes had a bad habit of looking ahead to the end, and so he already knew that the hero finally managed both to foil the communists and to buy a teddy bear for his little girl. Before long he began to get bored and put the book down. He finally fell into a sound sleep, content that he had at least located the base and would meet the Officer in Charge tomorrow.

"Ensign, your mission here is simple: stand by to stand by."

Lieutenant Ragis said this as though he had had a great deal of practice. He wore a slight absent smile and folded his hands primly in front of him, sitting straight behind his desk and peering shyly ahead through thin glasses. Wes listened in mild stupefaction as his new

OIC thumbed through his orders and continued speaking with only occasional glances at him:

"You see, the flight schools on both coasts are backed up *indefinitely*. Why that is is hard to justify, but in part it's a simple numbers game. We could sort out all the contributing factors retroactively and determine what should have been done, but the facts are these." He paused and waved his pen, as though he were ordering the facts into formation. "When you entered ROTC—mid-eighties, right?—the military was building up to unprecedented levels. Reagan was talking about a six hundred ship navy, for God's sake. And the manpower was there to do it. *And* everyone wanted to fly. I'd be willing to bet you and your whole high school football team saw *Top Gun* the summer after you graduated, didn't you?"

Wes winced and tried to think of a good answer, but the lieutenant kept talking anyway.

"Regardless, you've done well enough that you've actually gotten into flight school. Not that brownshoes are the only ones with this problem. Subs have recently gotten popular, and even the good old surface navy is jam full—I bet you had buddies with eye problems or who were business majors who were disappointed to find out they had to go to supply school.

"The bottom line, as they say, is that the navy you're actually being commissioned into isn't the one the planners were planning when you started. We can't even decide who the enemy is anymore, and the past year has been nothing but budget cuts, budget cuts, and more budget cuts. The army has even started letting people who got a full ride through college go because they can't find billets for them. We haven't gotten that far yet, though I'd guess we might in a few years.

"But to get back to you. For the time being, you're stashed. You and a couple of dozen other potential aviators, but we have surface guys in and out of here too. The ships usually find a place for them sooner than flight school does for you. Of course, your commitment doesn't start running out until you actually start school, so your lives are more or less on hold until you get in. That's why they're trying to open up more billets. But meanwhile, we're going to see what we can do to keep up your professional training—send you out to the firing range, arrange some base visits, maybe even run you through comms school—but you're more or less on your own for a little while. Enjoy it. There are worse things that could happen to you than being stuck in southern California with a decent paycheck and a lot of free time."

The lieutenant leaned forward and gave him a brief smile, at once placating and ingratiating and conspiratorial, but it did not last long. More than anything else he looked relieved to have finished his speech and to be done with Wes. He seemed mildly uncomfortable. At first Wes had the strange sense that this unease had something to do with his Institute background, but later he noticed that the lieutenant acted the same way toward all of the men under his nominal command. He had given Wes a brief history of his own career. From Connecticut, he had gone through ROTC at Georgetown, surface warfare officer's school, then three and a half years on a destroyer out of San Diego. What he did not say was that something had gone wrong on that sea tour, something significant enough to earn him as his first shore duty this plum assignment: Commander of the Temporary Personnel Unit. The papers on his desk all had to do with his ongoing efforts to have some mysterious letter of reprimand removed from his record and to effect a permanent transfer to naval intelligence, where he could sit at a computer and analyze data and maybe garner an assignment to an embassy alongside the Mediterranean. If he didn't succeed he was going to get out, move to the Napa Valley, and start a vineyard. But Wes would not learn all this until later, after the "professional training" generally failed to materialize and he began to wonder what the OIC did with all his time.

At least that first day Ragis had established an agenda for the day following, an orientation session in which the yeomen would lead newly reporting officers through a few hours worth of paperwork before showing them around the building and the base. "So tomorrow should be fun. Maybe you'll get to meet the warrant, who's sort of my acting XO around here." He grimaced. "A truly charming man." Then he opened the door for Wes, only to see another junior officer waiting outside. The lieutenant invited him in, and as Wes walked down the hall he heard Ragis' voice trilling faintly. *Ensign, your mission here is simple....*

After that week the lieutenant began assembling all new arrivals on Friday mornings when he would give the speech just once so as to better conserve his time.

Wes had heard the term *stashed* before, back at the Institute. In the spring semester his supervisors at the ROTC unit had laughed about it. During their first briefing on orders the chief yeoman, coffee mug in hand, had paced around a room full of midshipmen and prefaced his remarks with a brief aside: "Now, some of you guys'll get lucky, have a few weeks of smokin' and jokin' before your training starts." Their instructor, a lieutenant commander, smiled knowingly. Officer or enlisted, all the staff had at some point ended up with a few weeks or even months stuck between posts, officially on duty but in effect on leave. For them it was a well-deserved respite from sea tours in the Med or Western Pacific, from time spent shadowing Russian cruisers passing through the Dardanelles or pulling Vietnamese refugees out of the South China Sea. Those were the stories they had so casually revealed and lingered over, the sea stories; being *stashed* was something mentioned only in passing, an obscure fact of military life that Wes had never really considered until the past few months. And it was never something that he had understood as happening "indefinitely."

But it was happening so now for at least three dozen people, as he realized the next morning when he found the middle rows of the base's small auditorium filled with khaki-clad ensigns. He took his seat among them for two hours of administrative tasks before they were dispersed around the base for medical examinations and housing updates. It was afterwards that a yeoman, some flunky of the warrant, drove Wes back to the TPU and shepherded him into the office where he heard the words that would mark the real beginning of his new life.

For, years later, he would look back and see that was in fact where it all began. Because of the warrant's charge. And because suddenly he found himself not alone but with others.

◁ 3 ▷

Whatever awaited them, it would not come until all four had passed through a time which allowed them to know one another in a manner afforded only during lives lived under rare circumstances: war, or enforced idleness. One thing they had time to do was talk. That, and to speculate about one another. And so within a few months Wes thought he knew them all. Cullen he had sized up within ten minutes of meeting him—his overriding good cheer, his lust for pleasure but essential unselfishness. Cullen was always so much *there* that from the beginning his presence overshadowed that of John, whose more muted friendliness was lost in occasional bouts of detachment.

And Stick. Well, certain things should have been clear from the beginning.

Their first night together was spent on the balcony of Stick's apartment, barbecuing and drinking and looking out at the sun sinking into the broad Pacific. They were up in the hills in one of those white rows Wes had seen from the water, a long stucco-faced apartment complex in the shape of a huge hollow square. Stick was lucky enough to get one of the ocean view rooms on the top floor. Its red tile roof sloped in front toward the sea and in back toward the trim green lawn and brick walkways of the courtyard. The whole place had, Wes realized, the same essential layout as the central building at the Institute, but the soft grainy stucco could not have been more different from the austere grey stone of his old barracks. It was called La Mirage and within a week all four of them would be living there.

For that first night went well enough. Eventually, as many as twenty of their new comrades in arms jammed into Stick's apartment, all showered and fresh in civilian summer clothes. They came bearing meat: thick hamburger patties, soggy half chickens, glistening slabs of beef, the great arcing ribs of hogs—all tossed, one after another, over the seething flames. The grill flared and fumed like a battleship in the mild California twilight, its heavy smoke wafting up into a pale blue sky that faded to pink over the long westward ocean. They clustered on the balcony near the food, cups in hand, looking from the flames to the sea and back again. Some were boys from the Midwest or the mountain states who had seen the ocean only a few times during their brief summer training. When they caught one another's eyes, they inevitably grinned in amazement: how had they come to be in such a place?

Their host stood across from the grill and managed to not do very much but talk, leaning against the railing with his arms crossed and a sly smirk on his face. It was Cullen who grabbed the spatula and the sauce, who flipped, basted, and tossed, swatting at the food with a brush and hopping left and right in an easy shuffle-dance as he did so, talking and laughing all the while. Gradually the other ensigns drifted into a circle that took shape around these two—the poles of the little world that formed on the balcony. They had gone to Annapolis together, as had several others in the crowd, and stories of the Academy became the common stuff of the night. As Wes looked on silently at the group around him enthralled by these two talkers, his initial pleasure slowly gave way to a mysterious unease, a faint, unarticulated anger. He caught himself staring at Cullen and then turned to see his own reflection frowning back at him in the sliding glass door, and for a moment he dimly perceived within himself a swelling sense of inadequacy and envy.

But that was not what he felt when the talk came round to Danny Ahearn, a football player who had been discharged from Annapolis.

Athletes at military academies generally had a popularity that was
dubious at best—many regular members of the corps, at least when
they weren't attending games, felt that athletes received special treat-
ment and detracted from the real mission of the school. But Ahearn,
he gathered, was a special case.

"That guy was a prick," spat out a clipped Long Island voice from
the crowd. "Cockiest bastard I ever saw," drawled another.

"Yeah, well, we took care of him." The words came from the far
edge of the balcony, where Stick stood against a sky now black but for
the dim light of the stars. His smirk had broken into an open grin.

"Alright, Stick—what're you *talking about?*" Cullen was beaming above the flames at the other end of the circle, still shuffling his
feet vigorously, light beads of sweat and a streak of grease glistening
on his forehead. He pointed with the spatula and a wave of laughter
swept back from him toward the speaker.

"Well, *my boy* and I were on that little beach trip *together,* ya see."
Stick took a long drink and passed over his audience once with a sweeping gaze. Every voice grew quiet, and then he began.

"I never liked the guy either, but he was in my division, you know,
and he needed a way to get over to Ocean City. Fuckin' hotshot jock
but he ain't got a car. He had this cousin of his, a real *hotty,* who'd
come through that week with a whole posse of her little girlfriends.
They just finished freshman year at frickin' Ohio State and they want
to know if ol' Danny boy wants to bring a few buddies down to visit at
their damn condo. His jock buddies have mandatory study hours, but
he's got some kinda pass and needs a ride, so I say, 'Danny, I'm your
man.' I'd met this little piece when she was passing through, and I
know that if I can spend a weekend with *that* I'm doing it, I don't care
if the guy *is* a cock.

"So it's me and Kevin Rist—you know him?—and Ahearn. We've
got ourselves a case of Bud and some Jimmy Beam and we're goin'
down fifty in my Blazer. *Beautiful* day—middle of May, about seventy-
five, not a fuckin' cloud in the sky. Rist is driving while we're knockin'
a few back. I'm feeling pretty good except for Ahearn's mouth—guy
won't shut up about himself, you can tell he thinks we're in fuckin'
awe of him—when I realize he's *shitfaced.* He's been suckin' on the
Beam since we left, and he's a big guy and all, but the boy can't handle

his liquor. They let those guys out even less than the rest of us, so his tolerance is *nothin'*.

"Next thing I know young Danny is tellin' us we gotta stop. Tells us he's gotta take a dump—I figure he's gotta puke, but to this day I don't know which it was. Like it matters? Anyway, it's good timing, cause we're about an hour away and there's this little dive right off the highway, it's packed with people going to the beach and a lot of them are just getting *plowed*. So Rist and I pull up at the bar while our boy goes to the head. We have to lead him to it. Dude hardly knows where he *is*.

"'Bout this time some clown sitting next to me says hey, my girl-friend's sitting there. I say too bad—maybe I'd give it up for the girl, you know, but this guy's just a puss, and he's buggin' me. He keeps hassling me and I think about getting in his face, but *suddenly*—I got an idea, one that's gonna make my whole weekend a lot better.

"Ahearn's still in the head and I noticed it's one of these that's got a lock on the outside, too. So I stroll on over there, flip down the latch, and head back to the bar.

"Now it's loud as hell in this place, and I don't know if he started yellin' or what—once I looked over and saw the door shakin' like it's about to come off its hinges—but we keep drinkin' for a good ten minutes before he comes out. I just feel this damn, I don'know, *presence* behind me and he's there, frickin' red in the face: 'Who locked me in that stinkin' head?', he wants to know. 'Place fuckin' *stank*.'

"Meanwhile, things have worked out just *perfectly*. Pussboy's girl-friend is back in her seat, but he's gotten up and wandered off—for all I know, he was the one who had to take a piss and let Ahearn out. Well, Danny sinks right into his seat. The girlfriend looks just-a-*little-bit-scared*, but she tries to tell him the seat's taken. Danny's lookin' confused, and just then I see pussboy coming up from behind him. Beautiful!

"'Danny,' I say, 'I think this is the man you been lookin' for.'

"Well, that was about *all* it took. The pussman taps him on the shoulder and says, 'Excuse me, sir'—no fuckin' lie, he says *sir*—'I be-lieve you've taken my seat.' Danny leans back like he's about to yawn or something, and then next thing I know his huge paw is slammin' into the guy's chest and pussboy is sprawled on the floor.

"Now what Danny hasn't noticed is that there are two cops by the front door, looking for high school kids or whatever. One of them, this huge black guy, sees the whole thing. He grabs his podner and before you know it, they're on top of Ahearn. Meanwhile Rist and I are backin' toward the door. Next thing you know we're back in the truck and headed east. When we got down to Ocean City and found the cousin, she was a little let down to find out Danny's coaches made him stay on campus, but let me assure you gentlemen that she had a good time that weekend. A *very* good time—almost as good as I did, in fact."

Stick leaned back and rattled the ice around in his cup while the hoots of laughter that had punctuated his story let loose again, longer and unexpectant now. But there was something else—hesitation, even a few groans. As they laughed they looked at one another out of the corner of their eyes: is this alright?

A tall raw-faced boy from Oklahoma who had stood stoic throughout the whole story said it. "Y'all just ditched him there?"

Stick's answer rang out like a gunshot: "Hey, the guy was a prick! Would you have wanted him in your chain of command? We just did the Nav' one huge fuckin' favor. Just let him do what he would've ended up doing sober anyway."

"He was a bastard, alright," someone murmured, and then a chorus of voices joined in corroboration. Danny Ahearn deserved whatever he got. "And let's not forget the most important thing," added another standing next to Stick, a tan boy whose hair glistened with gel. "You got laid!"

The party was back on.

It lasted well into the night and the following morning, spilling out into the bars downtown and back up the steep streets again to the huge stucco fortress. But what Wes would recall most keenly about that night, other than the story of Danny Ahearn itself, was the Oklahoman who stood alone before the crowd and spoke his mind as the firelight cast shadows around his eyes and beneath his broad cheekbones. He was gone from them within two weeks, one of the few who were immediately packed off to some surface ship that had room for them. Wes never saw him after that. But there were times in the months ahead when he would look back with envy not so much at the charisma of those who had won over the crowd that night, but instead at the readiness of the lone dissenter.

John, too, might have dissented that night, but it had probably taken him too long to get his thoughts together. He was the sort who thought too much.

That was Wes's assessment of his new roommate within the first few weeks of their living together. On the Monday following Stick's party they secured a lease at La Mirage, though they were not so lucky as he had been: they were assigned a room on the rear ground floor with a view of the steep hillside behind them. The few pieces of furniture they owned had already been shipped to the base, waiting for them, and the next day they moved in. John worked steadily until midafternoon and then collapsed into reading on the couch; his room—which he had set up painstakingly—would never be orderly again. Instead of cleaning it he would either read or come up with some extraneous project that never quite came to fruition. At the end of their first week together, Wes came home to find him sprawled on their deck trying to build a bird feeder. Months later it still sat unassembled next to an open bag of seed that lay half-buried beneath a flock of hungry swallows.

What made John's apparent fecklessness all the more laughable was that he was always trying to be practical. He constantly made lists of things to do—painting his room, tightening the seat on the toilet, rotating his tires. But he would become so absorbed with such tasks that he forgot more important things, like going to medical appointments or depositing his paycheck. Once he missed a flight to see his girlfriend—a social worker in Chicago who seemed to be steadily losing patience with him—because he had bought her a plant and lost track of time while he was musing over how to pack it.

Their joke was that John spent his whole life doing Cs.

One of the few "professional development" sessions Lieutenant Ragis had actually arranged during their orientation week was an official film on time management that recommended the aspiring leader write out his tasks and divide them into As, Bs, and Cs, in descending order of importance. If you concentrated on the As and put the Cs aside—preferably in a locked drawer—you would, the film advised, often find that the Cs were unnecessary or took care of themselves. Such advice was beneficial not only in uniform but also at home: "For what is life," the narrator intoned solemnly, "but a series of tasks to be managed?"

John, they decided, had gotten his alphabet mixed up.

Aside from creating superfluous projects, he liked to read, but much of what he read was the least practical sort of thing imaginable. On his floor, next to *Preventive Maintenance 101: How to Treat Your Car Like You'd Like to Be Treated* and *Designing Hammocks*, Wes saw books by Dante and Plato. One afternoon he came in to find John stretched on the deck reading *Hamlet*.

"Shouldn't you be building us a hamster cage or something, ensign?" Wes asked.

John smiled. "Just pondering the biggest A of them all, sir."

He said things like that occasionally, too, but it was hard to take him seriously with his crooked grin and his shock of hair drifting around in the afternoon breeze. Before Wes could respond he was suggesting that they go to the hardware store and look at materials for some new bookshelves.

Wes and John were the readers. That became clear soon after they moved in, the two of them settling easily into the ground floor and not buying a television for several weeks. All Wes really cared to watch was the news and for that he went upstairs, where Cullen had moved in with Stick and the TV was always on. Wes had never liked to miss the news, and now that he had so much time on his hands he liked to miss it even less.

It was suddenly a big question: what to do with time?

They had been told enough at the start to know it would be a question, of course. Then it had not quite sounded real. Before long, though, the unsettled routine that would mark their days became apparent.

They were to report on weekday mornings at 0800 to the TPU where sometimes there were minor administrative tasks for them to do, and, at least at the beginning, maybe one day a week they would tour some part of the base. Since they were at a weapons station they had a good opportunity to familiarize themselves with the national arsenal, everything from rifle bullets to stubby torpedoes and anti-surface missiles, even the long slender Tomahawks that could be launched from miles out to sea and guided to targets far inland. During the week ships pulled in—sleek frigates and destroyers, stately cruisers, great hulking amphibious assault ships with their cargo of Marines—to onload weapons and ammunition. The ships sat at the end of the single long pier across from the TPU, looming up into the pale sky, belching and spewing streams of steam and bilgewater into the dark sea. After a day or two they would leave, usually in the morning when Wes was pulling into the parking lot and could only lean against his car and look at them and wonder where they were bound.

Then he would go in and see if Lieutenant Ragis had come up with something for them to do. In the early weeks he concocted a number of administrative tasks for the ensigns. They filed reports, installed new bulletin boards, drew up a Standard Operating Procedure for cleaning the building. But such responsibilities were eventually usurped by Donkers, who was determined not to let his time in this forlorn waystation hurt his chances for career advancement. Compared to most of the other ensigns, who somehow managed to come in every morning looking exhausted, Donkers was a dynamo, a bustling worker bee. He had excellent clerical skills. Before long he had taken over the yeoman's office, a fact that the mostly Filipino enlisted men who ran it alternately deplored (when he was creating work for them to do) and appreciated (when he was actually doing their work). When Wes would leave the building at nine thirty or so the yeomen were already outside taking their first smoke break, and amidst their grimaces and murmuring snatches of Tagalog he could make out only one recurring word: "Donkers."

For Wes would usually leave by mid-morning. Occasionally Ragis did arrange some activity for them, either on their own base or at a nearby one—a few times they went to a nearby firing range, emptying clips of ammunition into stiff cardboard silhouettes that stared dumbly at them as bright holes opened up in the dark profiles—but otherwise there was nothing much to do after morning quarters. Often the ensigns would sit and read the paper in the conference room, most of them fighting over the sports section while Wes painstakingly worked his way through the headlines. A few of his colleagues enjoyed following domestic news, gossiping about the morally dubious shenanigans of assorted political figures, but Wes inevitably immersed himself in international affairs, in war and rumors of war and the men who made the wars happen.

Sometimes these were the topics of discussion at the beginning of morning quarters—what was happening in the Middle East or Europe and what the United States should do about it. Inevitably, however, the conversation deteriorated so that by the end of the hour they were arguing about sports or women. Wes noticed that after a few weeks these discussions began to build in intensity, as though they were about the most important things on earth. He found himself getting caught up in them (when else had he taken so much time to think about these things?) but he maintained a certain level of detachment. He was still, he believed, sovereign over himself, and that was the mastery in which he took most pride.

Not everyone was. At the beginning of the fourth week Wes walked into the conference room to find a crowd of ensigns sitting around the table. Stick and a boy named Hooper were leaning over the fashion section from the previous day's paper:

"Look at the tits on *her.*"

"Yeah, but I'm an ass man. *She's* the one." Hooper jabbed his finger at the opposite page.

"No way, man. I'm not backing down. Blondie is the clear winner."

"Bull-*shit.*"

"I've heard enough from you, Hooper. You hear me? Enough!" Stick had drawn his own middle finger back with his thumb, and as he said this he released it and gave Hooper a solid thwack on the wrist.

"You ass," Hooper yelled, and quickly popped Stick on the cheek like a girl.

Stick straightened up, and his eyes grew dark and narrow.

"Whoa, gentlemen, whoa!" Cullen, red in the face, jumped in between them. "To each his own. Save it for the real thing. You two keep messin' with one another's faces, neither of you'll be getting any."

The crowd was hooting, their initial interest only deepened by the quick bloodlust. A few grew quiet after Hooper's slap. But one low chuckle kept resounding from the far corner, and Wes looked over to see the warrant, cigar clamped between his yellow teeth. No one was supposed to smoke inside the building, but Ragis was away and he had undisputed dominion over the place—hell, he smoked in his office when Ragis was there. He wore a look of great satisfaction. As he got up and walked to the door, his muddy eyes wrinkled: "You men are makin' me proud. Real proud." The yellow smile flashed at them, and then he was gone.

Wes did his real reading at home.

That first month he bought a couple of new histories. All through the long bright afternoons he sat on the couch and studied overlooked Revolutionary War campaigns in the South, mouthing the forgotten names of Morgan and Tarleton and Greene. At intervals he would pause and lie on his back, looking at the thin fan spinning lightly in the center of the ceiling, or out the deck's sliding glass door—always open now—at the steep hillside and the lone spindly eucalyptus tree that grew there. Light sea breezes rippled the leaves and grass, turning them up to catch the brightness of the sun, and the steady slap of the fan blades overhead mingled with the faint murmur that always sounded beneath it, whether from the sea or from the freeway that ran behind the hills Wes could not tell. One moment he was lost with Francis Marion deep in the ancient Carolina swamps, and the next he was floating in the eternal present of the airy Pacific afternoon.

At first this was pleasant. But soon enough the thick books wore thin and he began to feel not so much bored as anxious. He looked at the clock more often. At moments in the middle of the afternoon he would be overcome by a sudden feeling that he had forgotten something, some important task that had to be accomplished. He did not know what it was. He would look out at the tree, and for a moment it would seem to be on the tip of his tongue, but he could never quite call it to mind.

What could men floating in the present—"dangling men," John called them—do?

One option was self-improvement. While a few, like Donkers, devoted themselves to their careers, others fixated on their bodies, worshipping the iron gods of the weight room. A couple of them read. At least one of their compatriots, a boy from New Jersey named Smith, committed himself to mastering the stock market. He was the sort who took notes during the time management film. He always wore his black hair slicked over to one side and a pair of glasses with tortoiseshell frames, and at morning quarters he looked down his nose at the ensigns who cut up in front of the crowd. He was as earnest as a young preacher. Once he cornered Wes in the hall outside the conference room, wagging his finger and staring him straight in the face: "Those guys need to straighten up. You have a responsibility for running your life, you know." He pointed out the window. "It's like a business."

He then proceeded to offer Wes a series of investment tips. *What is time? Time is money.*

Self-annihilation was another option, one almost all of them chose on occasion—at least in its limited form, the one that came in a bottle. Drink was a tricky thing because at first it was just a pleasure, not an escape from time so much as a way of capturing and bloating it, of slowing it down and soaking every moment with joy. Their weekends were almost immediately shaped by alcohol and the pleasures which went with it, so that Saturdays and Sundays became rounds of golf and parties and trips, long holidays that began to stretch into Thursdays and Mondays and finally to meet in the middle of the week. One afternoon he found himself at a racetrack with the others—about half the ensigns were there—watching Hooper fall down three rows of seats and break his ankle. In a moment of jarring clarity such as sometimes comes amidst bouts of heavy drinking, Wes saw the mangled limb sticking up above a chair, saw a horse and yellow-clad jockey in the background, glanced at his watch and suddenly realized that it was 3:10 on a Tuesday afternoon. They were all roaring drunk and there was nobody else at the track.

When he got back to the apartment that night he drank coffee for a while and then could not fall asleep, so he sat on the deck and read. Later he wandered around to the front of La Mirage and looked out at the sea and the stars. He was alone but thought about the others now. He wondered whether they were celebrating their freedom or denying the fact that it would all end soon. The drink could hold time for awhile but soon enough, he already knew, it would only drown everything.

After only a month of this Wes felt the days and hours and finally the minutes begin to decelerate. It was as if his life were a tape that was getting stuck at the head, wound tight around the spools that should have been spinning him toward an ever-clearer future but were instead dragging him slowly across the gaping mouth of the present. He had the last thing he wanted, which was time to think about time. He could dream about the future, but when it came to facts he had only the here and now, his own past, and that of the three others. For the one thing they all had was time to tell about the part of the tape that had already run by—their personal histories, where they were from and how they had come to be here.

Cullen (William Cullen, but he always went by the last name) was the simplest of them, and maybe it was for that reason that he became the center they all revolved around. Even in the first week, Wes would come home and go upstairs just to see what he was doing. Being around Cullen somehow made him feel like it was alright to have nothing in particular to do. But it was hard to find him alone—Stick was always there with the TV on, trying to lure his roommate into watching a mid-morning talk show or a live broadcast of Australian Rules Football. And Cullen, easily entertained, usually went along with it, just as he would with John's projects. Those two were always collaborating on something. Building tables or chairs, putting together surf-fishing rigs. Cullen was the handier of the two. John seemed mainly a big dreamer when it came to these kinds of things, and they usually relied on Cullen when they actually needed something fixed.

He mainly contented himself with doing simple things around the apartment, but had come up with one completely impractical project of his own. He bought an old sailboat, not quite seaworthy, which he parked in a corner of La Mirage's lot and worked on at odd intervals. The boat had been advertised in the local paper, and one Tuesday afternoon they had all driven down the coast together to take a look at it. South of town and a couple of miles inland they came to a decrepit little house stuck back in an orange grove at the top of a dry hill; behind it the trees gave out and there was a broad view of the long coastline. When they knocked on the screen door a couple of mutts pushed it open, and behind them came the owner, a middle-aged man with a shaggy beard that reeked of pot and dog. He looked at their hair and asked if they were military and said he had been in Vietnam, or actually Guam, where he was a Navy radio-man and first started "doin' weed, you know," and he thought that was all pretty cool but he was glad it was over now and "you guys are the ones out there doin' it, you know, and I can just sit back and enjoy life like it's the real bowl of cherries, you know, like the saying goes?" Then he took them back behind the house where they saw a big tarp draped over something in the corner of the yard. He pulled it off and showed them a little sloop about twenty feet long that had mushrooms growing in patches on the hull. But Cullen hopped in it and walked around the mast and asked for a hose. He ran water over the boat for a while and climbed in and out and under it, and the owner kept talking to him and lowering the price, and Cullen fi-nally said he'd take it. Then the guy offered them all a beer, and they sat on the boat and watched the sun go down while Cullen and the owner talked about fishing and the mutts dozed at their feet. Soon enough their host had gotten out a bong, called up his buddies, and was telling the four of them to stick around because he had some ladies coming over.

It was only when the ladies turned out to be fat, over forty, and laden with more drug paraphernalia that they hitched the boat trailer to Stick's truck and said their farewells. The four of them drove out of the grove under the same broad moon their host had told them hov-ered over Guam twenty years ago.

That was the kind of thing Cullen always led them into, not by design but by nature. It was as if he were in fact the slightly naughty Boy Scout he looked like, with his boyish smile and clean-cut face, a mischievous innocent who camps out in the back yard only to end up kidnapping and maybe accidentally maiming one of the neighbor's cats. When Wes was with Cullen he felt like that was the kind of thing that might happen and it would be fine. Whatever they did, there would not be much harm done, and in fact not much needed to be done at all.

They could sit around and watch sports and talk and fix up sailboats and that was enough. It was like being twelve years old again.

Cullen came from a big family in a small city in southern Pennsylvania. He spent a lot of time keeping up with them, especially one older brother who had gone to West Point and was stationed with a tank unit in Georgia. After learning this Wes tried to imagine that maybe it was some kind of sibling rivalry that drove Cullen to Annapolis, but finally he could not. Cullen was too uncomplicated to be jealous. He was a baseball player, had even walked on for a year or two at the Academy, and one framed photo he kept on his desk—him in his uniform, arms around two teammates—seemed to capture his essential nature: the all-American boy. His family fit the bill, too. His father had started out as a laborer but was now part owner of a small construction company, and his mother was mainly a homemaker who volunteered sometimes at the county hospital. Their picture sat next to the baseball photo. Smiling, well-fed faces. It was easy to imagine them in their backyard, surrounded by pets and children while they handed hamburgers to their neighbors and shyly accepted compliments about the two boys they had sent off to serve their country.

Cullen had been at Annapolis the same four years as Stick, though they had not known one another. Stick had not come there in the usual way. He had a mediocre record in high school but had been accepted to the Naval Academy Preparatory School because his father had been killed in action—shot down over Vietnam—and received a Navy Cross posthumously. The Academy made some allowances for such cases. So Stick left his mother in southern Florida and made his way to Rhode Island for a year before going to Annapolis. The prep school taught him how to study, and he spent his first year at the Academy quietly, slogging his way through classes. But in later years he had become a figure of some renown, first for his clever malice in tormenting plebes—he had a special gift at bestowing nicknames, saving the worst for those who could bear it least. In the long grey mornings around the conference table Wes heard stories about one thin bespectacled blond boy who had entered with the class two years behind Stick; he was apparently brilliant, with near perfect SATs and plans to major in nuclear engineering, but after Bill Simonich became Plebe Semenbreath he did not last long. Stick fixated on the boy and pursued him, so the stories went, with the undaunted single-mindedness that Wes had already begun to recognize in him. It was a trait that had doubtlessly helped get him through school, enabling him to lock himself away with his books even when such pursuits were antithetical to his temperament. Though he did not seem bright, he clearly possessed a certain dull intelligence that served him well in pursuing his particular ends. He had fumbled his way through courses and had been briefly charged in a cheating scandal before being officially exonerated by an honor court. That was just prior to the Ahearn trial, and may in fact have saved Stick from being implicated in it: the Academy had suffered a spate of bad publicity and hoped to involve as few midshipmen as possible in the athlete's case.

It was largely Stick's perfect vision and peculiar charisma—he was good at getting along with those of his own or superior rank—that had gotten him into flight school. Like most of the Academy grads, however, who had all missed out on the general run of collegiate hedonism, he was enjoying his current break from training. All his skills were now employed in the pursuit of pleasure and women. After their first few weeks together Wes had formed a composite image of the tall figure—lean, hungry-looking, drink in hand—propping his elbow on a bar and introducing himself to a fuzzy succession of girls, always as "Stick." Wes had heard his real first name but never cared enough to remember it.

John seemed the least remarkable of them all, though in a way he was, from the beginning, the most distinctive. He was the only one who had not gone to a military college. Within their first month of living together Wes had pieced together his new roommate's background: his father was an army doctor, his mother a war protester turned English teacher. They had formed an unlikely couple when they met in the sixties, but it worked out, and they—with a brood of children large as that of the Cullens—spent a typical military career moving across the country, even living for a while in West Germany and Korea. When the time came for John to go to college he enrolled at a small liberal arts college in New England, but after his mother contracted cancer he transferred to the state college near his family's last post in the Midwest. When she died a year later, John enrolled in the campus NROTC program, went through a summer of training, and picked up a scholarship. He did it in part to help the family financially. But there were other reasons as well.

"I had avoided it before because I didn't necessarily want to live my dad's life," he told Wes one afternoon while he was sitting on the floor and putting together an aquarium. "So I went off to this artsy-fartsy school where I thought I'd learn something, but all I found was a bunch of rich kids wearing tie-dyes and snorting coke and driving European cars. Then after what my mom went through I just didn't want to go back to that, and I knew it would help to get the ROTC money. Plus I suddenly realized there were things I liked about the military, you know." He was fiddling with the water filter, trying to attach a tube to it, when he looked straight up at Wes. "Sometimes it's good to be told what to do."

Maybe John thought so because he had the sort of eclectic mind that seemed to make it difficult for him to concentrate on any one thing for long. Unfortunately, that included his long-suffering girl-friend in Chicago. Two months into their assignment he flew back to see her one final time. On a quiet Sunday morning when Wes was just realizing that he missed having his new roommate around, the apartment door opened and there stood John, home a day early. "Well, that's that," he said, strolling in nonchalantly. She had dumped him. Wes stood ready to offer consolation—and above all to hear the de-tails, since this seemed to be one of the few things that had actually happened to any of them since they had been there—but John sim-ply made a sandwich and began to read the paper. After half an hour he disappeared, only to show up eight hours later with wet hair and incipient sunburn on his fair cheeks. He had secured a part-time job as a lifeguard at a nearby public pool and had already saved one fat Pakistani boy from drowning.

That was a day when two things happened, and somehow John, the most feckless of them all, had been at the center of both. Not much else had happened to them yet, unless you counted Cullen and the sailboat. It was a gift, maybe—being able to make things happen. That was what Wes decided, and it made him a little jealous, jealous of

Cullen and even of his own roommate, who most of the time seemed unable to get anything done at all.

And it didn't help that both of John's things had happened on a Sunday. That was the worst day. It had always been the day when Wes could not help but notice time.

When he was a boy it had not been so bad. Sunday mornings he had been roused early, stuffed into a dress shirt, and hauled off to endure church, where he looked out the window or, later, at the girls around him. But time's rich reward came when he and his parents emerged into the day and drove past flowered lawns slowly back home to where the air already hung thick with the smell of roast beef. Sunday dinner: thick moist meat and soft potatoes with gravy that ran into the salty green beans and rice, the dripping yellow corn—all on the good plates, and the cool amber tea in a tall glass that the sun shone through when he lifted it up to drink. He would eat until he had had enough and then lie on his back beneath a window to watch the dust motes drift through the long slanting beams of the sun. There he could hear the *clink* of the dishes from the kitchen and the soft sonatas playing in his father's study, smell the burley pipe tobacco begin to blend with the lingering aroma of the meal. The motes danced slowly in the thick air above him, drifting and spinning like miniature planets. On those boyhood Sunday afternoons he was full and the world was full, and he could just be there, in time but not even aware that it was passing.

It was when he went off to college that it all started to change. His first semester at the state university he slept in Sunday mornings and was glad of it. When he woke, he and his roommates swapped stories about the night before, and then maybe later in the day he would do some studying. But there was a gap in the middle of the day that began to widen. And by then it was no different when he went home. Even before he left, his father had begun to take his history more seriously and started to devote his weekends entirely to research and writing. His mother would still go to church sometimes, but more and more often she just went out to the garden to pull up weeds. Wes would pass his father's study and see him bent low there, head in hand, framed against the huge bay window; outside was the garden, thick, overgrown, littered with streaks of green flung from his mother's hand.

She had quit cooking, too. The day lost all rhythm, and whenever Wes came home that year he just slept in and ate cereal and felt bored and hungry. So he mostly stayed at school until the aimless freedom there drove him out, too.

Later at the Institute there was order again, but even there he found a Sunday emptiness that puzzled and horrified him, an emptiness he had to fill up with exercise and reading, with a discipline that came only from himself.

One of the worst things about his new life, he realized, was that suddenly he was living the veritable month of Sundays, the time between times that was supposed to be full but was not. Every day was Sunday now, every moment pregnant with silence.

For a while the histories of the others filled that silence up, histories told and hinted at in bits and pieces over those few months. They were histories that were not even yet clear except for the fact that they had, like Wes's own, come to an indefinite halt in a dreamlike *now*.

What was so bad about leaning back free in the thin California sunshine? Nothing, Ragis had told them. But it was not long until Wes recognized again what he had known before, what had driven him to the Institute—that the mundane was inadequate. What was one to do in an untroubled here and now? With no future assigned to him, he could only reach backwards or outwards.

That was why he kept up with the news, a paper or two in the morning and then, when he came home before lunch, CNN. Within a month he and John had bought their own TV and placed it against the central wall that ran perpendicular to the deck's sliding door. Wes kept it on the news channel. While the rich noontime light flooded down the green hillside and painted the eucalyptus white, he would eat a tuna sandwich and watch images of Berlin or Jerusalem flicker across the glass screen. Still and ordinary as his life was, there were things going on elsewhere. Of that there could be no doubt.

One Saturday afternoon before he walked down to the ocean, he watched a journalist interview an old man in Leningrad, an old man about to turn eighty. He had been born when the city was St. Petersburg and a czar ruled the Russian Empire. He was a boy during the October Revolution, grew to young manhood under Lenin, fought against Hitler on the long steppes between the Oder and Moscow. Then he was thrown in the gulag for ten years because he had muttered something about Stalin. All that before he was fifty; now here he was, stooped and near toothless, and his city was about to become St. Petersburg again. Beneath a shock of white hair he smiled up with one black tooth at the American journalist, a black man named Shea who sounded not like the black boys Wes had gone to high school with but just like the rest of the news team. Shea smiled a perfect white smile at the Russian: "And sir, what will you do to celebrate your birthday?"

Then the broadcast cut back to Atlanta and a report from Hollywood about the summer box office.

After Wes turned off the TV he walked down to the beach and looked out across the broad sea. Somewhere across there, he knew, was Vladivostok (he liked the name: the relentless consonants, the hard os), homeport of the Soviet Pacific Fleet. He had studied it on a map back in his ROTC classroom, sitting by a window under the cool Appalachian pines as he marveled at the vast blue expanse that stretched out on the wall before him. Now he was actually there, by the great western ocean, and if he only knew exactly where to look he could gaze in a straight line toward Vladivostok, a line that did not cross land.

But what did that matter now? The great port was only an oily harbor littered with rusting hulls.

The Cold War was over. The reports had been ringing out all year in predictable phrasing: communism is collapsing the world over, a new flag flies in Moscow, Germans are tearing down the wall that has divided their country. A new birth of freedom in Europe. All this was true and Wes supposed he should think it was good, but instead he kept thinking of years spent studying the Soviet fleet. Not his own—he had not been at it that long, after all—but the years of men like Ragis and his elders, men who had devoted their lives to formulating a doctrine of war that was now suddenly irrelevant. The great enemy had collapsed and, it seemed, the wide world lay open before them. They would once again have to begin figuring out what to do with it.

Wes stretched out close to the surf. The tide was going out; still the waves rushed in to fling themselves on the shore, withdrew in slow cadence only to mount again in a long, tremulous roar. Gulls dove and wheeled against the glaring blue sky. He closed his eyes for a while and then opened them to look out to sea. A great seabird plunged headlong into the rolling indigo expanse before him, emerged again with a writhing fish.

The world he saw was new, clean, full of beauty. But he could only look at it for a moment before the question came back: what was he supposed to be doing here?

He turned his gaze back to the land and the houses, and there between him and the rest of the world was a group of women playing volleyball. He looked closer, and they looked good.

It occurred to him that, whatever had gone on before or was going on elsewhere, here and now there was a group of healthy young American women frolicking on a peaceful beach. Surely he had no reason to complain—surely this was a good time and place to be.

He sat up straight and looked again.

A tall, swarthy woman with long brown hair broke away from the crowd and chased a ball down the beach. After a few steps she scooped it up and loped back toward the net, stepping gingerly through the loose sand.

He had lived a long time away from women, and women, he had begun to remember, could make things happen.

Midway through that summer, when it became clear that the ensigns were at the TPU for the long haul, Ragis set up a security watch (what were they watching for? There was vague talk of Islamic terrorists, but since it happened shortly after Hooper's injury they took the whole thing as a half-hearted attempt to discipline them). Once every two weeks each of them would report to the building, sign in, receive a pistol, and spend four hours patrolling the TPU and the nearby docks. Always there was an engineer on watch at the same time, and sometimes these were enlisted women. This arrangement lasted until one night a fat ensign from Kansas was caught naked with an engineer in a training boat. He was discharged, and the watches were discontinued shortly thereafter. Ragis had apparently decided that Muslim extremists posed less of a threat to the ensigns than female sailors did.

That was not much, but it was one of the few events that happened that summer. It was a good story even if it was pretty sordid and not the sort of thing Wes wanted to be involved in. But anyhow it reminded him how things went with women around. Things changed.

Later he could see it clearly. In those first few months when they were thrown together, they could sit and talk about the past because it seemed like everything had already happened, maybe was happening elsewhere, but for them it had stopped. When August began they were still waiting. But then two things happened: Iraq invaded Kuwait, and the women showed up.

Part Two

August, 1990 - January, 1991

4

Wes saw her first.

Maybe the others had noticed, glimpsed her across the courtyard when she first came to stay with Elizabeth, but they never said anything. Even if they had—well, he was the one who approached her, the first to learn her name.

Cynthia had not been easy on him from the start.

They were standing in the courtyard. The last rays of the sun slanted down the red roof and into the bright turquoise water of the pool, itself lit from within and shimmering like a jewel. He had had a few drinks and was talking to her and wondering what to say as he went. It was not as though he and his situation were not ridiculous. So he was telling her about watching the ships pull in and out on their way to the Gulf now: "It's pretty strange being stationed at the weapons base, you know, it's really just an ammunition dump. It's — just a…"

"Powderkeg waiting to explode?" She arched an eyebrow and tilted her bottle at him. A quick smile broke out beneath her bright eyes, and he had the sudden sense that she had already anticipated anything he might possibly say for the rest of the night.

With four words and that look she had given him the impression that his whole life was a cliché. He did not like that, but later he knew that it was in fact what he liked about her—both that she could immediately see such a thing and that she could smile at him as if she had some secret knowledge of how it might be otherwise. For she said it not too brusquely, and her smile tapered off with a twinge of mercy. If she had been a different kind of girl she would have swatted his forearm with her hand and forced out a giggle; that was what most of the women he had known at home would have done if it had crossed their minds to say such a thing. But this one stood back with one arm tucked under the other and looked at him with wry sympathy before her eyes shifted to something in the middle distance, then grew unfocused and shiny. She lifted the bottle to her mouth, not to drink but to blow across the top of it, absent-mindedly, like a child trying to coax out its deep hollow ring.

He could not say how long they talked. They had stopped and she was gazing off over his right shoulder when he heard a booming voice call out over his left. He winced. Stick and Cullen were approaching out of the deep violet night that had descended around them, and he had just enough time to regret the intrusion before Stick leaned between the two of them and looked straight at Cynthia: "Well, ma'am, I see you've met the Colonel."

Cynthia immediately scrunched up her mouth and bent into herself as if to better inspect these newcomers. Later he would see that this was a habit of hers, one that made her seem to be always peering up at him. She was of above average height, but her posture hid it.

Cullen hung back a little, but spoke up when he saw Cynthia's perplexed brow: "Wesley here is our resident Southern gentleman."

"Well"—Cynthia was eyeing them all suspiciously, "he certainly has been polite."

The other three had recently dubbed Wes "Colonel Hammond," a title they pronounced with a syrupy mock drawl. At first he was surprised. He had never really thought of himself as Southern before, except occasionally around the few Northerners at the Institute, mostly boys from New Jersey. But now he sometimes caught himself talking and realized that his words came slow and deep. It was a strange feeling, as though he were listening to someone else. But because of the way he talked, and for other reasons he was not clear about, he had become the designated Southerner. Stick now tried to incorporate him into his pick-up routines. At first Wes didn't mind playing along, but he had begun to be annoyed by the triviality of it. And at that moment especially, he realized, he just wanted Stick—even Cullen—to go away.

But they remained and before long he had Cynthia even less to himself. It was the Friday night of La Mirage's inaugural "Gala Community Cookout." This was an event Wes and John had been gently mocking ever since they moved in, at which time they had been informed of its existence by Elizabeth, the on-site property manager. She was a thin, attractive Virginia girl, as enthusiastic as a cheerleader, who had first shown him and John their apartment, chatting and laughing and glossing over the drawbacks of the hillside view. She sold it to them and then disappeared for six weeks afterwards, but by July she had returned. Now she was everywhere. Earlier that day she had stopped by to re-invite them.

Out of the side of his eye Wes had seen her corner John on the other side of the pool earlier in the evening, and now that Cullen and Stick had arrived the two of them walked over. "The famous Cullen!" she exclaimed, walking up and hugging him around the neck so that the loose bottoms of her baggy pants pulled up to show her bare ankle bones. She had never met him before.

"Look at these guys! Don't they look great?" She was beaming now, directing her comments to Cynthia but looking them all over. "You can't have them all to yourself, woman. I'm just glad I beat Terri out here!"

John was rubbing his forehead while the rest of them appraised Elizabeth. She held a mug and was drinking not beer but black coffee, hopping from one tiny sandaled foot to the other as she talked. Stick opened his mouth to say something, but she beat even him to the draw.

"But I am forgetting my duties as your hostess, gentlemen. As the official spokeswoman for La Mirage, let me bid you welcome!" She held a surprisingly long arm out in salute.

"Well, thanks." Cullen laughed gently as he said this, but his glance was uncharacteristically wary.

"You're welcome!" She bent over laughing, spilled coffee on her toes, shook them dry, laughed again, then stood up and leaned against John. "WoooOOOOoooh! Don't worry, guys, I'm not a total geek! Just doing my job—and I love it! Not the people who run the place—they're OK, lots of cash but kinda boring—but living here, it's great! And now we all live here." She slowed down and took a sip of her drink. "Isn't this gonna be fun, guys? We're creating a little *com-mu-ni-ty*." She simpered and pursed her lips at them, then wheeled around to survey the rest of the courtyard before she suddenly yelled, "Hey—TERRI!—you gotta come meet these guys!" and jogged off to intercept a blond woman on the other side of the courtyard. The two of them stumbled into another cluster of people before they could make their way over. Across the glowing blue water they could see Elizabeth as animated as before, standing in the half-light beneath a heat lamp, rocking from side to side and bouncing her knees up and down. But there was something strange about her profile. Wes later tried to think of the word for how she looked—that was a thing he did not often do, but in the months to come he found that he had to tell himself the story of this night— and finally he knew it was *brittle*.

But then all his attention immediately went back to the woman next to him. While the rest of them were gazing at Elizabeth with a kind of awe, Cynthia was looking too, arms still crossed. Her face revealed nothing. When they all turned to her as if for an explanation she only shook her head and said, "That girl."

"She rocks!" Stick was delighted. "Look at her! She doesn't stop!" He took a big hit from his drink as he gazed across the pool with admiration. "We've gotta get her and her buddy back over here."

But before he had a chance to do anything she returned of her own accord with Terri, an attractive blond who had little to say. She was a willing listener, however, and Stick immediately took her by the ear while Elizabeth talked and beamed at the rest of them until Wes quit listening to what she said and just looked at her. She had a pretty face—not angular but smooth, with rounded features that reminded Wes of pictures he had seen of his grandmother as a young girl. Her smile was broad, though the edges of her teeth looked somehow worn and gray. It was easy to see her and Terri clearly because he was able to look straight at them, something he found he could not do with Cynthia. But she was fully *there*, a presence he found himself glimpsing at askance—what to *say* to her?

The question became more urgent when Elizabeth tugged on John's sleeve and pulled him aside. That left Wes and Cullen facing one another with Cynthia by their side. Wes tried to convince himself that it was good just to be able to talk to Cullen, whom he rarely saw alone; they joked about some things that had happened at the TPU that week, and that got Cullen going about Lieutenant Ragis and on from there into an Academy story. Wes listened appreciatively at first because he always enjoyed Cullen's stories but also because he was glad to have his friend fill up the silence while he stole glances at Cynthia, who seemed lost in her own thoughts. But soon Wes noticed that she was listening with an appraising eye, and it began to make him uneasy. He felt that he had to do something and so he began to answer Cullen with stories of his own. But while he was noticing her and feeling uneasy and wondering what to do, Cullen leaned over and looked straight at her and said the simplest thing:

"You must be getting tired of listening to us. Come on and tell us something so we don't get too full of ourselves."

And she smiled and joined in.

So that first night they were all there and ate together and went down into the town, and before the night was done Elizabeth ran into at least a dozen other people she knew. Stick disappeared with Terri. So Wes was left together with Cynthia and Cullen and John and that was good, but when they sat together at the end of the night and the bar was so loud that they could not hear one another well, he noticed that it was good talking to Cynthia or Cullen but not talking to John because that meant Cynthia was talking to Cullen. He knew it then for the first time: he did not like that.

The next morning he woke to the sound of war.

He was dozing, only half aware of the dim light that leaked through his bedroom curtains, when the roar of engines and the pulsing hum of helicopter blades pulled him from his bed. He sat bolt upright as a deep, standard American voice drowned out the machinery: "The Persian Gulf. Aboard the *USS Independence*..."

He stumbled into the next room where he found the TV on. John was sitting in front of a CNN broadcast. On the screen was Shea, earnestly grasping a microphone as he struggled to stand erect in the wake of a great Sea Knight helicopter that dangled over his shoulder, banking its fat body on two spindly rotors like a giant dragonfly.

"Anything new?" Wes asked.

"They sent airborne troops in from the East Coast last night. And they're calling up medical reservists." John looked at him glumly. He did not normally keep up with the news—Wes should have been the first one in front of the TV today—but he had been following this as closely as any of them.

They had watched it all on the little screen in their living room. It had been just a few days now since the Iraqi army poured into Kuwait, rolling through the desert oilfields and on down into the port city. Squat Soviet-made tanks circled through the streets of the capital; now more were supposedly massing on the Saudi Arabian border. The president had called a news conference the night before, just before they went to the cookout. His skin looked slightly discolored, and sweat popped through his makeup as he leaned against the podium: "My fellow Americans," he said grimly, "we are suddenly faced with a diabolical threat both to the security of our allies and to our own vital national interests."

It had not been a very good speech, Wes thought—this was no Churchill—but it was war talk and he knew it. So did the others. They had not talked about it much but they all knew: it might really happen *now*. Wes felt it the first day of the invasion, when he walked down to the beach to read the paper. It was a great mystery—there was no other word for it—a mystery how out of the silent, languid days of summer this thing had sprung, this thing (what was it? this event, this opportunity) over which they had no control and might come for them.

John sat upright with his hands on his knees and watched silently as the camera showed American tanks now, rolling through the sleepy, moss-draped streets of Savannah and into a transport ship. But soon enough he got up and went into his room to read while Wes stayed and lost himself in the images that flickered across the screen. They seemed somehow both new and familiar at once. He felt strangely animated, expectant. It was as if he, after a long absence, were finally on his way home.

"My brother's on his way there."

"What? Already?" Wes and John looked up at Cullen in disbelief.

He had come down at lunchtime. It was unusual for him to stop by their apartment, but there he was, in the middle of a Saturday afternoon, not working on his sailboat but stopping in to talk. He sat at the one small table across from Wes, next to John.

"My mom just called. They'd been on the phone with him this morning. He's gonna try me later today—actually leaves sometime next week."

"Mech Infantry, right?" Wes remembered.

"Yep." Cullen nodded.

"How's he doing?"

"Good as he can, I guess. Probably can't believe it—*I* can't believe it. When we talked last week he was just telling me about some girl he was seeing in Atlanta. And how sick he was of training."

"That's something." Wes paused. "Does he think they're ready?"

"Don't know. Shit, how much has he even thought about it? The real thing, I mean. Guess I'll find out more when he calls."

John had been staring down at the floor but looked up now. "What time's he calling?"

"After four."

"I was thinking about doing some fishing. What do you say?"

Cullen bit his lip. "Sure."

"Let's go, then." John walked back to his room and emerged a few minutes later with the gear. He always seemed a little clumsy with these things and was too fair-skinned to convincingly play the outdoorsman—even with his lifeguard job he somehow managed to keep a perpetual burn rather than a tan—but standing there with his rod and net he looked more at ease than he had all morning.

It was quiet in the apartment until Stick came by at mid-afternoon. He had been in Terri's apartment since last night and wanted to tell someone all about it. Wes did not ask for the details, but they came anyway. He was beginning to get angry—not with Stick for doing and telling all this, but with himself for being in a situation where he had nothing better to do than listen to it—when Stick finally stopped. "Anyhow, she's alright. And her friends are definitely cool," he said. "We gotta see more of them."

But they did not, either that night or the next. When Cullen got back from fishing his brother called and must have sounded fine, because he suddenly came down to the apartment with a grin and a swagger and asked, "Who's up for San Diego?"

At the beach he and John had run into two other ensigns who were going down the coast for the night. Someone somebody knew was having a party. Wes was getting tired of that kind of thing—they had done it a lot recently—showing up among strangers, wasting the night away. But when Cullen was in a good mood it was hard to resist him. So he assented and felt fine about it until John backed out at the last minute.

His absence began to bother Wes more and more as the afternoon went on. What could John have to do with himself that night? he wondered on the drive down. It made him feel like his roommate must know something that he didn't.

The three of them found the party down below La Jolla. There was a reggae band and Hooper and some other ensigns and a lot of students from San Diego State. They stayed up most of the night drinking, and then they passed out on the beach.

Wes woke at dawn and sat bolt upright with sand falling from his hair. There were gulls circling overhead and seaweed washed up in mounds down by the surf. A dead fish lay on the sand near his feet. He looked along the empty beach, the morning as gray and silent as if it were eons ago and he were the first mammal crawling out of the primordial ocean. It was almost peaceful until he felt a sudden pang of anxiety, as if he had slept through an important appointment. He thought for a while and he knew there was nothing.

When he turned and saw Cullen and Stick sprawled on the sand above him and the houses up on the bluff, he felt a little better. But he could not go back to sleep. So he went down and jumped in the cold water and then walked up the street to buy a newspaper.

When the other two woke he was ready to go home, but they wanted to spend the afternoon looking around. Finally they wandered into Tijuana for a few hours. It was too much for Wes to take in at once, this jumble of rundown, low-lying buildings and streets—everywhere short, dark people and the smell of burnt corn, children running out of alleys to sell Chiclets. Crossing the border again near twilight, he looked back and saw the houses and the haze stretching up over the hills and far away southwards; all the drive through San Diego, past its tall, shimmering buildings and manicured landscapes, he felt that other country stretching long and smoky, mysterious, behind him. Further up the freeway he saw the yellow signs with their silhouettes warning drivers to beware not of crossing deer or schoolchildren but immigrants: stick figures, a woman dragging a child behind her. Her hair blew loose in the wind, disheveled from the rush of her headlong flight. Wes was looking at her when he dozed off in the passenger's seat, but the women who ran through his sleep were the ones he had met two nights before.

And as they ran he heard Stick and Cullen talking about Mexico, about the clubs and the drinks and the women they had seen coming out onto the streets at dusk. He could not tell for sure, but he thought it was Cullen who said it:

"We need to go back down there sometime soon."

When they got back that night John was sitting on the couch and reading.

Wes collapsed beside him, exhausted but curious. "What have you been doing all weekend, ensign?"

John grinned. He had to know that the other three were formulating hypotheses about his doings. "All sorts of things." He closed his book—Pascal's *Pensees* (he was in one of his A reading cycles lately, Wes had noticed)—and thought for a second. "I saw Elizabeth and the rest today."

"Had the ladies all to yourself. Very clever." If it had been Stick or even Cullen, Wes might have felt a twinge of jealousy, but it was hard to with John.

"So a Saturday night and a Sunday and all you have to say is that you saw Elizabeth." He looked John over again—the usual light burn. He must have been lifeguarding. "And do you have yourself a date?"

John was up and walking toward his room, but smiled as he looked back. "I have one for all of us. Baseball game—tomorrow night." He shut the door to his room for a few moments before it opened again and he asked, "Oh yeah. How was San Diego?" as though it had just occurred to him that the three of them had been gone.

The next night was as fine a summer evening as they could have asked for. Coming down the freeway the long sky stretched pale and burnt orange before them, bounded only by the fine line of grey mountains off in the east. Behind the billboards, palms rose up black against the sharp dying light, their fronds lifting gently in the cool breeze above an endless succession of low dusty houses; lights began to flicker on in the dusk, enough to rival the stars that had already begun to appear dimly overhead. Just ahead, set up on a hill, rose the white bulk of the stadium.

Wes was trying to listen to the news on the car radio.

It was not easy with all the noise. All seven of them, the four men and the three women too, had crammed into Stick's Blazer. He had somehow ended up front with Stick while John and Cullen rode behind with Cynthia. Terri and Elizabeth were in the far back. This was a mistake, Wes soon realized, because the two loudest people—Stick and Elizabeth—were at opposite ends of the vehicle and yelling at one another constantly. The three in the middle were talking, too. They were even more distracting because he was interested enough in their conversation to try to follow it.

But just now he was trying to listen to the news.

That morning Ragis had not been at the TPU. Off in San Diego at a meeting, a yeoman said. But he would be back the next day and would call a conference with all the ensigns. What about? Wes had asked. Don't know, sir, shrugged the yeoman. "Presumably he has some important information to relay to us," Donkers cut in, appearing from behind a file cabinet and tossing a condescending look at

Wes. "But right now we have other business to attend to here, Ensign Hammond, thank you very much."

It was about the Gulf, Wes thought. There was so much going on now—suddenly you heard about it everywhere—that they were bound to get caught up in it somehow. He just knew it.

And so he listened to the news more intently than ever before because he knew it was no longer significant only in the abstract. Now, he realized, it might at last have bearing upon *him*. And so he listened.

But the noise around him! The others were not paying attention; they seemed like war was the last thing on their minds. Even Cullen, who had a brother already caught up in it, was lost in talk. He and John and Cynthia had been at it the whole ride out. Wes tried to ignore them and strained his ear to hear about these places he had never been before: Riyadh, Bahrain, Qatar. Were they really in his same world? A teenage girl in a red convertible sped past them as a reporter speculated on the future of oilfields in the middle of the barren Kuwaiti desert. The captain of the carrier *USS Independence*—now steaming toward the Straits of Hormuz—answered questions about possible missile threats while a smiling Asian woman handed them a bucket of chicken at the drive-through of an El Pollo Loco.

Just when the others began to pay attention, the radio cut to an ad for a new waterslide theme park outside Escondido.

Then they were at the stadium. Parked. Stick opened the back of the Blazer, where Elizabeth and Terri had been sitting on a cooler, and they put together some supper. There was a light breeze and the sky was beginning to fade to blue. All around them people were streaming in toward the game: old people, children, families. He sat and ate, and for a moment he forgot the news and just looked at the world around him. He began to enjoy himself. He got a drink and went to talk with the women.

And inside the stadium Cynthia sat down next to him.

"You a big baseball fan?" she asked.

"Not really. I can't ever watch it on TV. Too slow. But sometimes it's not bad sitting in the park and looking around."

She smiled. "Good. Me too."

John and Cullen sat on her other side, while Stick was a row below them with Elizabeth and Terri. Those three were raucous from the start, and Cullen was subject to occasional outbursts—he was mostly watching intently or providing game commentary to John—after the first pitch was thrown.

That left Wes and Cynthia almost alone.

He had already started to learn a few things about her. She was a journalist and came from a northern Kentucky town, near Cincinnati, but she had gone east for college. That was where she met Elizabeth, who had graduated a year before her. When she finished school in May, she had a job offer at home and another possibility in D.C. But before she made any decisions she set off on a cross-country trip with "a friend." (Wes's ears prickled: why was this "friend" gender-neutral?) They stopped to visit Elizabeth in San Agustin and Elizabeth already knew half the town and introduced Cynthia to an editor at the county's mid-sized paper. The paper had a job coming open, "a real reporting job. It's just covering local news, but the other two leads I had were boring. Copyediting work. They would've paid more, but I would've lost my mind.

"Besides," she said, looking at him askance in a way that made him want to move closer, "I thought it might be interesting to spend a few years looking at this California place." She sat up and looked straight ahead. "But only a few."

"What does your friend think about that?"

"What friend?"

"The one you drove out here with."

"The one—Staci?" Cynthia looked puzzled. "Why would she care? I think she's glad to have someone to visit out here." She threw him a quizzical look but suddenly broke into a quick smile and looked back out at the game.

He got up to get a drink and asked her if she wanted anything and brought her back an ice cream cone. Then it was his turn to answer questions. He thought she must have been a good reporter, because he felt like he was being interviewed. She sat and looked at him soberly, attentive but somehow skeptical. Her brow wrinkled as if she were weighing every word he said. Where are you from? What do you think of this place? The way she held her ice cream, he felt like he was speaking into a microphone.

Why did you want to go to a military college?

"Nothing else was good enough."

She frowned. "What does that mean?"

"I went to a big state school for a year and it just seemed useless. I wasn't learning much and nobody really seemed to care. My grades were fine and I was about to major in business, but when I thought about what I'd be doing, it just didn't seem worth it."

"Worth the effort of going to school?"

"Yeah—not that it *was* that much effort—and worth actually doing it, too. I mean, once I'd gotten a job. What was I going to do with my life? Sell some product I didn't care about. Help my bosses make a lot of money."

"So you wanted to do something noble. Something you really believed in?"

He sat up. "Well—sort of. Something hard, at least. Something that didn't seem so *ordinary*."

"So ordinary is bad." She licked her ice cream and looked at him.

"Well. It's not good enough. All the time, anyway."

"Well, what you're doing now certainly isn't ordinary."

"What do you mean?"

"Having all this time to sit around and do nothing and get paid for it."

She had not said it accusingly, but for just a second he felt angry. He did not just sit around and do nothing. "I don't just sit around and do nothing."

"What do you do?"

"Read. Think." He tried to come up with something else, something impressive, but he couldn't. Get drunk? "Go to the gym."

She smiled. "Sounds pretty nice."

"It's not enough. You're right."

"Right about what? I didn't say anything about 'not enough.'"

"I need to be doing something. What needs to happen is, we need our damn orders to come through."

"Well. I'm not saying you have to be doing anything. It's just a curious thing."

"What?"

"Your situation."

"It's not curious to me. It's pretty frustrating."

"I guess I can see how it would get to be that way." She turned and looked back out at the diamond. "Sort of like if I had to sit at a baseball game *all* summer." She smiled. "Or work a copyediting job."

Wes leaned back in his seat. He felt somehow irritated, but after a while he remembered that it had been a long time since he had really talked with any woman. This one, he could already tell, was worth talking to. He turned to look out at the field and the players and the crowd around them. He suddenly had a vision of how the two of them must have looked there—caught up in the middle of it all, doing nothing but talking—and he felt that that was enough, that he did not need to do anything else. He felt better than he had all summer.

When the game ended they were no longer alone. On the ride back, he could not help but compare the other two women with Cynthia. Terri was more attractive, he might have said at first glance, but what else? She did not say much and, so far as he could tell, would agree with anything you said. Elizabeth said a lot but it was hard to tell if she heard anything, and from the beginning she assumed all four of "the guys" were just great. One thing he already could tell about Cynthia: she was no flatterer, and she was keeping her own counsel about whatever she thought of them so far.

From the front seat he watched her talk with John and Cullen, and he tried to tell himself that she did not have quite the same manner with them that she had with him. But he really could not say. Cullen was doing a lot of the talking, sitting up and becoming animated and explaining the joys of baseball while she questioned him in her semi-professional way. But she was laughing, too. Surely this was nothing serious. And there was John in the middle of it all, just looking on as though he were enjoying the whole spectacle, not just Cullen and Cynthia but the others too.

He confused Wes sometimes. At times he seemed so utterly open that when you were talking to him you felt like you were the only other person there, but when he turned away he was off in another world and you could swear he had forgotten you existed. At least it could seem that way. Maybe that was what got the girlfriend fed up with him, Wes thought.

He had to give his roommate credit for one thing, though. It occurred to him only later, as the importance of that night grew steadily in his mind, that it did not necessarily have to happen at all—that given Elizabeth's gregariousness and Cynthia's reserve, the one might just as easily have latched onto a different group of young men and the other tagged along. Whatever came of all this, they had John to thank for it.

But just now he was not in a grateful mood. He could not even sleep well that night. He had two things to think about now: Cynthia, and the war that he had begun to hope might somehow bring him orders.

Already he had found out that he did not know which of the two made him more anxious.

After the game they had driven back to the apartments—looming up the hill on a clear night, La Mirage was pale and luminous and shadow-pocked as the moon itself—and walked the women to Elizabeth's room. But then instead of saying goodbye the whole group of them sat down in a circle and began talking. Wes was next to Cynthia again, but it was not the same now. He felt almost disoriented. Before long he found himself beginning to get restless.

Somehow the others started swapping stories about growing up—family talk. Cullen told them how his dog loved peanut butter and his brother used to hold him down and smear the stuff in his ears and then just keep holding him there until the dog came around and licked it out. He got so involved in telling the story it that he started wringing out an ear until he caught himself and broke into a broad grin. The girls loved it. And that got Elizabeth going about her own big brother and how, when she was in tenth grade and about to leave for her first prom, he had started cleaning all his guns at the kitchen table so her date could see them. She started laughing: "Eddie—oh, Eddie!" Her eyes were bright as she clapped her hands, holding her thin fingers and wrists up together. "I miss him!" Her brother had become a Marine, like their father, and was back on the East Coast with the rest of her family. "He never was happy until I started dating one of his buddies." Her voice dropped a note as she said this, and Wes saw the skin beneath her eyes droop so that they suddenly looked hollowed out.

"That was Tom?" Terri was looking at her inquisitively.

"Unn-*hunhhhh*..." Elizabeth was sliding off the couch as she said it. "Whew! Whaddayasay let's talk about something *else*, everybody!?" She was directly across the room from Wes and, as she plopped onto the floor, her eyes caught his. "Hi, Wes! How ya doing?" she beamed. She looked like she was smiling for a panel of judges.

Wes nodded and smiled but wondered what was going on in this girl's mind. He turned to Cynthia and saw her sitting at ease and soaking it all up with her sharp brown eyes. She is different, Wes thought—a watcher and a waiter like me, but she is content to watch and wait.

He had no stories of his own to tell, and so he only felt more and more lost as the night went on. There was a coffee table in the middle of the room and Stick had been sitting there, setting up props for some kind of drinking game. Now Elizabeth was chattering beside him. Wes could see where things were headed: he glanced around at the others—Terri seemed to be on the verge of falling asleep in her chair, John suddenly detached and thoughtful—and then at the clock. It was almost midnight, and they were just killing time. He thought about the news and suddenly saw the seven of them tucked away in their little apartment while the wide world raced on by outside. A wave of disgust swept over him.

He stood up abruptly and said, "Well, we'd better get on to sleep, don't y'all think?"

The others all looked at him with surprise.

"Yeah, another busy day tomorrow," said Stick, shuffling a pack of cards.

"You never know."

"Let us know what's on the news, you hear?"

Wes bit his lip. It irked him that someone like Stick knew him so well. Instinctively he turned to Cynthia and found her appraising him with mild curiosity, one eyebrow slightly raised. Over her shoulder was a full-length mirror. A young man—a boy, really—stared back at him from it, red-faced, his fingers curling in upon themselves.

"Gentlemen—and ladies," Stick said with a mock salute, "I do believe the Colonel is ready for battle!"

Wes walked out the door and left them all behind.

Back at the apartment he turned on the TV, but all he could find was a repeat of a story he had seen earlier. He got in bed and tried to read Pershing's *My Experiences in the Great War* but could not, so he just stared at the walls. The clock ticked. John did not come back. He imagined the others all together in Elizabeth's room.

He felt that he was alone.

But now there was Cynthia to think about, and as he looked at the walls around him his short time with her that night was already becoming something imbued with significance, a shining moment lifted out of the circle of days his life had become.

He already believed that more like it were ahead. All he had to do was wait.

5

Both had come that first week in August, both the women and the war. But when he woke the next morning and turned on the news, Cynthia seemed like a dream to him. The war, he knew, was real. You could see it right there on the TV screen.

He had a feeling about orders, was the first one to leave for the TPU. But Ragis did not speak to them that day. Or the next. On Thursday, when Wes had nearly gotten sick with waiting, the OIC finally called them together and delivered a sort of non-speech.

They had not all been together in the base auditorium since their first week. A few of the ensigns—some of the surface warfare officers—had been doled out to ships, and new arrivals had trickled in throughout the summer. But now that the bulk who had been there from the beginning were assembled again, it was easy to see that they had split into two distinct groups: those few, led by Donkers, who were taking advantage of their free time to hone their military bearing to a fine polish, and—the far larger group—those who were letting their hair get too long and their uniforms too wrinkled. Wes noticed this as he took his place with the latter group, and his sense of revulsion peaked when Hooper limped in on crutches and slumped into the seat next to him. "What's up there, Wes?" he grimaced, wiping his forehead. He had two days of stubble on his cheeks, and whatever pain he was feeling wasn't only in his foot. He smelled like someone had dumped a bottle of scotch on him.

Hooper was the worst of them, but as Wes watched the other ensigns straggle in he recognized that virtually all were hungover and more than one were limping.

Then the "meeting" began. Wes heard a wave of murmuring sweep through the chairs and he looked down toward the stage to see Ragis standing there, his mouth moving.

The OIC had wandered in some time ago—Wes had noticed him sliding in through one of the side entrances—and begun conferring with Donkers in a back corner. Now he had wandered down to the front and apparently begun talking without benefit of stage or microphone.

What was he trying to pull?

Wes strained his ears. *Unsubstantiated rumors*, Ragis was muttering, strolling around with his hands in his pockets and looking down at the floor as if he were holding a conversation with the ten people in the first two rows. *No basis in fact.*

What was wrong with him? Was the microphone broken?

There is some possibility—he had raised his voice!—*accelerated curricular progression. Only a limited number.* Was he walking toward the exit? *Preliminary reports will be forthcoming as they become available.*

The door shut behind him, and there was a long silence.

Wes stared down at the stage in disbelief. He caught Cullen's eye, two rows below him. "What was that?" he almost yelled.

Cullen shrugged. "Stand by to stand by."

He sat stunned for a few moments, until he heard a deep rumbling laugh behind him. He turned and saw a figure emerging from the back of the auditorium, a great craggy head. "Men—" the yellow smile flashed over them—"it just keeps getting better, don't it?" The warrant sauntered down the aisle and hopped on the stage with surprising nimbleness. He was chuckling to himself and muttering something about "the Officer *in Charge*." He lit a cigar and positioned himself in front of the podium. "Gentlemen—" he switched the microphone on—"Happy hour at the O Club will commence at 1500."

Wes drove too fast down the coast highway on his way back home.

Pulling out of the base, he looked over his shoulder and saw a wave of Marines rolling in toward the beach. Half a mile out in the ocean beyond them sat the squat hulks of four ships, well decks gaping open like huge jaws at their sterns; helicopters circled overhead, carrying more men ashore. This was Amphibious Readiness Group 4, bound tomorrow, he had already heard, for the Arabian Sea.

While he looked on from shore.

Stopped at a traffic light, he saw a young boy in the car next to him staring at his uniform. The boy's eyes made Wes feel embarrassed, like he had been caught telling a lie, and when he got home he stripped the uniform off and hung it sloppily in a corner. He had never felt his uselessness more acutely than he did now, and he had to do something to get away from himself. He turned on the TV.

What he saw there was not war but preparations for war. Training and encampment.

A reporter stood in the desert, in the middle of a ring of brown tents, interviewing an Army corporal who worked in the supply service. The soldier was from some small town in Missouri, and when the reporter grabbed him it was clear from the look on his face that he knew this was his big chance to be seen by the folks back home. Something happened to his voice as well. At the start, he identified his rank, unit, and specialty in standard military jargon, but as the interview went on he sounded more and more like Gomer Pyle. His face remained somber and serious as he finally held up an MRE for the camera to inspect: "Yessir. It definitely ain't Grandma's cookin', but it's got all your basic nutrients." Then he stepped back, took a bite, and smiled.

Here was a soldier on the brink of battle, mugging for the camera!

Wes sat back on the couch. He felt a little better. The men over there were just waiting, too.

As the months passed—summer becoming fall and then winter with hardly a sign to tell it in this place—they watched the troops wait.

The only thing that changed, so far as Wes could tell, was that their own lives became increasingly interwoven with those of the women. After that first week they were suddenly *there*, so much there that they somehow became even more present in their absence. When Cynthia left on assignment for two weeks in September, Wes found himself with an unexpected gift, something he had not had in a long time—a specific day to await, that day when she would be back among them. It was a strange feeling. She had, without even trying, presented him with a means to escape the eternal present in which he found himself awash. Time was anchored again.

He told her none of this, of course. She had given him no reason to believe that she would rebuff him, but still he never felt that the moment was right to approach her. It was a peculiarity of his that had manifested itself before with those few women he had truly been attracted to. The first times they talked were always free and easy, but to Wes those conversations themselves soon became a barrier to further talk—ideals not easily attained again, images out of some golden age that could only have existed in the distant past. There was that, and there was also the fact that he and Cynthia were never alone, but always with the others. If they were to recapture the purity of their first time together, there would have to come some perfect moment when they would be alone, when things would just happen and they would both know it. Wes could not quite articulate this faith, but it was in fact what he believed: at some point the moment would come when he would know what to do.

One Sunday evening he finally confessed this to John, who shrugged and said, "Why don't you just talk to her now?"

The matter-of-factness of this reply irritated Wes. He was already annoyed with his roommate because he had disappeared for most of the day—something he had gotten in the habit of doing. And now he was back with this brisk air of confident knowledge.

"Well, you're full of answers today, young ensign. Where have you been, anyway? I know you haven't been lifeguarding *all* day."

"Just taking care of things." He smiled. "Filling time. Nothing out of the ordinary."

"C's?"

"A's, B's, C's. Which reminds me..." He walked to a closet and pulled out his toolbox. Last week he had decided they needed some barstools for the kitchen, bought a hand-operated lathe, set it up on the deck, and proceeded to churn out rudimentary stool legs. Random pieces of lumber littered their front hallway.

"I can see where this is going." Wes got up and headed toward the door. "Just hurry up and get all this crap out of the hall!" Walking into the courtyard alone, he was not satisfied with either of John's answers. If the first had been too straightforward, the second was too enigmatic. John had been up to something on the weekends for some time now, and—though this was the first time he asked about it—Wes did not like the mystery of it.

He would not have admitted it even to himself, but he did not like the loneliness, either. As October turned to November, even his normal diversions had begun to fail him, and, in the dead pockets of time when they were not all together, suddenly everyone except him seemed to have something to do.

John would be gone and Wes would trot up the stairs to Cullen's apartment only to knock at the door and get no answer. Many times this would happen even as he heard the stereo and TV and video games within blaring all at once—Stick was a technology addict, a seeker after stimulation in all its forms, and he liked nothing better than to plug in as many gadgets as he could at one time—and a female laugh. Terri, and sometimes Elizabeth too.

Then, on his way back down, he walked by the rooms where the women lived. Elizabeth was always out somewhere visiting. She saw all the newcomers into their new apartments, lodging herself immediately into their lives, and even in this place where people came and went so quickly it seemed that after working here for six months she knew almost everyone. Wes wondered how she kept up with them all—too many people, he thought—but it seemed to suit her. Of them all she seemed the hungriest for companionship, and Wes often saw her scampering around the courtyard with other denizens of La

Mirage. At night he sometimes heard her frantic laughter echoing off the walls.

And Cynthia—well, many times she was off at her office. She was a hard worker, Wes had discovered, and kept herself busy. Certainly he couldn't just drop by her place.

But one time, by accident, he did.

He was passing through the courtyard and ran into her coming in from work on a Saturday afternoon. She looked tired, but when she saw him she invited him in for lunch. They stood around mostly in silence while she fixed sandwiches and he poured some Cokes. Sitting across from her, eating, at last he felt he had to say something. So he asked her what she had been writing that day and she told him, but while she was talking he just kept looking at her face and thinking about what he was going to say next, and so he missed the details. There was a silence.

Then he asked what drove her to write and she sat there, munching thoughtfully, and finally said she just thought it was important to get things down. Not that she was going to change things, necessarily—when she started college she had a touch of the crusader in her, but —no, she was realizing that she just liked to get things down, even everyday things. The paper she was working for now had her mainly covering features. Human interest stories. At first she thought that was fluff, but to her surprise she was beginning to like it. "Like this thing about the Sanchezes."

That was what he had missed—the thing about the Sanchezes. "So—everyday things. You don't want to break the big story?"

She shook her head. "I don't know. I guess that would be fine. But I'm not sure I *need* to break the big story anymore."

Her replies confused him, and so they sat there and stared at one another for a while. "Good question," she finally said. Her tone was encouraging, like a patient schoolteacher's.

"Thanks." He was feeling puzzled and probably looked it. It had dawned on him that they were actually talking, and suddenly the whole conversation seemed so fraught with significance that he knew he would probably have to think about it for a week. So he thanked her for lunch, and together they walked to the door, exhausted, and said goodbye.

So that had happened and given him something to think about. They would talk again, he was sure. But the time had to be just right to drop in there, and it never quite seemed to be, even when he couldn't find any of the others.

On a good day he could find Cullen out in the parking lot working on the sailboat. He had done some superficial repairs during the summer but now was spending even more time at it. Wes would go out and find him lathered in sweat, sanding, painting, caulking furiously. He seemed driven by something outside himself. Wes had talked about it with John—whenever you went out there to see Cullen, he was quick with a smile; but when you caught him alone and he first looked up at you, you could see the apprehension in his face, a shadow that seemed so out of place on his bright features as to make him look like someone else.

They knew he had to be thinking about his brother.

That was how Wes found him when he went out to the lot after lunch one Saturday in early November. There was almost a chill in the breeze, almost a hint that the season had changed, but still the sun beat down on the asphalt and the heat drifted back up around Wes's knees as he walked so that he was glad Cullen had parked the boat where he did. It sat in the shade beneath a clump of palm trees in one corner of the lot where the asphalt faded to sand. The boat looked so natural in the little grove that it could almost have been shipwrecked there, its own desert island, with Cullen—now emerging from the tiny cabin, beer in hand—the hapless captain.

Cullen squinted into the sun for a few seconds and even at a distance Wes could see his features brightening. "Ahoy," he heard—"Colonel Hammond!" Cullen disappeared again for a moment and reemerged with another beer as Wes approached the stern and drew up at attention. "Request permission to come aboard, sir."

"Permission granted. Grab a paintbrush, sailor."

It was a golden afternoon. Beneath the palms it was cool, but the gusty breeze tossed the rustling fronds overhead—it was a sound that made Wes think of fall—so that the bright sun shimmered and played around the boat. They seemed to float, half-submerged, in a pool dappled with light and shadow. The two of them worked only lightly, stopping at intervals to take deep sips of beer and look out between the palm trunks, down to where the sparkling ocean spread across the horizon. The lot and the streets around them were quiet except for children riding their bicycles through the neighborhood below. Their calls to one another sounded gently in the distance, drifting up occasionally only to be swallowed and lost in the long murmuring breeze.

After a few hours they put the brushes down, and Cullen leaned back against a life preserver to rest. Wes walked up to the bow, stretched out and looked at the palms drifting above him. They made a living roof overhead, and in the drowsy quiet of mid-afternoon he rested, blinked his eyes, slowly, until his mind went back to the summer when he was ten, when he and the black boy who lived behind him had built a treehouse in the little stretch of pines that ran between their homes. Freddy's mother cleaned house for the Hammonds once a week, but his father was gone and sometimes Wes's dad would wander out of his study and say things about his responsibility to set a good example for Freddy. But when the two of them were together they did not think about things like that. It seemed like all they did that summer was sit up among the trees and read comic books until it was time for school to start back. It was a time when he had nothing to do and felt good about it, and now, here, in this quiet place, it felt like that was not too long ago. His eyes were closed, but the palms and Freddy and the treehouse were all there, floating in a drowsy sea of sun and shade...

Then it was bright and Cullen was standing over him, staring off at the ocean, a clutch of papers in his right hand. "Letters from my brother," he said.

He had brought them out to the boat to read back over—only three or four. When he sat down and started talking, Wes hardly heard him. He was having trouble believing it. Eyewitness reports from the front, here in his presence. Watching Cullen shuffle the stack of tattered envelopes, he was struck by how much more *real* the letters—their physical substance—seemed than any of the dozens of hours of clips he had watched on TV.

Cullen began waving the letters around and trying to summarize them, but after Wes just stared intently he finally said, "Here, look at them yourself. He wouldn't mind."

They were numbered and dated, from the first few weeks of the deployment on. The first had been sent from a Saudi port town called Ad Damman. He and his men had been flown there to await their tanks, which were arriving via ship. They were part of the first American armored division to arrive in country. *We're sleeping on the concrete floor of a warehouse. Crammed in here, a few hundred yards from the dock. Don't feel too good about the layout. Better tomorrow when tanks arrive, then out to the desert.* Much of the letter was like that—quick, matter-of-fact, all the way up to the close. *I'm doing fine. Lots to check up on now with my platoon. I'll write again soon as I can—Joe.*

Joe. The simple signature jarred him. He had heard the name before, but now he would remember it for good.

The next letter was similar, written after Joe's platoon had established itself at one position in the desert and was standing by to shift to another. Wes read it eagerly, as if he himself were the one awaiting word in the wilderness. Something about the simplicity of the sentences—*Left Ad Damman, made camp in the desert. Nothing here but sand and camels. Tomorrow we train*—added to its authority. There were no wasted words.

The third letter was dated late September ("they get here about a month late," Cullen said) and was much longer. GREETINGS FROM PARADISE! it began, written out in capital letters like a postcard. The paper felt strange, gritty, and Wes looked back at the envelope. There was half a handful of sand at the bottom.

Dear Bro: We ain't in West Point anymore. Or even backwoods Georgia. This place SUCKS! OK, now I have to resume proper military bearing. We have established permanent base camp within a defensible perimeter...

There it was, after all—the Cullen sense of humor. It faded in and out of the letter, but by the time Wes had gotten halfway through he could tell that behind it was an intensely felt sense of responsibility and anxiety. *Training daily now for the possibility of an enemy offensive into Saudi.* They were not far from the border and would likely be the first targets of the chemical weapons attack the TV had been talking about. In the press conferences Wes had watched it was merely one of a number of offensive strategies the enemy might consider, but to Joe it was something else. *If I have to don a gas mask and a big rub-*

ber MOPP suit one more time, I'm gonna puke. It's not like this place isn't hot enough already. Of course, this is exactly what my guys tell me and I have to let them know it's for their own good. Let me tell you, I only halfway knew what it was like to be an officer before. But now you really realize that once something starts out here I'm responsible for all these guys. Now it's real.

Now it's real, Wes almost said out loud. Now it's real.

Sitting beneath the palm trees he could almost feel what it was like to be there, waiting, in the desert—a pure windswept place where anything could happen and the call to action was about to come. He knew that starkly present moment of possibility as he read, knew it even more so when Joe described his initial call-up. He had just spent a long weekend in Atlanta, drinking with his buddies and visiting a couple of girls, returned to base late Sunday night. The next day he thought he would be on liberty by noon—he was supposed to temporarily transfer command of his platoon to a senior ROTC cadet on summer training—and catch up on his sleep. But instead, the call came at 1130 for his entire division to go on standby. *I couldn't believe it. 24 hours before I had been completely goofing off. Now they were telling us we were about to deploy to the Middle East.* Within a week he was on his way.

> *Don't worry about me. I've got a lot on my mind, but I know what I have to do and am doing my best to make it happen. We're training every day and we've got enough people and firepower over here to handle whatever they come up with. I'll be fine and this'll all be over soon enough. Make the most of life in Cali! You know I'd be right there with you if I could. Soon as I get back, I'm taking a month of leave and hopping a MAC flight to the Left Coast so I can see some good sand. So keep your tolerance up and drink a couple for me. Take it easy—Joe.*

Cullen was reading over his shoulder. "Man," he said, "the thing is, he means it, too. About having a good time. He would fit right in with us out here. He was coming to visit at Thanksgiving. That was the plan before all this started. And now he's making it sound like he's not scared, but he's gotta be." Wes looked at him and saw his brow knitted and his eyes shuttered. "What a shitty deal he got." He crinkled up his beer can and threw it into the hold. "But that's what we're signed up for. It's just dumb luck that it's him instead of me."

Wes did not know what to say. He only knew that he did not like this sentimental turn. It wasn't that he didn't feel some kind of sympathy for Cullen. With no brother of his own it was hard to know exactly what it was like, but he could imagine. Still, he did not want any sentiment to cheat him of the sensation he had gotten while reading the letters, the feeling that he himself had somehow, vicariously, been lifted out of the mundane. He wanted to stay there, to believe in the possibility that he too could actually be yanked out of his lackadaisical life and suddenly galvanized into action. Even as he buried himself in the final letter (short again, mostly straightforward accounts of travel and training, sprinkled with a few doses of rough brotherly affection and more injunctions to Cullen to have a good time) he tried to ignore Joe's occasional complaints about training—how even at the time when it seemed most necessary it became repetitive and dull, how he was anxious for the final order to come. That was the part Wes did not expect. That even on the brink of battle, there was the boredom of waiting.

"Enough," Cullen said, finishing the last beer. "You've heard the man, now. He doesn't want us brooding on this too much. Let's go see what the others have on tap for tonight."

They climbed down from the boat together as the great hazy bulk of the sun sank into the sea, and Wes felt a twinge of regret at leaving. Of them all Cullen was somehow at once the most open and the hardest to get to know. He felt suddenly privileged to have shared the letters. It was as if he had been chosen, as if there in the little grove he had just for a moment taken the place of the brother Cullen was missing.

That was what he thought even as they walked up together toward the luminous white face of La Mirage and Cullen turned to him to ask, "Is Cynthia going to be lame tonight, or is she gonna blow off work for us?"

Wes had no way of knowing. He was sure Terri and Elizabeth were around.

"Good. Those girls are all cool enough." He paused. " But Cynthia—she's a good woman. She doesn't take any crap. And—she's got a way of making things interesting, you know?" He turned to Wes and smiled.

"I know."

November was a respite for Wes, a good time amidst the waiting, a time that stole up and caught him unaware with joy. It was a season when they were all together, and that somehow made the days tolerable. On weekends when they went with the girls on some local excursion—hopping the ferry out to Catalina, driving into the new wine country around Temecula, stopping at the overviews along Mulholland, just following the Pacific Coast Highway up the long, sloping arc of Santa Monica Bay—and the day was sunny and just cool enough, he could look out over the broad sweep of sea and sky and coastline and maybe for a moment he would sense it: the richness of place and happening, the fullness of life and time. He would look to Cynthia, near him, and she became the axis, the central mystery upon which that wide world turned, and then he did not care if orders ever came.

But with November came the holidays, too, markers in time that he found himself silently dreading, days meant to be celebration and respite from time now emptied out and become the very measuring sticks of its passing and disappointment.

Thanksgiving was a fiasco. Stick had taken up with some strange girls who had moved in next to Terri—"the hippy chicks," they were calling them—and invited them over to Elizabeth's for dinner. He was lusting after at least one of them, Julie, and to woo her had taken to wearing tie-dyes and blasting the Grateful Dead on his stereo. She showed up at dinner a little drunk and three different times started to tell them a story about how her old boyfriend stuffed a turkey with pot one year, but she never finished. Stick was no more sober than she was and kept rubbing up against her while she basted the turkey. Wes watched Terri and waited for a blowup, but it never came. She seemed oblivious as ever, sitting blandly at the little bar where Elizabeth and the other girl, Louise, were fixing Mexican margaritas and laughing like madwomen, spilling tequila all over the counter. Cullen was helping them. That left Wes and Cynthia sitting on the couch and smiling at one another in silence until Wes leaned over and said, "Well, we're missing our mystery man again, it looks like."

Cynthia perked up. "John? Oh. He's at his dad's, right?"

"He is?"

"That's what he told me. Helping him settle into his new place, I guess."

Wes turned away. New place? He felt mildly embarrassed. How did she know more about his roommate than he did?

Just then Stick and Julie fell onto the floor in front of him, arms around one another and whooping like savages. They were having some kind of wrestling match.

"Get him, woman!" Cullen was yelling. He had downed a few drinks himself and broken into his usual broad grin, dancing a little jig, bare feet sweeping across the carpet. "You can take him!"

The others were cheering too—Elizabeth hopped over the two wrestlers, coffee mug in hand, and started swatting the floor like a referee—while Cynthia and Wes looked on grinning. It was hard not to when Cullen was having such a good time. But as Wes watched those two roll around on the floor and heard the rest hooting and cackling, he knew that he could only take so much of this. Somehow John's absence made it worse; when he was among them they somehow became not merely partners in diversion but something more. Without him? Wes looked around at the others and knew that—with the exception of Cullen and Cynthia—here, on Thanksgiving Day, he was just killing time with strangers.

After a long weekend with no sign of his roommate, he found himself wondering if John was in fact any different, if he really knew him at all. Then on Sunday he suddenly reappeared, strolling into the living room looking particularly red and parched and disheveled.

"Where the hell have you been?" Wes asked. It was their joking tone, but underneath it he meant business. He wanted an answer.

"In the desert." John had walked into the kitchen. The sound of a running faucet ran underneath his reply.

Wes groaned. "And was there any particular *reason* for this little trip? Maybe you've been collecting cacti? Or is the tanning just better out there?"

John walked in gulping down a tall, silver glass of water. At last he pulled it away and smiled as a bright drop trickled down the crease of his mouth. He ducked his head, wiped it against his shoulder, and smiled again. "My dad's moved out there. Toward Barstow. Middle of nowhere, really."

"Helluva place to settle down. The Midwest wasn't good enough for him?"

"Well, he never had any ties there. He's just retired and, with the Army and all, doesn't really have a home. With Mom gone, I don't think he quite knew what to do. He used to come out here for training, you know, to Fort Irwin, and for whatever reason he's got some attraction to the desert." He took another swig of water. "He's always been a little eccentric. Apt to do strange things—like marrying a 'Nam protester in the middle of the 60s and bringing her to live on an Army base."

"I take it it runs in the family?"

John laughed. "Probably."

Wes didn't press any more, and they sat together in silence while John gulped down glass after glass of water.

So Wes already felt like a stranger when, the day before he flew home on Christmas leave, he went out to the parking lot to say goodbye to Cullen. It was overcast, and as he strolled toward the boat he could feel the breeze cutting his shoulders. He saw Cullen's head jutting up out of the stern and heard the sound of voices.

There was someone else out there with him.

"Ahoy!" Wes yelled.

Cullen looked up and paused a second before smiling. "Come aboard, sir!"

As Wes walked up to the side of the boat, he could see the other person. He saw her and then he looked again. It was Cynthia. She was wearing Cullen's coat, and in her hand she held a stack of letters.

Cullen was looking back over his shoulder and grinning. "Looks like I'm gonna make the news, Wes. Not on my own account. Our reporter friend here has been grilling me about Joe."

Cynthia quickly smiled up at him. "Human interest! I'm doing a story." She looked away. "On locals who have family members in the Gulf for the holidays."

"Wow," Wes said. He could not come up with anything else to say. "That's pretty good."

"So what are you up to?" Cullen asked, clearing a space for him.

The three of them talked about holiday plans. The TPU had dictated that half the ensigns needed to remain on duty at all times—"In case of emergency," Ragis told them above the outraged whispers and laughter that immediately filled the auditorium—and Cullen, unlike Wes, had been assigned the second leave period. He would not go home until almost New Year's Eve. Since Cynthia had been back not long ago and was covering for other people now, she wasn't going home at all. It would be a while before they were all together again, they said.

After a while Cynthia got up to leave. She said her farewells to Wes, wished him a merry Christmas. Then she walked off and looked back over her shoulder as if she had forgotten something. "Bye, Billy," she said.

Cullen smiled back.

Billy?

Wes had almost begun to think it would be good to go home. At first it was. The return flight was a voyage into a familiar from which he had been gone long enough that it was almost new again. After over six months in southern California, he looked out of his window before landing at dusk and saw as though for the first time the endless sea of pines he had lived in for so long. The earth rolled beneath him like a cool blue-green wave, the last rays of the sun glinting off the tiny citadels of glass and steel that rose in the far distance.

His parents. Waiting at the terminal. His mother kissing him on the cheek and admiring his dress uniform, his father looking him almost straight in the eye and offering him a firm handshake. They are glad to see him.

Home. Good food, a place to rest. His parents mean well. Sitting at dinner the next night his father asks, "So tell us more about your duties."

His mother wants to know which uniform he normally wears.

They tell him that he should relax. "That's what the holidays are for!" He tries. He sleeps late and goes with his mother to pick up a tree. He calls a few old friends, meets a couple of them out one night. They are working hard at their new jobs—accounting, engineering—and mostly they don't like it. Wish they were back in college, or had moved somewhere else, at least for a while.

"You've got it made," they tell him.

He begins to feel restless.

He wanders around the backyard, half-heartedly chopping fire-wood. The tall pines bend in the wind above him. He hears an engine in the distance and far away through the trees he can see the yellow sweep of a backhoe, clearing space for a new Wal-Mart. Home is a thick green place that is slowly being buried in asphalt. Those were the woods where the treehouse was, and back there where Freddy's family lived. The house is still standing, deserted now, the house where Wes first went to a funeral after Freddy's mother died. He was eleven years old and his parents were coming later so he walked back there alone past the other two or three rundown houses and the lean barking dogs. He was scared but he went up the steps and knocked and waited for the door to open. Inside there were only black people and the smell of good food, and in the middle room in a big box was Dayzeerae, or something that looked like her.

Now when the backhoe is silent and he walks back in the pines and looks at the rotting house it is like another country, the land of the dead.

His father has published a new book, an account of the life of Colonel Jacob Byrd, soldier in the Mexican war and a prominent leader in Jubal Early's cavalry before being shot outside Winchester, Virginia in 1863. "It was nice being able to use all the local archives," he says, sitting in the study one night. "To think"—he lights his pipe—"he grew up *right here*." He stares out the window into the dark. "The old Byrd plantation is just up 74." He smiles. "We could go out there together one day, you know."

Wes watches CNN and sees frozen holiday dinners being loaded onto cargo planes. The troops must be fed. He watches an Army platoon training for a chemical weapons attack.

On Christmas Eve he has a dream.

He is flying low over the pines and is worried that something is going wrong. Then his face is buried in sand. He is crawling out of the helicopter, stands erect in a desert. His arm hurts. There is smoke coming from over a dune, so he walks to the top of it and looks down. He sees a tank parked in a little grove of palm trees. Next to the tank is a soldier in a gas mask. He is holding a stick over a campfire, and on the end of the stick is a package.

The soldier calls to him, and he walks down. It is Joe. The soldier never says so, but Wes knows. Joe pulls the MRE off the end of his stick and opens it. There is a full turkey inside. They sit down and start eating the turkey and suddenly Cullen is with them.

They are eating and talking and laughing when a volleyball rolls into the campfire. Wes turns to see Cynthia stepping gingerly across the sand. She opens her mouth to say something.

"Billy?"

There is someone else in the dream. Wes does not remember until the next afternoon, but John is there, sitting high in the palm tree. He smiles down at them once or twice. Mostly, though, he is watching something in the distance.

On Christmas morning Wes receives a biography of Admiral Farragut from his father and a new set of choker whites from his mother. They go to church. Since he has not been in a long time, the hymns almost sound new and Wes starts to listen. The story is about camels and dreams and navigating through the desert. The minister ends by praying for peace in the Holy Land in this time of trouble, and "for all our servicemen." Wes's mother looks at him and whispers, "That's you."

Two days later it is time for him to leave, and he is ready. He has a window seat and looks down at the earth for much of the flight back.

As they pass over the Colorado he begins thinking of the sea and cliffs and manicured green lawns, but beneath him there is nothing.

It was easy to forget down by the beach, but he sees it now.

They are living on the edge of a vast desert.

When he lands, he takes the airport shuttle home and throws his bags into the apartment. John is not there.

Before he knows what he is doing he is knocking on Cynthia's door. No answer.

He passes Elizabeth, who is showing some newcomers around. He asks where Cynthia is. "Not sure, sweetie!" She winks at him. "Why don't you come see little ol' me?"

Then he is at Cullen's door, and after he bangs for a few minutes the stereo is at last turned down and Stick's head appears. "Yeah? Oh, hi, man." Wes can see the two hippy chicks sitting with Terri in the room behind him. "Wanna come in? We're just making drinks."

"I wanted to see Cullen about something. Is he around?"

"Nope. With the sailboat. He just moved it down to the city dock. That sombitch actually thinks it'll float!"

Wes walks, trots, the few blocks down to the main avenue that runs along the beach. Just beyond it is the paved boardwalk. He turns south toward where dozens of thin masts stick up at the municipal marina. He quickens his pace.

When he gets to the end of the main dock he sees the wind catching the sail of a little sloop that has drifted a hundred yards out. There is no mistaking the paint on the stern. Just then Cullen stands up to straighten the boom. A hand reaches up to steady him, and Wes sees a stream of long brown hair flying loose in the breeze.

Gulls wheel and cry overhead, dazzling streaks of white against the pale blue sky. Alongside Wes a young boy fishes from the dock with his father and pulls a strange, speckled crab from the sea. Its legs wave wildly above the worn planks. "What is that?" says the father with a slight foreign accent. The boy stares at it wide-eyed. He is too overcome with wonder to speak.

The father drops the crab into the sea. It lands with a deep *thwuuuunk* and fades back into the blue-green darkness. The water slaps together above it as the man smiles and turns to Wes. "A beautiful afternoon."

Wes stands on the dock and watches, silent, as the white sail becomes part of the horizon.

6

Winter settles in, though they know the passing of time not from sun and wind but from the television screen. Blizzards in Omaha, freezing rain in Ohio. Cars slide into snowdrifts, pile up in fields of ice along I-95.

Tomahawk cruise missiles—sleek, almost beautiful atop pillars of flame—erupt from a battleship. Planes follow, their blinking lights lurching steadily off the decks of carriers and out over the black Gulf.

A midnight skyline: the dark sky pulses yellow and green behind dull gray buildings. A journalist trapped in a Baghdad hotel room peers out his window and reports explosions to his anchor back in Atlanta. "Tom—it's spectacular out there," he whispers. "It's hard to believe people must be dying right now."

A general behind a podium in Washington calls it "Desert Storm."

When Wes first heard that the war had begun, he was at Venice Beach watching a man stick needles into his tongue.

A few weeks previous he had refused to go up there, had thought himself already bored with the day trips and even more ambitious travel schemes Stick and Cullen were beginning to devise. But as January wore on, things changed. He grew more convinced of the final insignificance of his life here. Sitting in his room one Tuesday morning, staring at the ceiling, he was ready when Stick came—ready for diversion, ready to offer himself up to the crowd.

So it was that he had come to pass a day watching strongmen juggle dwarfs, listening to women with shaved heads sing Nepalese folk songs, dodging the onslaught of a troupe of legless mimes on skateboards. All alongside the sweep of Santa Monica Bay and under the shadow of the purple mountains looming above it. Venice.

The four men and three women—Cynthia and Elizabeth had not come—hung together carelessly as they moved through the spectacle. Most of the morning Wes spent close to Cullen, but as noon approached he broke from the others and wandered alone past the vendors and the gawking crowds, glancing from time to time out to the sea. He stumbled into a ring of performers. Before him a man in a turban—his face a mask of concentration, the fierce countenance of one who daily stared death in the eye—doused a sword in gasoline, lit it, and leaned back to swallow. An Asian woman in a sari emerged from a tent and offered to administer a "natural enema cure": "You will feel clean again, as clean as when you were born. Fifteen dollar."

He began drinking margaritas before lunch and later had his picture taken with a three-breasted woman.

By mid-afternoon, he felt better than he had in weeks. This place had him interested. Walking through it, he knew that he had had enough of waiting, waiting and thinking about what would happen to him and what was happening elsewhere. There was something happening right here. Venice was a madhouse, but at moments it seemed an only slightly skewed reflection of something real, a riddle whose answer was on the tip of his tongue but just out of reach. He didn't even know what the riddle was. But drinking his drink, looking out at these sideshow freaks and the glorious Pacific afternoon, he felt he was onto something.

Sitting at a patio bar along the boardwalk, he told John all this and immediately felt foolish. Maybe he had been with Cullen too long —Cullen, who had taken more drink than any of them and then run off down the beach almost dancing with delight at the day and their freedom. Maybe it was all coming from him, this enthusiasm. Maybe John would have no idea what he was talking about. "Do you know what I mean?" he asked sheepishly.

"Yeah." John took a sip of beer and gazed out over the beach. A ship lay at anchor in the bay beyond. "I know exactly what you mean."

Wes felt relieved, and then suddenly more interested. John had turned to him with a level gaze and was beginning to speak. "Something I've been thinking about—" he said. But he paused, like a man who has a secret he is not sure he should share or doesn't yet know how to.

Just then a figure on a unicycle rolled up the boardwalk and began to rock gently back and forth in front of them. Lean, wearing nothing but a thin black swim thong, his body was almost entirely covered with tattoos. He flashed a yellow smile directly at the two of them. Then he tilted his head back, balanced a cup on his nose, and plucked from it a needle that he drove slowly into his extended tongue.

The television behind them spoke. "At 2:50 AM local time, U.S. warships in the Persian Gulf launched—"

At that moment Stick and the hippy chicks swarmed around the unicyclist on rollerblades, wearing tie-dyes and waving little American flags.

They came home that night to the TV, to flickering green-gray images recorded in the cockpits of warplanes, the spectral film narratives of what the voices on the TV called *precision bombing.* Late into the night and the next morning the four men watched, drinking and marveling at the technology and sometimes hooting when a building maneuvered square into the sights of a computer then sank beneath a curling cloud of dust.

When morning came they were all dozing on the couches of Cullen's apartment. Half-awake, tossing before the white glare of the muted television, Wes was not fully aware of the room's musty darkness until he felt a faint breeze and saw a dimmer light creeping from behind him. He got up and stumbled to the balcony, where John stood looking out at the gray Pacific. He turned to Wes with dark, heavy eyes, as if he had not slept at all.

In the coming weeks, those images would flicker in the background of their lives. But not even Wes would immerse himself in them as they all had together on that first night. After months of waiting for the war, he found its eruption unbearable because its commencement finally confirmed his own utter irrelevance to it. He became at once both fatalistic and restless, so certain of his fate that he needed constant distraction from it.

In his restlessness he was not alone. For what began that day in Venice would soon take them farther afield. Maybe the war somehow intensified their collective wanderlust, each finally driven by it to the same end, but January was already the month when the traveling had begun in earnest, the month when they could no longer sit still.

Had they, he wondered, simply all been together in one place for too long?

From the beginning the group had necessarily had its small alliances, its unspoken and special companionships. But now they had shifted. Where initially the four men had naturally formed a loose bond, they now broke with one another. Stick roamed free, sometimes with Terri, sometimes with the new girls. Elizabeth, too—when, careless socialite that she was, she was with them and not some other of the myriad denizens of San Agustin—at times seemed to fall under his sway.

To the uninitiated, seeing them all together at an outing or party, John would have seemed nearly indistinguishable from Stick, moving easily in and out of conversations with the women among them. But there was a difference. Whatever the outcome of his efforts, Stick was at bottom a predator, while John's intentions remained unclear. They were—so far as Wes could tell—mysteriously innocent. For that matter, John seemed equally at ease with any of them, man or woman. Wes had greater occasion to notice this because he found himself turning more and more to John, a circumstance he had not chosen but that arose indirectly because of the new bond of intimacy he most regretted, that between Cullen and Cynthia.

This was the bond that, almost as much as the war itself, he had sought to drive from his mind, but it somehow emerged most clearly when he sought to escape it. He came to know it most fully during their first extended journey of the new year.

The desert stretched before them, vast and clean. Wes had volunteered to drive Stick's Blazer—he had wanted something to occupy his mind—but now the landscape almost overwhelmed him. There were few roads, but here, between distant low-lying ranges that rose chalky against the long horizon, the open land was so flat and inviting as to seem an arena of possibility.

They had passed the hazy glitter of Palm Springs and then a small Indian reservation where a dark woman surrounded by silver and turquoise peered out at them from a tent. Then for a long time nothing, until a sign appeared. Joshua Tree.

"Joshua Tree, smoshua pee. What are we doin' out here in the boonies, man?" Stick was cradling a can of beer in the back seat. "Vegas, baby. *Vay-gus!* Turn north and we'll be there before happy hour."

"He won't let up, will he? He *won't let up.*" Cullen snickered as he opened a can of his own. "You'll get your chance, buddy. But hey—a little time out in the wilderness never hurt anybody. And a few days away from the booze will be good for us all." He took a drink. "So once this twelve is done, we're sobering up. Detox weekend."

Stick leaned forward. "John, your dad's not gonna mind if we're a little shitfaced when we drop by, is he?"

"He can handle just about anything," John said. "He'll probably have a couple with us."

This was John's trip. Venice had been Stick's, and after it the other three wanted something different. Since the women were all busy that weekend, it had seemed like a good time to go camping.

"It'll be just like the old days," Cullen said with a grin. "Just the boys."

They were stopping at John's father's house on the way.

He lived far out in the middle of the long flat plain that stretched between the mountains. The nearest town—on the edge of another reservation—was not even a town in the sense that Wes knew the word. Just a gas station and a store and a trailer park where some sprinklers darkened the dirt. He drove through it and dodged a dog that lay asleep in the middle of the road, and then they went ten more miles before they turned left at a mailbox. At the end of a long straight road, a smudge rose against the horizon. Soon it became a tiny grove of cactus and palms.

In the middle of the grove was a cottage and beside it a garden, partly shaded by a long canvas awning that ran off the house. Alongside a row of corn stood an older man in a clean T-shirt and khaki pants, smoking a cigarette and holding a hose. The new white cotton of his shirt and the silver rainbow sheen of the water shone bright in the noontime sun.

As they pulled up, he turned toward them but stayed where he was.

"John!" he yelled. "And your partners in crime, I presume." He smiled.

They walked out to him. Entering the garden, Wes saw that it was bounded by a series of poles on which were mounted a system of ropes and pulleys. He stepped gingerly among the rows of vegetables. Moving alongside the corn, he was surprised at how healthy the stalks looked. Deep green. Droplets of water hung glistening from the tassels.

John made introductions. His father was a trim, energetic man with an easy smile. He held the hose with one hand and shook with the other. "I hear you young men have been working pretty hard. I'm just about done here, so why don't we step inside. I've got a few cold ones ready to help you unwind from your stressful jobs."

They followed him toward the house. At the edge of the garden he stepped up to a post where a hand-crank was mounted and began to turn it. A rustling sounded over their heads, and Wes looked up to see the awning rolling out over the corn. "Careful to wipe your shoes before you step out of the garden. I'm not worried about dirt in the house—just want it to stay with the plants! Had to have two loads of topsoil hauled out here." Wes looked at his feet. The dirt was rich and black.

The inside of the cottage was bare but clean. In one corner of the kitchen stood an old refrigerator that the older man swung open. He pulled out bottles of beer and a long plate of filleted fish. "Trout," he said. "Caught 'em up the Colorado with some buddies." He led them back out the kitchen door to a little patio nudged between the house and the garden where a charcoal grill sat in the cool under the awning. Cullen helped him pick up a monstrous bag of coals. He dumped them in and lit them up.

"There," he said. "Now we're ready to go."

They sat in lounge chairs and talked freely while the coals settled down. Wes held his bottle and looked out over the expanse of land that surrounded them—they were on a slight elevation—and to the faint hills beyond. Rocks, cactus, air. Nothing. The wind rippled the tops of the palms, blew hot and dry beneath the awning. But from the garden came a kind of relief, as if the dark soil and the plants themselves emanated coolness and moisture.

John's dad had asked them about their homes.

"Grilling with charcoal—that's what my folks always do," Cullen was saying. He had been going on about his family for a while, but now he paused. "Now, what about you? Before the Army, I mean. Where were you from?"

He was laying the fish down on the grill. "Oh. Maryland—other side of the Bay from that little place where you boys went to school." He grinned at Cullen and Stick. "Or my father was, anyway. My mother was from Virginia. We wound up in between. But it's been a long time—hard to remember where home was, other than the Army."

"You ever get back there?"

"My sister ended up back there, outside D.C. Went to visit her a few times when she was still alive. But I don't recognize that country anymore." He had walked out into the garden and was standing alongside the corn, tugging at the stalks.

"So why'd you end up way out here?" Wes felt embarrassed at the straightforwardness of the question, but there was Cullen for you—right out in the open.

"Oh, just thought I'd do something crazy before they put me in the nursing home." He was walking back to them now, holding an armful of corn, and threw a smile at John.

"Good Lord," John said.

"Ha." His father stood alongside them, shucking the ears. "Nah, I've got some buddies stationed not too far north from here. Go see them when I want, have plenty of peace and quiet the rest of the time. Like it here—least for a little while. Something about the desert."

"So what do you do? I mean, knowing John, I thought you might have a nice little library, but I don't see too many books in there."

"Well—John got that from his mother." He smiled at his son. "I like to watch sports. And I've got plenty of little projects to keep myself busy."

"Sounds familiar." Cullen looked at John and they all laughed.

They brought the fish inside, boiled the corn and some beans, and sat down at a long plain table to eat. Their host sat at the head and said a prayer so suddenly and gracefully that Wes hardly noticed it. Then he lifted his bottle. "Well, gentlemen, here we are. Cheers!"

Wes was surprised at how good the food was. Fresh—the trout and vegetables exploded between his teeth, his mouth so awash with flavor that it almost hurt. All the others were silent. John's dad made some attempts at conversation, and Cullen mumbled a few replies, but mostly they just ate like starving men.

Afterwards their host took them into the next room. There was only the kitchen, a bedroom in the back, and this large den. Plain hardwood floor; small TV in the corner; whitewashed walls hung with photos. John and his siblings, among them a pale sister with bright brown eyes—"teaching in Phoenix now. Another reason to get me out this way," his dad said. A shadowbox full of medals. One photo of himself, much younger, in fatigues and stethoscope, standing beside a man on crutches in front of a drab green tent and a dark stand of trees. "Dong Tam. Surgical unit." He moved on.

Cullen stood looking at the photo. "What do you think about the Gulf?" he asked.

"Try not to. I'd rather watch basketball." His features wrinkled. "John told me about your brother," he said.

"Yeah."

"Well. God help us, this won't last long."

It was Stick who drove them back out on the road an hour later.

While John and his dad and Cullen talked, Wes, half-listening, had sunk into a rare contentment, could have stayed the rest of the afternoon. There in the central room where they all gathered, the blinds were cracked so that sharp blades of light pierced the cool darkness, glinted off the photo frames and lined up in clear succession along the far wall. Squinting his eyes and feeling the good food warm in his belly, he became drowsy.

In the middle of this house, surrounded by voices, he found himself unexpectedly restful, at his ease.

Then Stick sat across from him and began thrumming his fingers on a chair. His eyes had not been still all day, and as he began to fidget back and forth they finally sank into a dull glare. During a lull in the conversation, he broke in: "'Bout time to hit the road, isn't it?"

As they began to say their goodbyes, Wes ambled through the back of the house and got his only glimpse of the bedroom. It was even barer than the front, but passing through he saw a single photograph of a woman who looked like John's sister. Same eyes. The photo was older, black and white. The woman wore a bridal dress. High up on the wall above was a piece of wood with a bare human figure nailed to it.

John's father was waiting for him out by the car. "Beautiful afternoon," he said matter-of-factly, gazing up at the sky. "And you fellas are free! Make the most of it."

That night, atop a barren hillside that overlooked the long dry valley through which they had passed, they lay beneath a huge marbled moon. Bright stars hung round it, speckled against the deep black of space. A few yellow lights flickered down in the gray valley like a dim reflection of the brilliance above.

They had almost not made it there.

Roaring down the cottage's long driveway, Stick had begun to dig frantically through a box of tapes and turn the volume up on the stereo, wheeling the Blazer right at the main road.

"Wrong way, Stick. Campsite's *left*." John was looking at the map. He and Wes were in the back.

"Don't I know it. *Vay-gus*, baby! It's not too late." He grinned like a madman, looking straight at Cullen.

"Whooaaa there, sailor! You'll get your chance. But right now we need to stick with the Plan of the Day. Another weekend of hard drinking would do me in. What do you say, gentlemen?" He turned to the rear.

"Camp," John said. Wes nodded in agreement. Stick was beginning to irritate him so much that he was afraid of what his voice would sound like if he spoke.

"To the wilderness, then," Cullen said. Stick groaned but gave in, wheeling the big vehicle around in a wide U-turn that took them off the asphalt and into the sand. A fat lizard scampered from beneath their wheels and atop a rock where it stared, panting, its shiny black eyes following them down the road.

Then as later, hiking out into the flats in the late afternoon, it was Cullen who held them together.

Strapping on backpacks, they left the Blazer at a lonely wind-swept parking lot and walked out into the open desert. Small posts planted at intervals amongst the sagebrush and cacti marked their path. They joked for a few minutes—"We're lettin' *this* guy lead us into the boonies?" Stick said as John, smiling, pulled out a compass—and then for a long time there was nothing but the wind and their feet crunching the caked earth. Finally, Cullen spoke across the other two to John.

"Your dad's a funny guy. But cool. I mean, it's funny how he's living out there like a hermit, but he seems really social, too."

"Yep."

"So he's got his buddies that he sees sometimes. But what else? I mean, during the week. Is it just him and his TV and plants?"

"Couple a days a week, he volunteers on the reservation back there. Runs a little medical clinic. Some old nurses drive over from Palm Springs to help. You know." He paused. "Those people don't have too much else to work with."

"*That's* pretty cool." Cullen was beginning to sweat a little, looking down at the dirt. "And he didn't even mention it."

The deep blue sky grew brighter, orange and red, over the long hills to the west, but mauve and then purple before them even as the land itself fell into shade. There was only the four of them and the strange low plants and the range that rose ahead like a moonscape, then only their voices and the beam of a flashlight and the place where the stars disappeared behind the looming bulk of the hills. Finally there was the trickle of water.

"Creek leads up to the camp." John's voice.

They were tired now and quiet until they came at last to a place where there were scattered boulders and a stand of eucalyptus. The creek was narrower and faster. Where the flashlight shone, Wes could see grass along its banks. "Here," John said.

They set up tents and cooked a small dinner, then lit cigars and lay on their backs and looked up at the sky. It was so vast and clear as to be overwhelming. When Wes stood to go back to the tent for water, he saw at his feet only the small fire and the orange coals on the ends of their cigars and for just a moment felt dizzy. He was glad to lie back down on the solid earth.

"Jets," Cullen said. Where his finger pointed, Wes had to stare for a moment before he could make out the puny red lights—six of them—cutting across the sky.

"Going up to Twentynine Palms."

"Shit," Cullen said.

"What?" John turned to him.

"It's just like my brother."

"What do you mean?"

"Except we're not with a damn tank squad." He sat up. "My folks talked to him middle of this past week. He couldn't say much except that he was still in the desert. They asked him if the air war had changed anything, and he said no, except he saw all the damn lights in the sky every night, going in there and coming back out."

No one spoke. The jets passed out of sight, and Wes looked down in the valley to see faint headlights inching their way along the main highway they had come in on. Some trucker, hauling Coke or diapers or refrigerators to the Pacific. Wes imagined him—an overweight man, plagued by hemorrhoids, inching his way across the drowsy continent. He looked back up and saw Cullen's profile against the stars.

"Wonder when Joe'll see something happen," Wes said. He really did wonder, of course, and the long silence had somehow begun to embarrass him, but he immediately regretted saying it.

"God only knows." Cullen shook his head.

"Well." Stick was rolling off the ground. "We'll see. I don't want my man worrying too much about it, though. Things'll be fine. Besides," he said, pulling a little flask out of his back pocket, "I think 'Billy' here really has a little something else on his mind."

"Is that right?" Cullen said slowly, turning and smiling meekly.

"Or a little *piece* of something, maybe?" He turned the flask up.

"Come on, now," John warned, laughing a little but looking straight at Stick.

"Whoa now, Stick. You're running along the wrong tracks here." Cullen did not smile. "I'm not just playing one of your little tricks."

"Is that right? I saw you looking and talking up at Venice last week. Don't tell me you've been tamed, my man—we still got a lotta work left to do."

"That's enough."

"Hey—*serious*. Okay, okay..." He took another drink and leaned back into the firelight. "I'll back off. Besides, I'd bet there's *someone* else here likes hearing about it even less than you." His eyes moved to Wes. "Don't wanna cause too much trouble out here in the wilderness."

"Alright now, gentlemen. Let's settle down." John stood up. "The sheep up here are gonna start making noise around 0600, so we'd better get to sleep."

Wes made himself lie still on the ground as the others began to move. He had to let Stick pass. If he got up and faced him, he did not know what he would do. Stick had done the worst thing to Wes that he could have done. He had tried to humiliate him.

Cullen waited. It was just the two of them now, looking out into the valley. Something howled in the distance. Wes thought of a coyote loping home with a rabbit dangling from its mouth, yellow eyes aglow.

"Hey," Cullen said. "Don't worry about that jackass. He's just about three sheets to the wind, and say what he will, he's the one who can't stand being away from the women." He smiled. "We'll kick his ass together next time he sounds off."

Wes smiled back, then stepped toward the tent he shared with John. The last thing he saw outside was Cullen, stretching, his long arms reached upward as if to pull down the luminous constellations overhead.

Gazing at the dull canvas over his head while John dozed next to him, and then all the ride home, Wes turned what had happened the night before over in his head. Cullen—too innocent to hold a grudge—had forgiven Stick by morning. Whether Wes could was another matter.

Stick had broken the rule that the others observed silently. He had spoken about Cullen and Cynthia in front of him.

Had Stick not been the one responsible, he might have thought that it was just as well. Why should they all act as if he did not know? It was insulting in its way—as if he were not man enough to take it. And, of course, he *did* know.

In the weeks after he first glimpsed the two of them out on the sailboat, Wes could see Cullen and Cynthia slowly beginning to change. In company with the group, they refrained from obvious affections but silently gravitated together, each watching the other peripherally, exchanging sly smiles and glances. But it was when he was alone with either of them that Wes could most tell. Passing him in the courtyard, Cynthia was friendly but would then duck her head and move on. There were no more lunch invitations.

He had known that was coming and envied Cullen enough for it. What he was not prepared for were the changes to Cullen himself.

He might have expected the mounting inaccessibility—with the boat no longer out back and Cynthia's apartment so close by, Cullen was harder to get to than ever—but there were other changes, too. When he was with Cynthia he looked calmer, more relaxed than ever, and she less skeptical, even delighted. It was obvious: they were happy together. The only pleasure Wes could take in thinking it was that it was such a cliché, more so even than his own life must have sounded when he had first met her.

There was something else. Whether it was Cynthia and what she might lead to or his brother or both—Wes could not know for sure— Cullen seemed suddenly pulled toward extremes, at moments (mostly with her) ever more at ease, almost serious, at other times seeking diversion with an ever growing intensity. It was as if suddenly Cynthia and Joe and maybe even something else were presenting him with a choice, a choice he alternately pondered and sought refuge from. Wes not only watched but eventually felt it, became swept up in it himself, as Cullen somehow both disappeared more frequently from their ranks and emerged more firmly than ever as their leader, a dauntless daredevil captain in the frantic pursuit of pleasure that their lives had long been tending toward and now became.

For all that, it was not Cullen but Elizabeth who set them the next step toward their final end. Three days after they returned from the desert, she hosted what she chose to call, in her half-mocking promotional manner, a "beachside bacchanal." And it was there that she turned herself for the first time to Wes.

In the middle of the broad strand that ran not quite half a mile beneath La Mirage sat three great rings of stone. There Elizabeth—who had taken the day off to prepare—led the four men to find driftwood for bonfires. The day was overcast; gray birds circled overhead. In the middle of the clouded afternoon Wes looked down the beach to see Stick and Cullen moving along the waterline, hunched over, kicking aside clumps of seaweed, clutching sticks under their arms and occasionally lunging at one another like warring hunter-gatherers afoot in the primordial surf.

When there was not enough wood and what they had found was too wet to light, the five of them drove to the grocery store to buy artificial logs. Elizabeth hopped into the back seat between Wes and Stick. "Alright, hunky cavemen," she said, laying a hand on each of them, "you two have to keep me safe tonight. There's no telling what might happen at a *bacchanal*." She drew the name out with a kind of ironic relish. Cullen laughed out loud—"This girl is ready to go!"— while John just smiled back at her from the front passenger seat. She gave him a long wink.

The guests began arriving at dusk, following the bonfires and the row of tiki torches Elizabeth had lit to guide them down to the gray sea. She had invited not only her usual circle of acquaintances but also the entire contingent of ensigns from the TPU, and they were arriving in full force. When enough had gathered she leapt atop one of the stone rings and stood there, her thin frame dark against the flames. "Gentlemen!" she said, hoisting a cup, "...and *ladies*," she simpered, "welcome to our *bacchanal*!!" She thrust one arm out over the crowd and almost lost her balance.

Wes saw Hooper appear next to him, gazing at Elizabeth as if he were a child discovering some exotic animal on his first trip to the zoo. "What is up with *her*?" he said, flames playing off his face. Donkers—how had he gotten here?—stood close behind him, aghast.

Their hostess had regained her footing with a hand from John. "If you've been watching your TVs, you know that right now it's *freezing* back on the East Coast... and if you're like me, you're glad just to be here in wonderful, sunny, southern Ca-li-*forn*-ia." She clicked her teeth and beamed at her audience. "So while we're all here—dashing naval officers...members of the La Mirage community... friends!—let's, all, have a very, good, *time*." Her voice took on a singsong lilt as she finished, and both her arms had risen gradually so that they were now over the level of her head, her slender body so rigid that with a set of wings she would have looked like a statue of Victory.

The crowd stood silent for a moment before breaking into hoots and applause. She beamed back at them and took a swig of her drink before Cullen stepped up beneath her and lifted her onto the ground as easily as if she were a mannequin.

"She's drinking."

The voice over Wes's shoulder made him start. Cynthia had somehow appeared behind him, but when he turned she was not even looking at him—just staring straight ahead at the bonfire scene.

"Yep," Wes said. "More than coffee, it looks like." He thought a hard moment before he came up with something else to say. "Cullen's got ahold of her now, though."

"She's in no shape for drinking." She took a step forward and was lost in the crowd.

His eyes followed her for a moment before another voice interrupted. "That a friend of yours?" A short pear-shaped figure had sidled up next to him. Donkers.

"Her? Yes." He paused. "Of ours."

"First party she's thrown?"

"Party? Oh—Elizabeth. Well, no. She lives for this kind of thing."

"You and Cullen seem pretty buddy-buddy with her."

"Yeah. She helps run our apartment place. She's always inviting us to things."

"Party boys."

"Party boys?"

"You know. I know *you* know. I guess I don't expect much different from Stick and Cullen. They'll skate as long as they can. You, though—I'd expect a little better performance from you."

Did he need Donkers telling him this? "Well, Ensign Donkers, I'd be doing a little more if our Navy would call on me. But as it is I don't seem to be real necessary to the war effort or anything, so I don't see much else to do."

Donkers pursed his lips. "Could be doing something. Lot to be learned from just following the air war. Lot to be learned even at the TPU office. The yeoman's job isn't the glamor side of the Navy, but it's there. And some of us know how to make the best of a bad situation."

"Well, you sure have been the golden boy at the TPU, but you seem to be letting your hair down a little right now, don't you? I mean, what are you doing here?" It was the first time he had seen Donkers out of uniform. He had on a garish green Hawaiian shirt and a pair of khaki shorts that hung down like Bermudas.

"Just having a Coke." Donkers lifted his cup. "See ya," he smiled, and slipped away. Wes saw him walk to the edge of the crowd, pull something out of his pocket, then hunker down close to the sand. A tiny penlight gleamed in the gathering darkness.

As the evening deepened and Wes wandered from conversation to conversation, he found himself talking only half-heartedly and more and more sunk in his own thoughts. Donkers was a bureaucratic little fool (was he taking notes— filing reports on them? As if Ragis cared). More pathetic than Hooper, in his way. Still, his remarks stung. Donkers was partly right. Beneath the drink and the chatter in which he immersed himself, he knew it, and knowing it, drank more.

In the round of the night that gradually became not ordered progression but jumbled images—laughing teeth, dancing arms, coals glimmering deep red against the darkness—his eyes turned more and more to Cynthia and from there to Elizabeth. Cynthia hung close to her, keeping Cullen, too, in a sort of loose orbit. But in the midst of all the people Elizabeth moved among, it was John more than anyone that she clung to, so that when they were all together Wes could lean close to him and say, "Looks like Miss Elizabeth has taken a liking to you, sailor."

John shook his head with a frown. "She's pretty messed up."

"I may be getting there myself."

"Looks like it." He turned up his own drink for a second. "That's not what I mean, though."

Just then Elizabeth leaned in and put her arms around the two of them. "My boys!" she said. "What are my two favorites up to over here?"

"Why, praising our hostess, of course." Wes was feeling better. Elizabeth could do that to him.

"You two are so sweet," she said. "Not like that Stick. He's all trouble. A *bad* boy." Her cup dangled in front of them. Coffee.

"You need all that caffeine to fulfill your duties?"

"Ha! Something's gotta keep me goin'." She gave him a swat on the cheek and flew off to another group.

Cynthia walked up in her place. "Alright," she sighed. "I'm worn out, and some of us have got to go to work tomorrow. And at least she's not drinking. Can I turn her over to you guys?" She only looked at John when she said it. Cullen lingered behind her, silent, his eyes still but restless beneath. Wes knew the look—it had been locked on him before, though it burned deeper now—and it meant that Cullen was ready to stay out with them all night. But when Cynthia walked off into the darkness, he followed her.

Later, alone, Wes found Elizabeth suddenly clinging to him and when she began to speak he was ready to listen.

"It's so good to have you here, Wes."

He nodded. "Well, thanks."

She had turned her face up to him. "You seem like somebody who knows what he's doing. You know what I mean? It's a simple thing but there aren't as many as you might think, you know? Like John, too.

But he worries too much about me. I don't need people to worry about me. I need people to be my friends."

He nodded. His side hurt where she was leaning against him—she was unbelievably light, but he could feel her shoulder bones sticking into him.

"You can be my friend, can't you?" She looked toward the crowd and did not wait for an answer. "And you. You're—*gallant.* I can tell. Like my dad. Real gallant, old school. And it's only someone like that you can be a lady with."

He nodded again, though he was not listening so much as watching and trying to assess her. She was not drunk after all. Still there was something different in the way she had looked at him and now was looking out of the circle of fire and into the darkness that masked the sea. He could not say it then, but later he knew it. Elizabeth always seemed to avoid conversations with just one person. She was forever in company with a group or running from one group to another, but here and now she had slowed down. For the first time Wes was seeing her seek herself in the mirror of another, and somehow she had chosen him or at least what she thought he might be.

She tightened her grip around his waist and then turned directly to him in a way that made him start. Behind wet eyes ringed with darkness her features were clear and finely drawn, and for a long moment he did not know whether to turn away or speak or pull her face up to his. He felt suddenly relieved when she tilted her head, released him, and slipped suddenly into her old expression. "John's coming! And the others. Yay!"

He took a step back and looked behind him. Against the feeble light of the dying bonfires, silhouettes approached from out of the thinning crowd.

"One heckuva party, don'cha think?" she asked, talking to him as if he were ten people. "I'm worn out with hostessing. Been doing my best, even though I feel a little full. Too much to eat!"

Then the group was upon them and they were back in the familiar.

When Elizabeth soon ran off to talk with other guests he felt ready to go up to bed. He left the others and walked out past the remnants of the crowd and took the long way down the beach. He moved farther from the light and the voices, saw the moon broken in pieces on the

sea, heard the waves rolling in unbroken succession from east Asia.
He was thinking about the war and what Donkers had said, and he
looked to the ocean, one great body of water lapping at the shores of
Kuwait, he knew, even as it lapped here. Beneath the great web of stars
he felt utterly alone and of little account.

Then he heard retching sounds behind a trashcan. Someone sick.
Repeatedly. A small figure appeared and trotted back toward the fires.
When the moon came out from behind a cloud he could see that it
was Elizabeth.

The light he had seen in Cullen's eyes that night began to burn
brighter.

In the weeks following the bacchanal, with Cynthia hard at work
on a story, Cullen led them all out nearly every other night. Presumably he spent the nights in between with her—Wes knew it but tried
not to think about it. And whenever Cynthia was busy, Cullen suddenly began to appear in their doorway in the early evening, never
quite setting foot inside but standing in the doorway, leaning across
the threshold with a cigarette in his mouth. He had taken to smoking,
at first without conviction but with a kind of dilettantish absentmind-
edness and only later a furtive need, popping open a can of cheap beer
with one hand and dangling a cigarette in the other, wearing an old
T-shirt and ragged shorts and a pair of flip-flops.

"You look like hell," John said to him one day.

"Damn straight," he laughed, and lit a match.

"Boy Scout gone bad," Wes said. It was what he looked like—tawny
hair disheveled, tan face obscured in a cloud of smoke, clean features
hidden by the upturned beer can. "Why don't you quit hanging on
our door and just come in?"

"No can do. I've come to bring you two ladies *out*," he said, looking at them half-seriously and taking a long drag on his cigarette. He
coughed.

"Good God. You don't even know how to smoke that thing."

"What's your girlfriend think about your new tobacco habit?" John
said.

"My *girlfriend*. Nice." He laughed and flicked a butt out on the concrete walk. "She thinks I'm a nut. But, fortunately," he grinned, "that's part of what she seems to like about me. Can't say I see what motivates her." He looked like he was going to say more, but then he glanced at Wes and stopped. "Enough talk. Happy Hour at the Box starts in thirty minutes, gentlemen. Who's with me?"

It was almost always the four men—John sometimes got away with one of his absences—and three or four of the women. They walked down into the strip of bars that ran along the beach, dark crowded places where the music was too loud and the air reeked of cigarettes, to the Old Ox (the "Moldy Box," Stick called it) and a dance bar that served rum drinks and a place called the Shellback where young accountants and law students and waitpeople eyed and groped and talked at one another beneath huge mounted fish, surrounded by coffee-tinted photos of old ships and grizzled seamen. It was there that they always ended the night, Cullen sinking into a corner booth too drunk to talk and Wes not much better but clear-headed enough to survey the scene and be dissatisfied. Across from him, inevitably, were Stick and the hippy chicks—they worked through a temp agency and never had any clear commitments the next day—and sometimes Terri. The women hung onto Stick like they were drowning.

One of them, the bigger one whose name was Louise, would sometimes come over and sit by Wes and talk about how she wanted to chuck it all (*chuck it all*, that's what she'd say—what did she have to chuck?) and follow the Dead. She vaguely aspired to an acting career. "Everything here's so fake. On screen I could be real," she told him once. But so far she had only landed a role as a gun moll in some half-assed gangster farce that was being staged in the cocktail lounge of a Ramada Inn out by the freeway. She would talk to him for a while and then, after a few drinks, sigh and lean against him and blink her empty blue eyes up at his. Meeting them he could only turn away and fall prey to an immense sadness. This heavy girl from out of some Midwestern cornfield—he pictured her grandfather riding a red tractor and wearing bib overalls—now far from home and fallen into the clutches of Stick, a world as debauched and foreign as that of any Persian satrap. For with Terri still hanging around and Julie now Stick's regular lay, as he told them often enough, he seemed to be presiding over a virtual harem. One time Wes had gotten annoyed enough with his pseudo-hippy posturing to ask him what the hell a military officer saw in all this Woodstock crap, and Stick just grinned and said, "Free love, man. Free love."

The girls didn't even seem to mind one another. But even though two of them were attractive enough—Terri harmless and slow, the sort who was always wearing fuzzy sweaters and smacking her gum and reading *Cosmopolitan* without knowing any better, Julie dressed like Janis Joplin but dumber and better-looking and probably meaner—Wes did not really envy Stick the women. He only grew to dislike Stick's mounting smugness. He had been hungry and now he looked almost full. That self-satisfied grin ... this dumbshit who thought he had it all. A dumbshit. Once or twice, looking across the table at him, Wes felt tempted to reach over and slam his face into the bottles piling up beneath it.

Worse, Stick seemed able to gauge and enjoy his anger. Occasionally he taunted Wes, though he would misjudge how best to do so. For some reason he tried to get at him through Elizabeth. She always came with them but usually wandered off talking to others, ever the crazed socialite, running around the bar and hugging acquaintances until she returned to their circle at the end of the night. Then if John were with them she might seek him out, and occasionally she might turn to Stick himself. But often enough she would come to Wes and lean on him, looking and feeling thinner than ever alongside Louise. Then Stick would get up and come to them and start rubbing her back—as if this would upset Wes, who by this point in the night usually felt nothing but disdain for the whole lot of them, himself included. Rather than making him angrier, Stick's ploy only emphasized the ridiculousness of their situation, pushing him beyond disgust and into a kind of bemused numbness.

In the face of all this folly, why, he asked himself, did he persist in keeping company with them?

He had two reasons. In part it was because the crowds and the noise and finally even the anger were preferable to the empty introspection he felt himself condemned to most of the day. But it was also Cullen. For despite the fact that he had destroyed whatever dim hopes Wes had half-articulated to himself about Cynthia, Cullen could still, in her absence, somehow summon up the simple sense of boyhood, near brotherhood, that they had before. It would come seemingly unbidden, the two of them at the bar, Cullen telling some joke or just talking about going home, missing the East Coast and wanting to go back to live near his family but near the coast too, dreaming about running a little marina for a living, tending to boats and selling beer.

And had Stick known anything he would have known that what made Wes angriest was not whatever doltish designs he evidenced toward Elizabeth, but that Cullen did not share his own anger. How could Cullen be what he was and still countenance someone like Stick; how could the two of them share the same world?

Always in the bar there was a TV with the war on. It had come in the slow season after New Year's, and now it was like a football game or something. There was never any volume but perpetually the war shimmered there, harsh and bright as the desert itself, above the dim haze of smoke and chatter. It was like a torch held aloft over a congregation of ghosts, a beacon lighting their way out of the ephemeral and into a world of substance. So it seemed to Wes. Then he would turn to see Cullen, hunched over, lighting a cigarette and turning his face away.

Even there, half-drunk and sitting in a beachside bar, Wes could tell that the war was doing something to them. Distant as it seemed, it was somehow responsible for his own predicament, the knowledge of his own inadequacy that grew deeper every day. It was what justified Stick's headlong and heedless pursuit of pleasure. And it was behind whatever was happening to Cullen. They had all been affected. And subtly, silently, they were being torn, sundered, driven to the things that were to come. Watching them all gathered in seeming friendship around the table at the end of those nights, he might have known that something had to break.

Part Three

February - April, 1991

7

February had always been to Wes like a long Sunday—a time between times, the month when nothing happened, four long gray weeks meant to be endured rather than savored. But now maybe they all felt it. Maybe it was at least in part the fear of February that drove them to the kind of near perpetual motion they were about to embark upon.

Surely there was more to it than that for Cullen, whose brother was enduring not the time between times but what seemed to be the last time (he'd told him in a low voice one night at the Shellback—one of those moments Wes was always hoping for, both placing him vicariously on the field of battle and binding him closer to Cullen—about his brother's last letter, some enlisted man in his tank reading aloud from the Bible and praying a lot and talking about "the end time"). And Wes's own frustrations with the war were clear enough—to himself, at least. But what was it that finally drove Elizabeth to him? And what was driving John to the things that possessed him by the end of the month?

How strange that, this year of all years, February was the month when things began to change for good.

The first of the month, Lieutenant Ragis took a thirty-day leave and placed the TPU in standdown. The ensigns now had to report in only on Wednesdays. The rest of the week they were on liberty.

Cullen and Stick pulled out the maps and rallied the others, and then they were off.

They planned it so they would circle back through San Agustin in the middle of each week. That still gave them time to cover plenty of ground, to move in great looping figure eights out from the southern coast to the far inland reaches of California and beyond—north along the seething coastline to Big Sur and back down the dusty San Joaquin Valley, down again to San Diego and along the barren border, curving up past the Salton Sea and slowly westward again, then out to Havasu in Arizona and north to Vegas and at last through Death Valley back down toward the sea.

After the frenzied neon glare of the casinos, the Valley was a place of stillness and quiet, a jagged white landscape as stark and geometric as a skeleton picked clean. When they drove out of it, Wes, hungover and sipping icewater, looked out through his open window to see a large sign welcoming them back to the main road. Eisenhower Interstate System. Five stars formed a pentagon beneath the letters, white against the green sign, a shield emblazoned above them in red and blue. Then he remembered the story of the general and the roads, how after the first big war young Colonel Ike himself took a road trip cross country. It took him two months to drive from D.C. to San Francisco. With his advocacy the interstate system was born in the wake of World War II, partly to help mobilize troops in case of an invasion.

That invasion was going to be communist, of course. But now that was all over. Now the Soviet Union was dying, there was a war on in some oilfields half a world away, and here they were burning up fuel as they sped through the desert trying to forget both it and themselves.

It was all a joke, Wes thought, and Julie and Louise were the punch line. They had bought a Volkswagen van and were trailing the men across the state, Stick riding with them most of the time while the others drove his Blazer. That was fine with Wes. But he knew they were back there listening to their music and the girls were smoking pot—if Stick wasn't careful he was going to test positive from second-hand smoke—and acting like it was the goddamn sixties. They loved the whole hippy thing except that they didn't give a damn about the war. When they had a hot radiator in Barstow, the whole lot of them stopped and the girls started drinking beer and playing pool with one of the off-duty mechanics and told him they hated Saddam as much as anybody. "Fuck the ragheads," Julie said, sinking an eight ball and cradling the stick between her legs in the middle of the hot dirty garage. She was sweating lightly, long blond hair pasted back across her forehead, her tie-dye damp and sticking to the tips of her little breasts. The man she was playing with had a couple of teeth missing and a few that were brown and a big smear of grease down his cheek, and he was staring straight across the table at her. She looked back at him, unwrapped some French ticklers she had gotten from the bathroom, and slid them around the top of her beer bottle. "Tasty," she laughed, turning the bottle up. "I've got to try one of these on the other end." Another mechanic had quit working on a Buick and was staring at her while he wiped down a wrench with an oily rag. Then she and the pool player walked behind the garage, and a couple of minutes later she came back around the corner stuffing a little bag of something into her Guatemalan purse. Their van was ready and the owner, a fat bald man who looked like he had a cancer on top of his head, walked them out with a big grin on his red face. "You ladies stop by any time you're back this way, now."

Through the whole thing even Elizabeth, who had taken a couple of days off to join them for this trip, stood between Wes and Cullen in silent wonder. Now she shifted from the van to the Blazer as Wes took the wheel for the last stretch home. "Whoo!" she sighed. "Those girls are something else. You think it's a Midwestern thing?" she said, putting her hand on his leg. She had taken to doing that lately. She looked frail sunk into the passenger seat next to him, bony legs—they were bony, there was no other word for it— tucked up beneath her but still sticking out from the skirt she had had to wear because of the heat. Normally she wore some kind of loose slacks. There was something else different about her, though. She turned her face to him and he knew it. She looked exhausted. "They keep talking about heading up to Berkeley next. What would my daddy say? Or my sorority sisters? Not the kind of scene for a proper Virginia lady." She batted her weary eyes at him. "But between them and Stick, those girls'll probably have their way."

That was how they came to be in the city of St. Francis when the ground war started.

It was a trip that came at the end of the long muted week when he first suspected what John was up to.

February was winding down and Ragis was still not back yet, but they had decided, against the protests of Stick and Julie, to slow down for a few days so that they could do laundry and pay bills. These sorts of mundane tasks, their insignificance, always made Wes feel worse than watching the war or even knowingly diverting himself from it. He was all the more irritated to see his roommate—who had only taken part in half of their trips anyhow—seem to find a kind of simple pleasure in them.

It was a time when he necessarily found himself turning to John. Deprived of Cynthia and Cullen alike, repulsed by Stick, he might naturally have confided everything to his roommate; but he found that whenever he came close to doing so, John would reveal something that threw the conversation into disarray.

It was four on a Tuesday. They were in the apartment with the glass door open and the TV on, feeling the breeze blow in from down the green hillside and watching the aerial annihilation of an Iraqi convoy—explosions, smoking vehicles, stick figures scurrying into the sand. Wes was saying something about himself when John looked up from his latest project and spoke:

"I don't think I'm meant to be shooting at anybody."

Wes frowned. "Well, you picked a hell of a profession to sign up for, then."

He felt irritated. It was just like John to start talking about this kind of thing out of nowhere, and he felt a sudden wave of disdain sweep over him. Sitting cross-legged in front of the TV and hammering together a miniature chair, John looked like a boy playing with his father's tools. On the screen behind him now, a mock tank smoldered atop a sand dune while Apache helicopters swarmed overhead. Army officers stood milling about in the distance.

"I guess you're right about that." He picked up a nail.

"What in God's name are you building?"

"A chair."

"I can see that. What's it for?"

"The Chaplains Charity Drive."

The Chaplains Charity Drive. A chaplain named Commander Kuwelski—Father Kuwelski, John called him—had come by the TPU to solicit donations for it. "Wasn't that over a month or two ago?"

"Better late than never. Somebody'll be able to use it."

"Good Lord. You've been getting softer all the time. You should take up with Julie and Louise and start a little love commune."

John laughed.

"You and Stick. Between the four of you, you can start the goddamn sixties all over again."

"That's not exactly my speed." He drove home the last nail and stood up. Then he tested the strength of the chair with his foot. It held.

"You and me both. But everyone else around here seems to be having a regular lovefest."

John looked at him. His brows came together so that he looked both sad and perplexed. *I know you told me so way back when,* thought Wes. *But you better not say it.*

John looked at his watch. "I've gotta go. Be back around dinnertime."

Wes nodded. He wasn't going to give him the satisfaction of asking.

The chair stood in the middle of the room while John washed up. Wes picked it up and tugged at the joints. Firm.

John grabbed it from him as he went out the door.

The next day he went by the TPU in the morning to check in and then drove alone to a near deserted beach at a state park just south of them. He went on a long run, swam for a while, and stretched out in the sand to dry in the noonday sun. Then he bought some tacos at a beachside stand and sat on a bench by the boardwalk. He looked to the sea and saw a little dark man with a stick and a bag, walking alongside the surf and picking up garbage. Gulls circled overhead; a great tanker moved slowly across the horizon. From this distance it looked tiny and he could not tell which way it was bound.

That evening he came back to find his apartment dark and quiet. He went out to the pool in the dusk and found Terri there, sitting in a lounge chair and reading *Cosmo*.

"Hi," she said. She was smacking on a piece of gum.

"Hi."

"Where've you been?"

He told her.

"You've been getting some exercise. Good job."

"Gotta do something."

"I'm fat."

He protested dutifully. Actually, she looked pretty good in her bathing suit.

"Out here you've got to work to look good. Can't stay bundled up like back home." She was from Ohio.

Wes was looking at the cover of her magazine. It said something about orgasms.

"Oh, I see you. Can't let you in on all our secrets." She snatched it up. The glossy pages slapped against one another in the evening stillness. "You're a big reader, aren't you?"

"Not really."

"You seem kinda deep to me. Like Louise. She and Julie are so—political, you know?"

"I guess." Sometimes he saw Louise reading *Rolling Stone*.

"Those crazy girls." She was looking at him pretty steadily.

"Y'all spend a lot of time together, don't you?"

"Well. Sometimes."

"So Stick and Julie are kind of dating now, I guess?" He had a sudden urge to see if he could get a rise out of her.

"Sort of, I guess. They're not real possessive people though, ya know?"

"Hm."

"So cool. I mean, I've had a lot of boyfriends, and it just gets kind of old. It's nice just to be kind of relaxed about everything?" She had picked up a California way of lilting her voice so that a statement sounded like a question, *y'know?*

"Hmmm." He had leaned back in his chair and was scanning the inner walls of La Mirage. There were lights on in most of the rooms—dozens and dozens of them. Who were all of these people? What was going on in there?

He tried to make out Cynthia's room, but it was sunk in a corner.

"You kind of keep to yourself." She had pulled out some nail polish and was leaning toward her toes.

"Hm. I suppose so."

"It's not like we wouldn't like to see more of you." She was squinting at a toe but threw him a little glance and a smile. "Not just Louise."

"Well. How about that?"

"Then there's Elizabeth. Course, she's in the loop already. And then Cynthia says we've got to keep an eye on her."

"Yes." He wondered what she meant but not enough to ask.

He had already determined that it was best just to look at her and not to listen—so long as he only heard the lilt of her voice she was not so bad—but still he could not help but overhear a few things. She was a dental hygienist (he already knew that) and liked her job fine. She was making good enough money and having the time of her life in southern California. "I'm making good enough money, and I'm having the time of my life in southern California," she said.

The stars brightened slowly overhead. People moved in and out of the shadowy walkways in front of the apartment doors. After a while they saw two figures walking slowly across the courtyard. They stopped beneath one of the lights surrounding the pool and stood there talking. Cullen and John.

"Hi guys," Terri yelled.

They walked over at an easy pace and came into the light.

"What's up?" Wes asked.

"Not much," Cullen said. It was hard to tell the way the shadows played around his face, but he somehow looked serious.

They talked for a while and Wes thought something looked funny but Terri said it.

"Do you guys have *dirt* on your foreheads?"

John laughed a second, then stopped. "Ashes."

There was a brief silence. "We were at Mass. Church — Ash Wednesday." Cullen stood a little stiffly as he said it.

"Oh, church! Wow."

"Well—it's not like I'm a regular." Cullen paused and looked at his watch. "Getting late. I'm supposed to give my parents a call. They're supposed to hear from Joe today." He looked at Wes. Wes didn't know what to say and so he just nodded, and then Cullen and John walked off.

Terri sat up in her chair and pulled a foot beneath her. "Bad light," she said after a minute, fingering her toes. "What was it about the ashes?"

"I think it's a Catholic thing."

"Ohhh." She let the foot go and leaned back again. "I'm not Catholic. I'm that other thing. What do you call it?"

He pursed his lips. "Protestant?"

"Yeah! Or — noooo," she said. "Church of… church of… something, I think."

The last trip was Stick's. He insisted that they all squeeze into the van for the drive to San Francisco, and the whole way up the great green valley and across the golden hills that rolled down to the Bay Wes had to listen to it:

> *Sometimes the light's all shinin' on me*
> *Other times I can barely see*
> *Lately it occurs to me*
> *What a long strange trip it's been.*
>
> *Truckin'*
> *I'm a goin' home*
> *Whoa whoa baby back where I belong*
> *Back home*
> *Sit down and patch my bones*
> *And get back truckin' on*

He fumed in the back for a while and wanted to blame it all on Julie and Louise — acting like it was 1968, the year most of them had been born — but finally he knew he could not. It had been building for a long time now, and they weren't the only ones. Even back home he and the other cadets would go down to the state university and see lots of kids in hippy gear and Birkenstocks, strumming guitars and playing hackeysack and that kind of thing. At bars they'd talk with girls like that. Some of his buddies even bought into it a little to get their attention, just like Stick now, wearing the clothes and talking the talk, sporting tie-dyes with their crew cuts and nobody saying a thing. "It's not like we're anti-military or anything like that," a girl told his old roommate once. "We're just into being mellow and people doing their own thing. So if that's your thing, I guess you gotta do it, right?" His roommate had taken this as a good sign, bummed a cigarette from her, and proceeded to spend the night at her apartment. On the drive back to the Institute the next day he kept doing a little shimmying dance with his shoulders and saying "Make love, not war."

But here they were now and there was a goddamn war on and they were doing this crap. It didn't seem right.

No one else seemed to mind. John was driving and grinning and even singing a little — *sometimes the light's all shinin' on me* — while Elizabeth sat across from him, wearing a baseball cap pulled low on her head and laughing and waving at people out of the big glass window that stretched out across the broad front of the van. Behind them were Julie and Louise, Stick sitting in the middle with his arms around both, and behind them Terri and Cullen and Cynthia with a cooler in the middle. It was the whole lot of them, drinking and singing and cutting up like a bunch of kids on a schoolbus, and Wes just sitting in the back, having a beer and trying to forget everything.

He had almost decided to lean over and start talking with Terri when someone else sat down beside him.

"You had enough?" Cynthia said.

"What's that?" He had to look again to make sure it was her.

"You look like you've had enough."

"I'm fine."

"It is a bit much."

"What is?"

"It's just a bit much, that's all." She was looking straight ahead at Cullen's back.

The music was loud around them and so they didn't talk much more. They just sat, Cynthia growing quieter and more sunk into herself until Cullen turned around and leaned back toward the two of them:

"Hey! What is this, loser's corner? You two need to liven up a little." He grinned at both of them for a second but then his eyes met Cynthia's and softened. "What is it?"

"Nothing," she said. "You doing alright?"

"Fine," he said, though his bright features had darkened.

"Good," she said. "That's all I'm worried about."

"Hey," he said, sliding next to her and putting his arm around her shoulders, "don't you worry about me. You just need to unwind a little, miss." He looked up at Wes and smiled awkwardly. "This woman's been working too hard."

"It's alright, Billy," she said. "It'll be a good trip. We'll have a good time." She turned to Wes and leaned back into a sunbeam that was slanting in through the back window. "Never been to San Francisco!" She had broken into a hard, sudden smile, and with the golden light on her features and her chestnut hair falling across the pained brightness of her eyes, he could only face her for a moment before he had to turn away.

The group in front was growing more raucous. When Cullen went back to them Cynthia lingered with Wes. "I don't mean to be a pain," she said. She leaned close without looking and said lowly, "It's just that his parents didn't hear from Joe the other day when he was supposed to call. And they think that could be it — that something's coming." There was a shout from the front. Cullen and Stick were wrestling with one another across the seat. "He doesn't say much about it to us all together, but he spends half his time worried sick. All this — he's just trying to hide from it." She sat back for a second and stared straight ahead. "I mean, I know he would have told you himself if he had the chance." She stood up and began to move forward, but then looked back at him once more, a little sadly. "Because I know you're his friend."

So that was it. While she was there he had allowed himself a kind of understated pleasure at her presence — and more than that, at the feeling that they were sharing something, co-conspirators — but it was all gone now. He sat silently for a minute and didn't know whether he wished more that she had come to him for some other reason or that it had been Cullen himself who had told him.

But suddenly Elizabeth was tugging at his sleeve and Terri making a space for him to sit, and he had another drink and saw out the window a great sparkling reservoir and the sweeping amber hills of what the map called the Diablo Range shimmering gold against the coming sunset and he felt alright. He had worried and felt bad enough and now he let a kind of lethargic peace sweep over him as the music played:

> *Set out runnin' but I take my time*
> *A friend of the devil is a friend of mine*
> *If I get home before daylight*
> *I just might get some sleep tonight*

But when he saw Stick's leering face mouthing the words, he felt a dull rumbling pain that he knew was not just disappointment but anger.

That night they detoured to Santa Cruz to see some people someone knew from college and so it was almost noon the next day when they rolled into San Francisco and lost themselves there.

Wes had never seen anything like it. All the drive in he was gaping childlike out the window at the looming skyline and the great ships out in the Bay. Then they were in the city itself, up and down the great hills, each one a new vista of crowded streets and high bright-windowed pastel houses, shops and restaurants marked with the cryptic curving scripts of Asia, walkers set high against the deep blue of the sea and the white of sailboats. They checked into a hostel in Haight-Ashbury — Julie and Louise had insisted on it — and walked the streets where every bar and café they passed was foreign and alluring enough to draw them in and might have held them forever, but finally they hopped on a trolley and climbed to the top of a hill and then the top of a tower and saw it all spread out before them, the wharfs below, the hills and houses across the bay that the girls said were Berkeley, the rich towering cliffs of Marin County and the arcing twin-spired bridge to seaward and the great rocking ocean-traffic passing in and out around the walled solitude of Alcatraz before them. The Pacific loomed beyond like a great abyss, but the arms of the earth curved in at the bridge to seal the bay off, a world unto itself.

They walked the streets down to the wharfs and saw the fat harbor seals basking there in the sun. Then, climbing back into the city, they stopped for coffee and whiskey, sat at a long mahogany bar lined with gleaming brass and looked out at the gray clouds rumbling in from the sea and the crowds walking dressed heavy in black on the sidewalks. They passed up through Chinatown — this place nearly Asia itself, small-framed men and women with night-dark hair and smooth saffron skin carrying groceries and smoking cigarettes in the streets — and on back to Haight. Then while the others napped he and John and Elizabeth and Terri were in the van again and out across the Golden Gate, up onto one of the Marin cliffs and looking west over the crashing sea where only a jagged cluster of islands stood like small lonely sentinels in the distance. The sky had cleared and the last dying light of the afternoon was pouring in through the remnant clouds like powdered gold. There in the trembling brightness, leaning hard into the buffeting wind, they stood atop the edge of the continent and stared down the rocky green coastline where it tumbled into the sea.

They ate the sandwiches they had brought with them and then the women, cold, went back to the van. The two men stayed to smoke cigars and look out at the Pacific.

Standing beside him John was quiet, and when Wes asked what it was he muttered something about the sadness of coming at last to the sea, "coming at last to the end of America."

"You're drunk, aren't you?"

"A little." He grinned. Terri had driven them out while he drank in the back with Wes.

Wes drew on his cigar and spat. "So you're not observing your holy season, or whatever it is, very devoutly, now, are you?"

John glanced at him, grimacing lightly, then flicked his cigar at the ground. Ashes fell at his feet. "Well." He looked away again.

"I heard Elizabeth asking you about it."

"She's just interested in the fasting part."

"Or she's just interested in you."

"She's just interested in the fasting part. The last thing *she* needs."

He paused. "What do you mean?"

"You know," he said, shuffling his legs back and forth. He was starting to shiver. "I mean, it's pretty obvious, isn't it?"

He thought for a second. "That she doesn't need to go on a diet?"

"That's a damn understatement."

Wes could just make out a long horn drifting in on the wind. A massive cargo ship, its black sides streaked with orange rust, was steaming slowly toward the bridge beneath them.

"What else?" Wes said. He was thinking about Elizabeth now. Things that had lingered in the back of his mind. The spindly legs tucked up beneath her skirt, that night at the bonfire.

John looked at him. "She's messed up. Some kind of eating disorder. Anorexic. Bulimic. One of those."

"Jesus."

"Yep." John was pulling the hood from his jacket over his head.

"Damn." He took up his cigar again. "Makes sense, I guess. I mean — I believe it, now that you say it."

"Yeah. Well. Cynthia's known for a long time. She's trying to look out for her."

"Cynthia knows? Of course Cynthia knows. Why am I always the *last* one to know?"

"Have you been paying attention?"

Wes winced. John smiled when he said the words, but they came abruptly. With his hood up he looked like he was delivering a real rebuke, some kind of inquisitor.

But even as the words began to puzzle and even irritate Wes, John suddenly broke into a little dance, shuffling his feet lightly across the rich green grass. "Getting a little chilly up here," he said under his breath, so that Wes could think, *it's just the cold that's getting to him.* "Time to go."

The bridge rose like a cathedral before them, and Wes's eyes began to follow its great cables upward. But as they sped across it toward the rich green lawn of the Presidio, he looked back down and saw a sleek gray destroyer easing into the bay. Sailors in dress whites stood at parade rest along the rails to let the civilians know they were ready for battle.

He could not look for long.

And when he turned away and saw Elizabeth smiling next to him, he knew for the first time that the darkness at the bottom of her glittering, friendly eyes was hunger.

As they parked the van they heard music coming from the hostel. There was a party going on in the lobby.

"Dudes!" Stick yelled when they entered. "Where have you been?"

Behind him stood Cullen, the three women, and a group of strangers.

There were maybe ten of them, male and female, all drinking wine and smoking clove cigarettes and maybe something else — a cloying sweetness hung in the air — and mostly dressed like the hippy chicks except that a couple of the females had camouflage pants on. In the middle of them sat a couple of coolers and a massive boombox blaring the sound of a single guitar that alternately screeched and warbled across the room. Faint voices hooted in the background. The tune was vaguely familiar, but Wes could not quite place it.

He cornered Cullen, sipping a beer in the corner, and asked what was going on.

The story was that the newcomers were all enrolled at some big state university in southern Minnesota and had left there two weeks ago to go to Mardi Gras. They had such a good time in New Orleans that they decided not to go back. When they had started wondering what to do next, one of them said he had heard that the Dead might be playing in their old hometown the next week.

He was wrong, but that hadn't stopped them from driving to California. They had a van, too, and were reading aloud from *On the Road* and *The Electric Kool-Aid Acid Test* the whole way there. Their ringleader was a guy named Del, from Missouri, who stood over by the boombox dipping snuff and hanging on Louise. The two of them had run into one another at the ice machine a few hours earlier. That was how things got started. Now there was a plan afoot for them all to head out into Haight and party together.

Stick and the hippy chicks were completely swept up in it, of course, and Elizabeth had immediately leapt into the midst of the strangers and began to introduce herself to as many people as possible. And Cullen — talking with Cullen Wes recognized anew the feverish stare that had been lingering there on and off for weeks now. Cynthia was eyeing them carefully. He saw Stick and Julie dancing with some of the strangers atop a big coffee table in the middle of the room and then he knew there could be no question: they were stuck with these people.

"Haight! Haight!" Stick was yelling, and the whole lot of them picked up their drinks and began to surge toward the door.

As he fell in step behind them, Wes finally recognized the tune that had been playing over and over on the boombox. The Star-Spangled Banner. Del appeared beside him, and when Wes asked for confirmation he grinned and showed the black tobacco stuck in his teeth. "Damn straight. Hendrix. Live at Woodstock. Figured you military boys would like it. Kicks ass, don't it?"

It was dusk outside and they made their way down the street, carrying the music with them, stopping occasionally so that some of the women could dance while the men yelled at passing cars. At one point they came upon a group of bald people in purple robes squatting on the sidewalk around an American flag. The flag was covered with splotches of red paint and flew from a wooden staff that had a baby doll impaled on it. They were singing in a strange tongue when the group passed them by. One of Del's cohorts dropped his pants and wriggled his ass at them.

The first bar they turned into was called Zarathrusa's and since he knew they were going to be in this crowd and he would rather not think too much about it, Wes ordered two beers and set about catching up with the others. He started talking with Elizabeth and then Cullen, and before he knew it a few hours had passed and he was in a booth with one of the Minnesota girls. She had sidled up to him and said something about someone named *Nee-chee*. He had no idea what she was talking about, but she was pointing to a photo of an angry-looking bearded man that hung on the wall and going on about some class she had taken. "I mean, some of it's pretty depressing, you know. But no rules, man — no rules. I mean, I think we've just got to live for right now, you know, live life to the fullest? Like this trip. Wow. Fuckin-A." She was slurring her words and her eyes looked like they were about to close. "I mean, I'm kinda into philosophy. Too bad I'm probably about to get booted from school." She spilt a little of her wine on the table, and then he felt her hand move against his leg.

He was feeling his own drink now and just starting to wonder what he should do about her when he heard a loud noise behind him.

The place was full of mousy-looking men with goatees and women in black sweaters. Some of the women were holding hands with one another and, because there was no meat on the menu, he had guessed that they were vegetarians. Most of this crowd had just been drinking coffee and looking soulfully at one another when their group first poured into the place and started ordering beer. Even then he had half-noticed the disdainful looks they received from the crowd, and now when he turned around he saw them scatter in horror as Stick and Del flew out of the booth behind him and landed on a table. (Later Elizabeth would tell him how it had started: Julie between the two of them, an arm around each, nobody seeming to mind for a long while until there were more drinks and the two men leaned close across her and started talking. She could not see where Julie's hands went then, or hear what they were saying. But after a few minutes their voices were louder, and when Julie got up to get another round of drinks the men were next to one another and Del put his finger in Stick's collarbone and then Stick leaned over and planted his hand in Del's face.)

Now there was a table overturned and chairs splintered around it and in the middle of a plate of hummus Del's head was covered with blood and tobacco spit. But then his arm was around Stick's neck, the two of them sloshing in the spilled drink and kicking at the air while the bartender yelled and John and Cullen leaned in to pull them apart. The other patrons huddled in the corners, looking angry or frightened. Suddenly there was a siren outside and Wes thought, *how could they have called the police already?*

But when he looked out there was a crowd in the street and, grabbing Stick's arm to drag him out of the bar, he saw that something larger was going on.

In the middle of the road was a bonfire, people dancing around it and chanting. He heard a voice behind him yell "Party!" A *slosh* sounded alongside him and he felt something wet on his cheek. A purple-clad figure — stooped and robed and bald like an old man but with the features of a boy — stood beside him, holding an empty bucket. A few feet away a parked car was dripping with red paint.

Music was playing from somewhere, and other people who had come out of bars and cafés were milling about. Some of them were joining the robed dancers, hurling their limbs in the air and laughing, but others were angry, yelling. The only word he could make out was *death*. A body fell across his feet, struggled to get up. A voice was yelling over a bullhorn from behind the bonfire. More sirens. Something hit him in the back. He turned — one of Del's friends, rushing at him with a bottle. He ducked and lunged toward the boy's gut, but someone grabbed him from behind and they were separated by a rush of people that suddenly poured across the street. Dogs barked. An orange-haired girl with a nose ring put her face in his, screaming — her tongue split by a row of metal studs that flashed in the light — and by the time the words reached him he already knew it.

The ground war had started.

The first thing he thought of — it surprised even him — was Joe.

In the rush of faces and the sirens and the firelight he circled, looking for Cullen. He saw Louise's back, glimpsed Del, still bleeding from the nose, and some of his cohorts, yelling and struggling toward the bonfire. He saw John across the street, standing atop a garbage can and gazing over the scene with a look of immense sadness as though he, too, were searching, for Cullen or for someone else he could not find.

Soon he found himself at the edge of the crowd and alone. He felt lost and tired and he knew that the strong drink in his head would not last for long. With the news of the war's onset it was coming — solitary and thoughtful, he would fall easy prey to melancholy, to the renewed recognition of his own superfluous place in the world.

That was when he felt someone beside him. He turned and saw Elizabeth looking back with a smile that was wide and inviting, that stretched out from beneath her bright eyes and into her famished cheeks. Her fingers slipped between his, and when she squeezed his hand he squeezed back.

His room at the hostel was on the third floor, a long narrow space not much bigger than a closet, with a bunk bed tight against the wall and a window cracked to let in the cool bay air and the distant sounds of the night. John was still gone, but somehow he and Elizabeth ended up in the top bunk anyhow.

She had started kissing him on the walk home, the two of them stopping to lean against buildings and sit down on steps. It was fine there with the sounds of the street fading behind them and a taste of salt drifting in on the breeze. The city's lights had dimmed, and overhead, framed by the rooftops, the stars were bright enough. A slice of moon hung amidst them. At one point they lay down on a bench and, her head resting on his shoulder, he watched the blinking lights of an airliner drift across the spangled blue-black void. He imagined it bound north, for Seattle or Alaska, and somehow this made him happy.

He had felt it then but up in the bunk even more: her frailty, her body a thing of bones and taut skin. With his arm around her he could have counted her ribs. As the drink wore off and they lay there in the tangled sheets he slowed himself, knowing now what it was he was doing and making his hands stop, instead just stroking her long spiny back and kissing her sometimes on the cheek. She slowed too and finally just clung to him, wrapping her arms around his back and her leg around his, pulling him to her in an embrace that was hard and long and surprisingly strong. Her sharp hips hurt where she pressed against him.

"Well," she laughed. "Here we are."

"Yep."

"Oh, my. What will everyone think?"

"Hard to say."

"Not that they all have to know. Don't worry." She rolled onto her back and gave him a little sock in the chest. "Guys are as apt to talk as girls, you know."

"Some guys."

"Some guys! True." She laughed. "Oh, I could kick myself for that whole Stick thing. That's about as stupid as I've been in a long time. My God. He's such an ass — but sweet too. But it's not like he doesn't have his hands full already."

She paused.

"Oh, Lord. You're being pretty quiet. What are you thinking?"

"Oh — nothing." Stick?

"Don't try to fool me." She socked him again. "OK. Geez Louise. Let's just drop it. My fault. Big mistake. Talking about it and doing it, I mean. The party had just taken too much out of me. OK. But you're different." She paused and rolled back towards him. "I mean, since I met you, I've known. You're kind of the strong silent type, aren't you? Yes. That, and something else, too. You know? You're a *gentleman!*"

Her face was beaming into his. He felt strange, as if he were in the other room eavesdropping on this conversation, but still he had to smile back at her.

She squeezed him around the back again. "I mean, the whole best kind of Academy grad. It's so nice! Like home. My brother and his buddies. That was how I ended up out here, you know? Funny how that is. It started at home but took me away." She had turned her eyes to the ceiling so that he felt even less present.

A siren whistled by outside.

"My family was so into it. I mean, Tom was practically one of us already. At the house all the time on the weekends, hanging out with my brother and my girlfriends and me. He didn't even notice me at first, of course. I mean, I was just a dumb high school girl, and he was this good-looking plebe. First time he came home with Eddie — my brother — we were all sitting around shelling crabs in the back yard. He was from Colorado and didn't know how to do it and I had to help him. Right then I knew I liked him. Knew it! But I was too young for him and he couldn't get off campus much then, so it went nowhere. But then I started school in Richmond and it wasn't too far away, and so Eddie brought his buddies down sometimes on the weekends, and when I was a sophomore I set them all up with my sorority sisters sometimes. Then one night after Tom had dropped his date off he came over to see me. Me! I had been waiting for a long time and then, just like that, it happened."

He was listening, as if at a great distance. He noticed that her voice had changed. It had grown soft and wistful, but there was something else. It had slowed, become more coherent. Then he knew it. She was talking not to a group but to one person.

Was it to him or to herself?

A sadness had entered the room — covered it, coated it with a film thick as if it had been waiting like a gas cloud outside and slowly leaked in. He sensed it and sensed further that he had a duty to show her some kind of sympathy. But all he really felt was curiosity. And at the same time he was beginning to think about himself. He was beginning to see himself and these people he was stuck with, and what he saw made him angry.

"Oh, it was so great. The next two years. He'd come to see me or I'd go up there, and I loved it — being in the middle of all those guys, and me with him, the best looking of them all. The formals! Oh, so great. Before the last one at the Academy my grandmother was there and saw me in my dress and him in his uniform, and she said it was like when she was a girl — my granddad had been a middie, too — and it made her feel so good. She thought her world was gone, and there we were, dressed up and smiling and keeping it going, like we were walking into a fairy tale or something.

"I mean, I was happy enough myself then — but she died a year later and then, right then, looking back on it, I was just as glad to make her happy. I was doing what she and granddad had done and it all seemed right.

"We were going to get married. That's what he said when he got orders out here — told me to just hang on. He kept flying back to see me that last fall. God, I would've dropped out right then to be with him, but my dad said no way. And then in the spring when he came less and less, I kept myself too busy with the sorority to notice, and after graduation I just packed my bags and drove out here. I mean, things had cooled off a little, but there was no doubt in my mind. When I showed up everything seemed great. He was waiting on the street for me, and grabbed me up in his arms! and we walked down to the beach — he was just a few blocks from La Mirage then, down by the Shellback — and we sat by the boardwalk and watched the sun set. The Pacific! Here we were, out West — a new life. It all started so good."

She rolled back against him. He felt his shirt tighten against his stomach as she grasped it between her bony fingers.

"So stupid, so fucking stupid. There I was living in his apartment, cooking and cleaning and having no clue. He was home a good bit, but sometimes he'd be gone for a week or more, on maneuvers. That's what it was most of the time, anyway. Looking back I guess I'm lucky for that — if it hadn't been for that I wouldn't even have gotten a job. I mean, I just got bored enough that I had to do something, and La Mirage was there. And I was good at it! Working with people. *People*, Wes! You know what I mean? I was never great with numbers or words, but my mom always said I was a people person, and she was right. And aren't people the most important thing?"

Between her grip and her profanity, she had gotten his attention again. He nodded. Who was he to say that people weren't the most important thing? He smirked to himself in the darkness.

"So when I found out, I was ready. My own job, and, since it was with La Mirage, my own place to live, ready for the taking. It was just as well, I thought. I mean the whole thing kind of woke me up, you know. When I caught them there — him and his little Filipino girl, the kind that's always hanging around the officer's club — I just walked out of the room and looked around the apartment for a second and it sunk in: I was *living with him*. I mean, it seems obvious now, but I had just never thought of it like that. Living together!

"There were a few vacant apartments at La Mirage and I just went there and took one and asked permission later. I went there and I cried and curled up on the floor and slept until I was hungry, and then I went to Jack in the Box and had two cheeseburgers and three milkshakes. Later I felt like I had a brick in my stomach and couldn't sleep. I had just spread a sleeping bag out on the floor and stared up at the ceiling. My grandmother had died just a few months before and — it was the weirdest thing — I started thinking about her watching me. I mean, it's not like I believe in ghosts or anything, and, I mean, what — was she supposed to be in heaven? Was that it? Sounds silly. But I just felt sick because of what he'd done but also because of what I'd done. It wasn't so much that I felt guilty as I felt *embarrassed*. Was I an idiot? Didn't I know that there are some things you just don't do? I was trying to imagine what she would have thought if she had known — would she have been angry, or disappointed? Or just sad? That her fairy tale world was gone after all.

"But then I knew I couldn't think about that too long. I mean, it's not my grandmother's world anymore. The same rules don't apply. Do they? People don't seem to know. I mean, isn't it pretty much make up the rules as you go? What are you supposed to do?"

She paused and stared at him. "What was *I* supposed to do?"

Through the wall behind him he had heard a faint movement. The adjoining room — in the silence he could just make out the rhythm of the low voices. Cullen and Cynthia. When he heard Elizabeth pause he knew he was supposed to say something and suddenly the words were in his mouth. "Why not go home?"

"Home. They didn't know what to make of me, had been mad with the both of us ever since I went California. Now what would they think? It was too much, too embarrassing. My mom's got some of her mom in her — sometimes even more so, I think — and she would have gone off on me. And what was really there for me, anyway? Here I had a job and people I had brought into La Mirage. Things to do. And then he was just a few blocks away, just a few blocks. And he had his little tramp, but we had years between us, and could a few months or whatever it was get rid of that?"

She stopped. "Sounds stupid, maybe. Listening to it now, it all sounds kind of stupid. But who's to say I haven't done the right thing? He's gone, but here I am with a life of my own, and why not live it here. You know? I mean, I feel good. Most of the time I feel good. But it's hard to *know*—to know whether you're doing the right thing. I mean, how do you confirm it? Is there someone you can go to to ask? Sometimes I think it would be better if it were laid out for us. So many possibilities. I mean, when I was a little girl there was my dad.... Then in college it didn't even seem to matter, you just got through and had a good time on the way and figured everything would just fall into place. But now here I am, and I don't think my parents even know what's going on anymore."

She leaned up closer against him. "Shouldn't there be a simpler way — some way? I mean, it's not just me, is it? You seem like you know something." She looked into his eyes and began to fiddle with his hair. "But what about you? Don't you ever wish someone would just tell you what to do?"

He hardly heard her now. His mind had drifted somewhere up toward the ceiling and was looking down on both of them in silent disdain.

He was in a soap opera. It had somehow come to this: he, Wes Hammond, cadet, Institute graduate, commissioned officer in the strongest military the world had ever seen, was living out a soap opera. There was a war going on half a world away — brave men facing death in the desert at this very moment — and he was stuck in California in the middle of a pack of incestuous hedonists. And he was going along with it! Becoming one of them! Sharing women with the likes of Stick, wallowing in mindless diversions. What enraged him was not the sordidness but the mediocrity of it, this sleepwalking life into which he had allowed himself to drift.

Elizabeth's skeletal frame loomed over him. "Are you listening to me?"

A metallic crash sounded out on the street, followed by loud voices.

Still she waited, but when he said nothing, she raised her head and stared toward the window. "The street party must be over. Lots of people milling around out there. Random." She hopped down from the bed and looked in the mirror, tugging at her blouse.

"God," she said, glancing at his reflection as she straightened her hair. "Sorry about the diarrhea of the mouth, I guess." She turned on the water at the little sink, then thrust her hands under the stream and began to wring them. "I guess you're up on my life story now. More than you needed to know, I'm sure."

More yelling erupted from the street. She lurched over to the window and looked out. "Del! Hey guys! Up here!" Her voice was grateful.

Wes turned on the bed so that he could see. In the middle of the street he recognized Stick and Del, arm in arm now, singing. An overturned trash can lay in the street behind them, some of Del's compatriots tussling over it.

"Hey guys! Alright! Is the party over?" Elizabeth's back was to him. It was her old voice.

Then there was another voice in the street, somehow familiar.

He began to climb down from the bunk.

"Guys!" Elizabeth yelled.

"Hey Elizabeth!" It was Stick. Walking up to the window, Wes could see him whispering into Del's ear.

"Hey Elizabeth!" Del screamed. Then he broke into a wide grin. "We're headed out to get some grub. You wanna share a big, fat pepperoni pizza wi' me?"

Elizabeth laughed nervously and started tucking her blouse in.

As Wes took his place beside her he saw it. In the shadows across the street a figure was moving. Lanky, bobbing, it emerged beneath a streetlamp, bottle in hand, wandering without apparent design into the midst of the others.

"John!" Elizabeth yelled. Her eyes grew brighter, her cheeks softened. "Hey, John!"

He did not answer but instead moved forward into the group, head thrown back and gazing up at the stars.

"Oh, my God," Elizabeth whispered, inclining her head a little but not looking at him. "He is *plowed*. Thank God he made it back OK. He's such a goofy drunk. Oh!" She reached out and grasped Wes's elbow, then released it immediately. "Look at him now!"

John had fallen down in the middle of the street. There were no cars but suddenly there was a crowd — not only Stick and Terri and Del's crew but others, too, the purple dancers and a boy with a Mohawk and the girl with the studded tongue. They were silent now but moving, moving fast, away from the sirens and into the night, and for a minute John was lost in their midst. When the crowd broke he was still there, kneeling, head thrown back and gaze fixed up at them or maybe beyond them. He threw his arms out and with a kind of half-grin on his face — was he doing this for himself, or for the crowd? — he began to yell.

"Haight! Haight…I look around me, and all I see is Haight!"

The voice was plaintive — almost a wail — and when John paused to gather his lungs in again and looked out at his listeners, his face looked so forlorn and pathetic that it seemed almost ready to break forth into a smile. And they were laughing now, all of them, Stick and Del clutching their bellies and pointing, the crowd passing by with catcalls and snickers and stares.

From their window, Elizabeth looked on with a smile of embarrassed wonder before she ran out of the room and down to the street as the voice started up again.

"Where is love?"

Wes stayed at the window, looking down on them all now, all but the two in the room next door, and glad that he was not among them. The whole lot of them staggering about on the street, wasting their time away like fools. And his roommate: what was he? The biggest fool of them all?

"Haight! Love?"

The words drifted past him and up into the darkness where countless shimmering stars turned slowly in their ordered courses. Then, as he looked back down at the figures strewn across the street below, there was only silence. In the stillness of that moment he felt more keenly than ever both his own insignificance and the rush of anger that went with its recognition. But even so he was overcome with the sudden sense that he was approaching an unseen boundary — that, at last, he was about to be involved in something important.

$$\triangleleft\ 8\ \triangleright$$

It had all been in motion for a long time now but years later, being a man and the kind of man he was, he would have to look back and come up with a cause. Because he did not take fiction seriously it did not occur to him at first; but one day he would think that if you were looking for at least an immediate cause for what happened in Mexico you might go farther off the mark than blaming Hemingway.

Cullen, sauntering across the courtyard, breaking into a solitary dance, sweeping his feet lightly across the soft grass in the bright noontime sun.

"So, *aficionados*" — the accent was terrible — "are we ready for the bulls?" Waving his beach towel like a cape.

Stick, beside him, pacing, hands folded behind his back, a coach in a locker room, a general before his troops.

"This could be it for us, *muchachos*. Now, we've been livin' pretty good. But are we ready to go that final step? Are we ready" — pause — "to take life by the balls" — again — "and make it scream?" He kicked the dirt. "This could be our last chance."

That was how it began. The final time, the days that were to be their last both in the passing and in the knowing, the end they had begun moving toward at the beginning of the long summer that already seemed lost in the great flood of years.

That Friday he was the first one at the TPU. He came because he could not sleep any longer.

He came because he could not sleep any longer, but once there he could only sit half-slumped at the conference table in the lounge. A coffee maker steamed fitfully against the far wall, intermittently enshrouding the lone clock that hung above it in thick gushes of white. The vapor faded, clung to the glass face, sought itself out again — trickling slowly down the surface, gelling into thick drops that both obscured the steady hands and seemed to make their passing more inexorable as if the clock itself were powered by some great unseen boiler which drove the slow blades relentlessly through the dense silence of time.

On the adjoining wall, a bearded officer glared out fiercely from a poster. Behind him gray ironclads steamed against the pale sky. Letters overhead and beneath — DAMN THE TORPEDOES... FULL STEAM AHEAD! Admiral Farragut's exhortation, his charge not only to his own crew but also, some public affairs bureau had decided, to those who came after him.

Or was it an accusation?

For Wes's part, he felt sure he could take Mobile Bay if only someone would tell him to do so.

He tried not to think of his father.

The morning paper lay open on the table before him. Troops embracing families above the gray tarmac. Ladders and fuselage and flags in the background. COMING HOME.

It had been over for a few weeks now. The ground war — fast, uncompromising, incisive — all those adjectives the CNN general used, pointing to diagrams and maps for the cameras, the color of sand and rock in his uniform as he stood before the sleek blue curtains and the rich polished mahogany of the podium. And the war itself: tawny whirling treads, grim helmets protruding from tank hatches, and dust—yellow-brown, thick, erupting beneath the vehicles, trailing them for miles, lingering in low ocher clouds just above the surface of the vast pitted earth. The fluid haze of heat drifting off the sand, invisible, a wrinkle in the atmosphere; flashes of bright orange and gold, then black, the deep billowing nighttime ebony of burning oil, not from wells now but from smoldering hulks of enemy armor.

The TV caught it all. Computer-generated targeting information. Jeeps pouring into Kuwait City, flags streaming behind them. Thermal sighting images. Tank turrets. Prisoners with arms held high in the air.

Skeletons strewn on the ground.

Iraqi, mostly. But still they looked. The whole one hundred hours, without saying it, they had all looked for Joe.

It began on the ride back from San Francisco. Except for the radio news, the van was silent. Even Stick and the girls cared enough not to talk, or maybe they were just exhausted, but either way they listened to reports the whole trip while Cullen and Cynthia sat in the back, huddled together, in retreat. Wes turned once to see him rocking in his seat, she leaning in against him. He felt something. But he did not know what to say so he sat alone and looked out the window. Only John ventured back there. Otherwise people kept to themselves. In the front there was a kind of empty reverence, as if Joe were already dead.

When they got back to La Mirage Cullen disappeared into Cynthia's apartment and they did not see him again. Only occasional reports from her. That was how they knew, on the morning after the last day of fighting, that the call had come, that his time of darkness had begun.

The door to the conference room opened. Two ensigns entered. Donkers, and Smith, the investor, each holding a stack of folders. They nodded, sat at the far end of the table, opened their files, stared down their noses. Haughty — Wes could feel it — the two ensigns with the highest opinions of themselves. And why? What had they done? Donkers had kissed what little ass there was to kiss here, shuffled papers for the better part of a year. Smith had made a little money in the stock market. He was already talking about which MBA schools he was going to apply to when his commitment was up. Wes looked at him — the slick drooping hair, the tortoiseshell glasses — with half-hidden disdain. He rattled the paper and stuck his nose back in the international news.

The steam rose; the clock spun.

Then, as morning colors sounded, he felt a presence over his shoulder.

Stick was there. Behind him, a huge pitted face and a yellow smile loomed, half-visible, along the edge of the cracked door. The warrant.

"Morning, gentlemen," the face said.

They murmured back.

"Orders are comin'." The smile and the dark eyes grew broader, leering, watchful. "Got to enjoy liberty while you can, men. If I was you I'd be out of here right now." A grave nod, a parting smile.

Stick stood by the closed door. A long silence settled in the room, broken only by the long wail of a horn. An ammunition ship, getting underway.

"Orders are coming," he said to Wes.

"Believe it when I see it."

The rumors had abated somewhat since last August but had been a steady part of the background noise of their lives for so long that they could never be accepted immediately. Precisely because of the waiting and the long hours of speculation and diversion that went with it, the very idea of receiving orders had steadily been surrounded by and at last become encrusted with unspoken layers of meaning; to the ensigns, their potential arrival had come to signify, in different degrees, both threat and promise. Most immediately they meant the end of this life, the life of carefree ease to which they had become accustomed. To many of them orders simply meant the beginning of something new, a respite from the boredom to which they were inevitably beginning to fall prey. Maybe they would bring good, maybe bad. But regardless, most felt it was time for a change — any change.

To Wes orders had become something even more, something almost spiritual. The day when he would finally receive orders loomed in his mind like a bright doomsday, an occasion for purging and transfiguration, the culmination of that design of self-annihilation and rebirth that he began five years ago when he entered the Institute. But precisely because he was the one who had made the most of orders — because he had hoped for too much, too long — he had become hardened and doubtful. He was not about to allow himself to be duped again. "Believe it when I see it."

"It's affirm this time, Mr. Hammond." Donkers closed a folder. "The CO has me double-checking personnel records right now, making sure everything's up to date. We think we might hear something as early as next week."

"Affirm." He paused. "Hmmm. I'll believe it when I see it."

"Well, Billy Cullen believes it, and he's ready to go." Stick leaned over the table and into the space beside him. "Just got off the phone with him — he had to call in to the XO, said he wasn't feeling too good, couldn't make it in today. The warrant just loved it, man. Hell, he knows Cullen's been on a binge, couldn't care less. He'd just as soon join us, far as I can tell. Anyway — let's get on back. Ol' Billy C's still on the upswing, in the mood to celebrate, and he's got some kind of plan in mind."

"That's right, boys. Play while you can." Donkers didn't even look up when he spoke, just kept his head down next to Smith's. Their poses were conspiratorial, his tone pointed and accusatory. He might as well have said it: *there'll be a reckoning soon.*

The white doors of the TPU swung open on a cobalt sky. A great black-purple expanse of ocean — endless, long as the horizon itself — stretched out beneath it, mirrored it darkly. They could see the ammunition ship drifting away from the pier now. It looked tiny, vulnerable, a toy that might at any moment be swallowed up in the immensity of the sea.

He was following Stick out to the parking lot.

"Fuckin' geek," Stick had muttered as they walked into the hall. "Before all's said and done, I've got half a mind to take care of that little son of a bitch. But he's probably not worth the effort, you know?" He spat into a trashcan. "Got to conserve my energy for bigger and better things."

Wes dropped half a step behind, not wanting to get too close. He felt something thick at the bottom of his lungs, low and smoldering. He did not know whether he was angry at Donkers for being a prick or for being right, or at Stick's predictable foulness, or at himself for being stuck in a position where the two of them mattered.

Then they walked into the sunlight, saw the long sea, and heard laughter below them.

Figures seated at the picnic table in front of the TPU. Four men in uniform. John and two of the yeomen who worked at the admin desk, Bilbao and Martinez. Filipinos. Bad English, bright smiles. They had grown up poor, starving poor, outside the naval base at Subic Bay, and Stick liked to recite his own abridged version of their family histories. "You know their mamas and sisters were taking cock for cash. Sucked and fucked half the Seventh Fleet." But they had made it out. Here they were in the California sunshine, American citizens, grinning like men who knew they had been saved — smoking and joking on a Friday morning with the broad Pacific between them and the past.

The brim of the fourth man's cover glistened in the light. A senior officer, a commander, smoking in the early morning with two E-4s. It made no sense until he took the cigarette away from his face and Wes saw. It was the chaplain, Kuwelski, slim and bright-eyed. He must have been in his forties, but he carried himself like someone much younger. His uniform did not fit quite right. He waved to the ensigns, then turned back to Bilbao and Martinez and said something in Tagalog. The three of them laughed.

John rose, smiling, and intercepted them on their way to the parking lot.

"Practicing your Filipino, ensign?" Stick was smiling too, but only on one side of his face.

"Just fooling around. I've got a few words down, though."

"Kind of fucked up. I mean, that stuff's not allowed shipboard. And they've got a senior officer talking that shit to them?"

"He doesn't really know much either. Just jokes around with them a little. What's the harm?"

"Hunh. Weird. Kind of a goofy guy anyway. Guess he doesn't have much else to do."

John laughed. "Depends on how you look at it. He's got more to do than us."

"Oh, little ensign — we've got plenty to do. Just you follow us on back, because I've recently spoken to Billy C and I do believe we're about to embark on a weekend to remember."

John hesitated a moment, scowled. "Hmmm. Another big trip, I'm sure." Then his features brightened again. "At least he's feeling better. Alright. You guys go ahead. Be right behind you," he said.

He walked quickly back to the table but as Wes drove off the base he could see John's car following them back where the empty road curved along the edge of the dark sea.

In the courtyard of La Mirage Cullen stands holding a cheap wineskin that is half-full of Budweiser, a beach towel draped over his shoulder. When he sees them he begins to wave it like a matador.

"My friends, the bulls are waiting. You must make yourself worthy of the bulls." He holds the wineskin out.

Stick takes it, drinks, passes to Wes.

If Hemingway were to blame, who was to blame for their reading Hemingway?

The books were mostly John's. But that would not do. John, after all, lightly disparaged them, refused to take them too seriously. It was Wes who dug them out, put them into the hands of the others.

After San Francisco and the war, something had come over him. He had been essentially alone for a long time but now he again began to seek out solitude actively. Sick of the lot of them, of diversions and complications alike, he had sunk into himself and grown silent. Stuck with time and unable to read history — it only depressed him now — he turned to John for books.

He had begun surreptitiously, sifting through the bookshelves during his roommate's absences, making his way through the little library. It that was broad, unorganized, eclectic: the manuals on carpentry and auto repair and the mysteries (John liked mysteries) intermingled with volumes of Aristotle and a book about not a university but the idea of a university by someone who had four names, one of which was the name of a bird. There was a book by Kierkegaard, whose name alone was enough to put him off, and one with seven stories about a mountain. He found the dog-eared book by Pascal, whom he vaguely credited with inventing some kind of primitive computer, and remained concerned by the title — was it all in French? — but picked it up and flipped it open. His eye found an underlined passage:

> *When I have occasionally set myself to consider the different distractions of men, the pains and perils to which they expose themselves at court or in war, whence arise so many quarrels, passions, bold and often bad ventures, etc., I have discovered that all the unhappiness of men arises from one single fact, that they cannot stay quietly in their own chamber. A man who has enough to live on, if he knew how to stay with pleasure at home, would not leave it to go to sea or to besiege a town. A commission in the army would not be bought so dearly, but that it is found insufferable not to budge from the town; and men only seek conversation and entering games, because they cannot remain with pleasure at home.*

The corner of the back cover said *Philosophy/Religion*, and this was not what Wes was looking for — flimsy stuff that pretended to be serious but never really amounted to anything. He returned the book to the shelf with a toss of his head. What he wanted was a way to imagine himself out of his life for a while, and for that he needed entertainment, escape. Fiction.

What he liked about the first novel he settled on was the realism. It was a short book about a prison camp in Siberia, and he was drawn in by the historical accuracy — the author had been in a *gulag* himself for ten years — but the end was a letdown. A day had passed and not much had happened. There really wasn't even much about Stalin and the Cold War and all that. It just ended with the main character, a prisoner, talking to some other prisoner who had a Bible hidden in the wall by his bed. Then they went to sleep and there was going to be another day just like it.

This confused and disappointed him.

John was just finishing another Russian book, a big one, which he said was very good, and he offered to share it. But Wes was impatient and it looked too long and too old so he started searching the shelves again. That was when he found Hemingway.

Within two weeks he had read all the books. They went fast. He liked almost all of them, but especially *For Whom the Bell Tolls*. It was good because of the history, because it was somewhere else, Spain, and because the war happening there was like the twentieth century in miniature. It was the 1930s and already it was fascism and communism and here in the middle of it all this lone American. The hero. It ended with him alone and wounded, thinking about his grandfather in his own country's Civil War, wielding his gun in the tall mountain pines, about to die but still killing.

"Now that," he said to John when he finished, "is a good book."

John shrugged. "It's alright."

"I guess you prefer that Russian stuff. What is it again?"

"*The Brothers Karamazov.*"

"What's it about?"

"Three brothers — or four brothers — and a bad father. And some monks."

"That's it?"

"One of them kills somebody."

"Who?"

"Read it yourself," he said. "I can't give everything away."

If John was bored with Hemingway, he was the only one. Suddenly even the others wanted to read. Because the books seemed to be mainly about drinking, shooting guns, and screwing foreign women, even Stick liked them. And Cullen — when he emerged from his time of darkness, he grasped at them like a man struggling up out of the sea might grasp at a stiff broken plank tossed about on the surface.

Something was happening to Cullen, something Wes could not fully understand. It had been coming for a while now — he couldn't help but sense it, he and John talked about it and they knew even the others had to notice too — but the outbreak of the ground war made it certain. Whatever had been building up inside him was close to the surface now; suddenly he looked washed out and shaky, less like a boy and more like an old man. This much they could see. But maybe only Cynthia could know for certain what it was, or at least all of it.

When they got back from San Francisco and Cullen disappeared inside her apartment, Wes knew that he could only be in there bent over and thinking of Joe. This is what he imagined, and this is what John confirmed when he came out on the second night from that place where Wes somehow felt he would now be an intruder, no matter how much John told him otherwise. It was obvious that Cullen wanted to be alone, apart from at least some of them — clearly (Wes took a certain satisfaction in thinking this) from the roommate whom he so often innocently tolerated and went along with and even embraced, but, Wes assumed, from himself as well. It was obvious that if he wanted to be with anyone it was Cynthia, and Wes felt sure that he did not belong with the two of them.

There was that, and then there was something he did not really want to recognize: it saddened him immeasurably to see Cullen, of all people, having to be serious. Himself, fine. But Cullen? It went against everything he was or seemed to be, everything that had long made Wes seek him out in the first place. He had counted on Cullen to compensate for his own seriousness and now he could not do so.

The truth was that, alone in his own apartment with the war on, Wes nearly forgot all of them. From time to time he tried to make himself think of Cullen and Joe but the images on the screen came and went so quickly that he found it hard to associate them with anything else he knew, with any part of the mundane world around him. They had an existence all their own, belonged to some plane of reality fit for neither Cullen nor Cullen's brother nor himself, a place where gods and heroes dwelt.

Alone in his apartment with the TV on it was easy to almost think this. Then, the day after the fighting ended, John came with the news.

He was leaning against the sliding door, his hands clenched tight at his waist as if he were pressing them hard against one another. The lone tree waved bright against the hillside behind him.

"Joe's wounded. It's bad."

Wes sat back and stared at him, silent.

The TV had not prepared him for this. The pictures were of Iraqi bodies and American flags, and when the anchormen and the generals and the politicians talked about casualties the words *staggering* and *unprecedented* were always attached to *low*.

"Cullen's having a hard time with it. Real hard."

His parents had called that morning. At first the details were indeterminate, made more frightening by their vagueness, but as the week passed they came in a steady stream by satellite message and phone, from the Gulf to Washington to the family in Pennsylvania and from there to California. The tank had been hit on the last day, crippled, two crewmen dead and Joe critically wounded, bleeding from the chest and an arm that had been bound up with a tourniquet and still might have to be cut off. Waiting for a helicopter. Bleeding in the desert and then in a tent and finally in a hospital ship in the Arabian Sea.

Wes heard the words, but finally the event and even its full effect on Cullen remained unknown, something he could only infer, guess at, reconstruct from the scattered disparate pieces.

Imagine.

Cullen himself bent over double now, physically sick, trying to schedule a MAC flight over there (Wes knew this) but it's impossible. Locked in Cynthia's apartment, she taking a week off from work, the two of them in there together. The phone calls coming and the news getting worse. Him emerging into the light one or two afternoons, seeing Wes and wringing his hand but not able to talk much, looking at one another but unsure of what to say. Then back in with her, the two of them retreating to that dark place and — what? — waiting and sweating and cursing and praying and holding one another.

A week of this. The two of them in there, John the messenger, Wes on the outside, alone with Stick and the others (but who were they?).

A week of darkness.

At last the good news came, the only way that it could, slowly; the second week, the news that the depths had been plumbed, the nadir passed, that on the other side of the world there was healing.

Things got better and slowly Cullen emerged into the light.

But even when he came out something had changed, was still changing, something in him and maybe her too. When he came out the fever was back in his eyes, brighter than before. Wes did not know it now but later he thought maybe he did: it was as if Cullen had somehow with his brother actually taken a good glance at it, the ancient unspoken mystery, the threat or promise or whatever it was of the end of days, and what had you made of them? He had shaken and danced his way along the edge of the old abyss of carrion and bones and night, the ubiquitous uncertain silence lurking beneath the loud world, heretofore unstudied, now tentatively recognized, glimpsed if not confronted, then half-turned from but still shading the world to which he returned, its darkness somehow making the trembling furtive life he found there more radiant.

What would he do with it?

Cynthia had already answered that question for herself, maybe, abyss or not, her knowing in a different way than Cullen could, she with the answer ready while he was still formulating the question.

Wes half-sensed it then, but he would not even begin to understand it until much later, and then only with the help of John and the years themselves, what they had done to him as well as to Cynthia and Cullen and all the rest.

Now all he knew was that Cullen had seemingly come out of that dark anxious week only somehow to be still living under its terms, terms Wes did not have a language for. The strange mixture of elation and lingering despair that marked him when he learned that his brother would live was heightened by the news of that Friday morning, the news that next week might bring orders. But it had been there all along. Already he was a man close to frenzy.

The week after the darkness, early on the first morning that Cynthia goes back to work, Cullen's smiling but fidgety, wandering into their apartment and grabbing *The Sun Also Rises*. By nightfall he's done, parading back in, beer in hand and cigarette in mouth, waving the slim bundle of paper in the air. "This is it. This is it! This is the good shit!!" Throwing it at John sleeping on the couch and demanding more.

He consumes the books, keeping easy pace with Wes, devouring them, loving the travel and the women and the sports and the drinking. "Intensity. You know, that's the thing about all these people," he says, leaning beer-breathed across their table. "They know it won't last forever, but they plan to make the most of it. Let the good times roll. Intensity," he repeats, looking Wes long in the eye, all at once a *carpe diem* poet and a coach leading his team into the fourth quarter. He takes a drag on his cigarette and coughs.

The bulls. He reads the other books but it's still that one he keeps coming back to, the veterans and the women and the festival. The running of the bulls. Wes can see that it's not the heroism, the stoic facing up to and dealing out of death, that gets Cullen. It's just the festival—the ultimate party. This is what the bulls are to him. He is obsessed with them, joking but obsessed all the same.

John laughs, wags his head, not a scoffer but in his eyes Wes can see he's tempted. "This party business. OK, but I mean, that's ridiculous. Can't you see that the whole thing's a kind of failed pilgrimage?" He's half-smiling, lighting a cigarette to humor Cullen, the two of them sitting and talking about the novels over beers at three in the afternoon like some kind of alcoholic book club.

Wes watches them with clear detachment, as if he's at a tennis match that he's not really interested in but attends because he has nothing better to do.

"Can't you see those people are all miserable?" John says.

Cullen pauses, stares at him, laughs. "Those people know how to have a good time. Put us to shame." He takes a long drink. "And, you know, we can't quite make Pamplona. But Mexico. Mexico just might do."

When the final Friday morning comes, Cullen is ready. San Francisco had been Stick's trip. Now, at last, it is his turn.

Wes and Stick and John strolling into the courtyard. Cullen standing by the pool, bright-skinned above the dusty stucco, golden, glowing in the noonday sun, then ambling over, glassy-eyed, a broad pained smile on his face. Hungover. In this light Wes sees what a strange version of his former self he has become. He still has the easy athletic build, the dirty blonde hair of the All-American. Only closer inspection reveals that a small paunch — well-defined, somehow, but paunch nonetheless — is beginning to slide over the sides of his swimsuit, that his strong bronzed hands are trembling, that his hair actually does have a good deal of dirt in it.

He produces the wineskin, waves the beach towel at them.

Breaking into a solitary dance, sweeping his feet lightly across the soft green grass in the bright noontime sun.

"So, *aficionados*. Are we ready for the bulls?"

He throws a sidelong smile at Stick.

There is Hemingway, but there are other reasons too. San Francisco had been Stick's trip and at times Cullen seems driven by some strange need not only to keep pace with his roommate but even to outstrip him. That is going to be hard to do now. But if it is going to be done, certainly it might be in Mexico.

Stick smiles back, takes the wineskin, rallies the troops. "This could be it, *muchachos*." The smile broadens — knowing, deeply knowing and deeply pleased.

They are on their way.

They are on their way, about to pack what little they will, with only one obstacle between them and the final trip. One obstacle, and a revelation.

Cynthia is home for lunch, seeing the four of them in the courtyard together, the wineskin, looking them over. Knowing and skeptical all at once.

She hears the plan and does not bother to hide her disapproval. "Billy. Why are you doing this?"

Behind her Stick looks at Cullen and mouths: "Billy?"

Cullen smiles, looks at the ground, swinging his bare right foot slowly back and forth, casts a wary sidelong glance at her, then peers up at Stick. He begins to dance his makeshift jig, bare feet sweeping over the grass, and even she laughs as he bounds across the lawn. Sunlight streaking through his hair and across his shoulders. He stops shortly, winded, beginning to sweat at the brow. The air smells of beer.

She takes this as his answer. "You know I can't go," she says, angry but a smile already playing beneath her lips. She too is still caught up in it, the relief of Joe's recovery, in that and maybe in some happiness that only the two of them might know, something that had taken root in the darkness.

"Sweetie, I know you'll be locked up in your office all weekend. Typing away. But can't I have a little fun?" His arm is around her now, the two of them moving toward her apartment. He will convince her. They have no doubts.

"If they promise to take good care of you." She is at a distance now and looks back, but the only one who meets her eyes is John.

They are on their way.

An hour later they are in the Blazer, running south through the dry canyon that points them toward San Diego.

"What'd she think about orders?" John asks.

"Orders?" Cullen has been unexpectedly silent, staring out the window.

"Yeah. I mean, there's a possibility they could split you two up."

He waits. "It's just a rumor."

"More than a rumor this time, buddy," Stick says from behind the wheel.

"Right, right. I know. Anyway, we didn't talk about it." He pauses, looks forward. "We had something else — "

They are pulling onto the freeway now, Wes in the front passenger seat, John behind him, Cullen beside John so that Wes can see him turning back toward the window as he speaks.

"There was a message from my folks on her machine."

"Yeah?"

"My brother." They had learned in the past week that Joe's platoon had fought a major battle in the open desert and been in the process of destroying an enemy airfield when they came under attack on that last day. But the details of his wounding had remained unclear. "They're still not sure, but they wanted to let us know before the media talk hits. Fratricide. There's a chance what hit him was friendly fire."

There is a silence. An eighteen-wheeler roars by them, rocks the whole vehicle.

Wes turns in his seat. "An accident. He goes through all that, and an accident. A stupid mistake." He feels confused, let down.

"Shit," Stick says.

"One of his own buddies." John is looking absently out the window. Then he turns forward, staring at Wes and at the back of Stick's head, lips pursed as though framing a question that goes unasked.

Palms wave on either side of the road, a triumphal arch marking their path into a new country.

"Yep. Friendly fire." Cullen repeats it slowly, as though he finds the words themselves strange and dissatisfying.

◁ 9 ▷

They bought a bottle of tequila outside Del Mar and by the time they got to San Diego Cullen was singing the refrains to the only Spanish songs he knew — *"La Cucaracha," "La Bamba,"* and *"Feliz Navidad"* — over and over again. They finally shut him up by telling him his antics were going to prevent them from being allowed across the border.

That was a lie, he said when they got there, the U.S. cars easing steadily southward through the gates beneath the red white and green letters that said M E X I C O and the tricolor flag with a bird and a snake on it. What kind of a fucked-up country has a snake on its flag, Stick said, and just to argue Wes said something about *Don't Tread on Me*, but Stick wasn't having any of it and the two of them were raising their voices when they got to the booth and a short fat dark man glanced in and they too had to shut up.

The seconds they waited were loud with the rhythmic clanging of metal. The pedestrian crossing to their right —a series of revolving gates, metal bars welded perpendicular to the spinning central axis, loose pipes and plates hanging crosswise against them —ringing steadily to mark the entry of the Americans into their sister republic, Californians and Eastern tourists come for an afternoon of sights and shopping, students and Marines and sailors come for the drink and the sex and whatever else they were forbidden or had to hide at home, to them the whole bright shadowy country a whore that spread her legs for dollars.

And already as they waited they saw the line of cars leaving: backed up against the border, long, gleaming dully in the hot mid-afternoon sun, not the easy stream of vehicles coming in with them but what looked like a vast exodus, a few Americans going home but mostly the masses trying to get out, swarthy, the blood Indian and Spanish, small-statured, ebony-haired and mustachioed, cheap jewelry and air fresheners and statues of Mary swinging from the mirrors of their ancient dusty rusting cars.

And already as they entered even the light seemed different — bright but grainier, a thick enshrouding yellow, and so much of it, coming up off the brown stucco and the dirty sprawling concrete.

Poor people in dusty clothes. Hags, children. Squatting on bright blankets with their wares. A young brown girl held aloft a dirty plastic package, waved it at them: "Chiclets! *Chicletos!*"

They were in.

There was a strip right off the border, the first easy stop, the place the cabdrivers called *El* Main Street. It was a broad boulevard of bazaars and tamale vendors and dance clubs and its real name, they learned as Stick tried to negotiate the Tijuana streets, cursing and honking and shaking his finger, was *Avenida Revolución.* They went there first for drinks.

They had done this once before, long months ago. Wandering up and down the street, climbing to a rooftop bar for a beer or a margarita and looking at the crowd below, then descending back into it, in and out of the little shops with the velvet paintings and the burlap ponchos and the carved birds, the owners yelling prices at them in bad English, and on to the next drink. It began like that this time and it was alright until they were on one of the roofs and the drinks had started to slow and Cullen looked across the street to an open-air dance club where a college girl was riding a mechanical bull and said, "This is bullshit. These games."

He suddenly grew mock-serious, striking a heavy pose, his voice thick with a gravity that buried the snicker beneath it. "We are here for the fights, not to play games with these children. The bulls await us. *Si, aficionados?*"

John looked weary, rolled his head toward the sky. "Not this bullshit. Not the shit of the bulls, but the bulls themselves."

"*Si, amigo!! Si!*"

They paid a waiter for directions and then they were back in the Blazer, the ride suddenly unfamiliar now, away from the border and deeper into the city. It was much larger than Wes had imagined. The glare and crowds of the tourist district faded, their path sticking to the flatlands, the main thoroughfares, where the traffic followed no discernible pattern and the signs were strange in shape and word. Even from there he could see that this was a city built on hills, rising and stretching away to the east, littered with endless small houses that seemed to be stacked on top of one another. So many people, so near to them, unseen all this long time. Wes had not felt it amid the hawking spectacle of *Avenida Revolución* but here for a moment he did — the shock of different lives, of what was either a new world altogether or a sudden vista, unanticipated, on the world they all somehow shared in common.

Going south they were cut off by a bus, thought they'd missed a turn, left the main road, made haphazard circles while Stick cursed and turned hard right to avoid a tractor and finally took them onto a low sunken road that looked like a creek bed. It ran through a row of ramshackle houses made of wood and mud. They were lined with tin and newspapers and their yards were mostly dirt. There was a strong bad smell and no breeze.

Stick honked at some stray children and took the first road leading up.

There were no street signs, and Cullen seemed to be having a good time drinking in the car and waving at the people they passed so they kept climbing. They were going up a long incline and soon the houses were made of concrete blocks. Simple terraces and stairs emerged along the hillside, connecting the homes to one another; tubs of soapy water sat outside; a small fire flickered and smoked in one yard, again in another. The road made a crunching sound beneath them, layered with gravel now. A chicken ran in front of them. The hillside flattened and there was green grass and a fresh breeze, rundown stucco houses that looked like they might have been on the outskirts of San Agustin. They were all looking out the window at some boys playing soccer in a field when John yelled and Stick hit the brakes. The road had ended and they were on the edge of a small cliff.

They got out to look.

Before them lay the city and beyond it the sea. It was late in the afternoon now, approaching dusk, and the rolling settled hills around and below them were shrouded in the gauzy charcoal haze of what must have been hundreds of small bonfires, smoldering trash piles or outdoor hearths billowing up strands of thick black that widened and faded to gray. The houses sat squat and full among the hills, all of them together still less a city than a village, a vast teeming village, even the small cluster of office buildings and the miniscule bejeweled airliners circling in the thick smoky twilight and the glaring lights of San Diego to their right bearing witness not to an alien modernity but to the real presence in this strange world of the unlikely, the bizarre, the inexplicable. It was like a dream and its center lay in their view not to the north but to the west, the long flat surface of the sea a silver and blue sheen beneath the coming night, the sun a bloody burning disc poised just above the water. Between it and them rose a cluster of islands, small from here but bold, erect, not low and flat and the color of leaf and earth that Wes knew from home but a rich and somber purple, the solidity of rock soaring up from the unplumbed depths before them and toward the sky it could not but fail to reach. They sat rich and solitary off the coast there, alluring, taunting, a realm sunward and visible but finally beyond their grasp.

And just before the islands, where the city and the land came to an end, they saw the squat low cylinder of the bullring in silhouette against the sea.

"Good God!" Cullen yelled. "Would you look at this!" The breeze was picking up now, fanning the grass, and he moved across it, bottle in hand, sidling back and forth before the cliff's edge, hopping and skipping and once or twice nearly falling, a man in a state of joy and confusion.

"It's something," John said, his mouth listing open. He was looking to seaward but kept one wary eye on Cullen.

There was a silence. "Yep," said Wes. "This is a different place." It was true. It was taking his mind off himself. He began casting about for words, trying to go further. "Something different about it. All of it. Even the smell. Even up here, there's a little bit of the ocean, but there's something else. That smell that's all over the city, it's like — the tamales. Corn, but burned. Burnt corn. And…something else."

"Piss," Stick said.

Cullen laughed, turned, pointed at Stick. "OK. Leave it to my man here for the reality check. I guess. OK." He gathered his chin up, smiling, took a drink, dropped his mouth back into the manly depths of *gravitas*. "Enough. We are not *turistas* but *aficionados*, and we have come not for the shit of the bulls but for the bulls themselves. We must see to them, my friends."

As they drove back down the hillside and toward the sea — they took only one wrong turn, a dead end where a waiting pack of dogs snarled and circled the Blazer until it backed out — Stick's laugh rang out again and again. It made Wes feel slighted and angry. The laugh, and not only the way Stick had cut him off just now but something else, something that went deeper. It was as if Stick were stealing everything away. He had insisted on driving from the start (John had volunteered to drive so Stick could drink but he said no), insisted on leading the trip even though it was Cullen's. Even now the two of them were up front, Stick joking and Cullen following his lead. Wes was suddenly seeing all this, growing angrier, and at last he looked across to John for some kind of confirmation. But they were passing back along the creek bed and through the houses of the poor, and in his roommate's face he saw only a muted sadness.

By the time they reached the bullring the horizon had deepened to purple and black and all they could hear was the tolling of an unseen buoy and the crashing of the long Pacific waves against the land.

There was just enough light to make it out looming black in the night against the dim starlit sky, and still it had to be half-imagined, massive and circling and empty like photos he had seen of the Colosseum in Rome. They drove through the parking lot by the sea and shone their headlights along the wall for signs but they found nothing until they lit up an old woman sitting on a blanket in a recess beneath a great shadowy tableau. She held her hand up against the light until they turned it from her. They got out and gave her some coins and she told them that they had come on the wrong weekend. *Domingo de los Ramos, Semana Santa.* Stick and John knew a little Spanish, translated. "Some religious bullshit." "No fights this week." She nodded to them as they walked back to the car, smiled at them with broken teeth, mumbled words that no one of them knew but some other tongue that was old and near-forgotten, some language of the night.

"*Compadres*, do not lose faith. We keep meeting with the shit of the bulls but those who have *aficion* will find the bulls themselves. They will purzerveer." Cullen was leaning hard into the back seat now, bleary-eyed and breathing beer. He did not put much stock in what she said, maintained a boozy faith that something would turn up tomorrow. But as for now: the tourist strip was too far away, and they had seen all that before anyhow. "We will not return there and dance with the little children, *amigos*." No, Stick responded. It would not do. He had a better idea. They would find a donkey show.

Wes had heard about them from the warrant. They were well-established in legend anyhow, part of the common fund of sexual mythology bequeathed to all the ensigns from diverse sources within the higher and lower ranks alike, but the warrant had spoken of them most eloquently if that was indeed the word for it, these remnant rituals of an earlier, darker time, woman and beast together on a low stage before a prurient congregation assembled in witness as if at some primitive and depraved sacrifice.

They never found one. By fate or bad luck or chronological happenstance — the police had cleaned out the shows some years ago, someone told them at last — they only spent a couple of fruitless hours wandering the streets and paying taxis to escort them to dark places that never held what the drivers promised. The cab was always gone by the time they had parked and Stick gone in, Cullen trailing him and laughing as if he did not really believe he were here, John sitting casually defiant in the Blazer, arms crossed, ready to wait alone for a long time, Wes himself standing halfway across the street and unsure, not excited but curious as to whether human beings were in

fact capable of such things. That a woman could so completely rein-
vent herself as to do such a thing—he almost admired the discipline
of it.

So they ended up in a strip club for an hour, paying too much for
small drinks and watching in boredom as the women strutted on stage
and collected dollar bills and finally took their tops off. Eventually
Cullen disappeared and Wes turned to see him talking with some
other Americans, heads shaved like Marines, at the bar. They were
the ones who told him about the new resort village to the south and
that was how the four of them wound up at some vast oceanside club,
a restaurant and bar open to the breeze and set atop a cove where the
beach had been built up into a massive dance floor with miniature
versions of the *Niña*, the *Pinta*, and the *Santa Maria* erected in the
middle of it, dancers parading on the decks. The *Santa Maria* was
still under construction and occasionally a large wave would wash
up around its base, sending the dancers there — tourists all, Americans and at least one Swedish nanny from San Diego that the four
of them were trying hard to impress — scurrying and splashing into
one another.

The place stayed open long after midnight but by the time they
got there the crowd was already at its peak and soon began to fade. It
had not taken Stick long to find a promising group of girls to solicit
lodging from — they were there for a volleyball tournament, staying
in a condo owned by one their fathers, and their judgment seemed
impaired by something other than alcohol — but within an hour or
two they had suddenly slipped off into the dark. So the four of them
ended up back in the Blazer, pulling off to one side of the parking lot,
leaning the seats back and opening the hatch and managing to sleep
a good bit of the remaining night away in various states of contortion
on the edge of the great roaring ocean.

In the morning Cullen was the first one awake, wrenching at Wes
and John beside him, dragging them out of the car and then running
down to the sea and hurling himself into the surf. Wes felt horrible,
musty-headed and sore, and the sight of the waves and the gray morning sky did not cheer him, but when he saw Cullen coming up from
beneath the water yelling and splashing like a boy he went down to
the sea.

The water was cold but good — it woke him, brought body and mind alive and together again. He blew the salty water out of his nose, shook it from his hair, looked at Cullen, and they laughed.

John and then Stick came too, the four of them circling one another, treading water, heads rising and falling with the steady rhythm of the sea. They were putting together the events of the night before and finally came back to the bullring.

Cullen spat out a trickle of seawater. "It is fine. It is just as well, my friends. TJ is a bad place, it lacks *aficion*. The real bulls we will see in Ensenada." In fact he did not know if there was a bullring in Ensenada and if there were he had no reason to believe that the season would be otherwise there, but he could not be deterred by such considerations. He swam to shore, leapt into the car, and pointed south along the coast.

The highway was almost empty and ran through a world that was starkly beautiful. The road ran along and often precariously above the edge of the sea, it and the westward sky grown brighter now, the water a deep rich blue in the distance but lighter, near transparent, along the broken shoreline. There the long dry land yielded to the thick wavering green of sea-growth, moss-haired rocks and yellow kelp drifting cool above the pale sand. In the blue distance the islands — the same they had seen at last twilight, closer now — watched lordly over all like drowsy beckoning sentinels that blocked out the horizon beyond, gatekeepers marking the entrance to some further world that lay hidden and as yet unseen.

On their left rose a landscape grim and austere. The earth climbed dry and steep from the water and rolled abruptly eastward to a long line of brown hills, cresting beneath the open blue sky and the hard glaring white of the great windswept clouds. From studying the map Wes knew what lay beyond: there, just over the line of hills, was the desert. It was that close. And for all the barrenness of the land it was really nothing but southern California itself made stark, stripped of freeways and housing developments and convenience stores, the world they had lived in for the past year now bare before their eyes. Where earth and sky met there was something more, indistinct at first, but once, rounding a corner, visible. Figures — moving, human. And other shapes that did not move but stood stolid and unyielding against the slow-tumbling clouds: cords of wood piled atop the hills, bonfires as yet unlit, at their center a great soaring cross.

Around another corner four men with guns stood in the middle of the road. Two wore black jackets and baseball caps and carried machine guns in hand, the other pair cowboy hats and mirrored glasses, rifles slung across their backs. They stood in front of a black truck that was parked across the road and stared at the Blazer until it stopped. When they had glanced it over one of the men almost smiled and waved Stick on with the barrel of his gun.

"*Jee*-sus," Cullen said with a wheezing laugh. "What was *that?*"

Occasional houses and villas appeared now, a little ramshackle settlement on the side of a hill. Patches of green rose out of the brown earth. And, as they drove, newspaper stories of the Baja drug wars — suppliers and dealers, feuding cartels, a mass killing at a ranch along this road — began to emerge from their memories.

"What a fucked-up country," Stick said.

"Where?" John turned toward the window.

"What?"

"Supply and demand, supply and demand. All that stuff's on the road north."

"I repeat: What a fucked-up country."

They drove on, beneath another hilltop cross, and then another, past a ranch where a dark man and a smiling girl stood with a white horse alongside the cool rolling expanse of the sea. There were no signs and the land was so open and desolate that for a moment they feared they were lost but then there was nowhere that they might have taken a wrong turn.

Around a corner where the road suddenly narrowed among stony hills a great yellow-eyed goat waited atop a rock, chewing slowly and thoughtfully. He watched the Blazer approach and pass beneath him and then, with a toss of his tousled grassy beard, he hopped down and began to trot along the edge of the road, a tight gourd of fat swinging between his long muscled legs.

At the end of the narrow passage Ensenada lay spread out before them like a kingdom that was theirs for the taking.

They checked into a hotel in the middle of town, took a long nap and then went to a rooftop restaurant down by the harbor for lunch and drinks. It was the best time of the day for Wes. He felt fresh and awake and he was realizing, almost despite himself, how much he had enjoyed the morning.

It was a simple thing he sometimes liked — driving with music on and the windows down — though it was better when he was alone. The openness of road and sky had made him recall his first drive west and how strange it was then, back when this all began, because on one hand he wanted orders but on the other he reveled in his freedom. By now he knew or at least suspected that maybe what he really wanted from both was promise, the promise of great things ahead, the important, the extraordinary. And this was why he was finding Mexico more alluring than he had imagined. He had not expected much — a vast theme park, ragged and dirty — but it was a strange country after all, thick with the promise of the foreign. For moments riding through that Baja landscape he had been able to feel himself Cortez or De Soto, the beauty of traveling this new ancient world only heightened by its rawness and vague threat. And so he could almost believe that Cullen was onto something after all, the danger and the courage of the fight properly not the end but only the means, the heroism after all only the vehicle for *afición*, for passion, the passionate and rich feeling and love of beauty that culminated not in the fight but in the festival.

There on the rooftop looking out over the harbor, the islands still dimly visible on the far horizon, he had a margarita and then another one. He could see a good deal of the city from here. It was much smaller than Tijuana, a fishing town, really, and they had walked down through the bazaars from their hotel. There was less noise and traffic here, few Americans. Wes saw a man leading a mule through the street below and thought *this, this is it*. They had left the false glitter of the border behind and come into the real. Still there was a boy selling Chiclets in the plaza below, but when Wes looked out over the drowsy rooftops and to the sea beyond — a small lighthouse adorned the cluster of rocks at mid-harbor, boats skirting it with nets aweigh — he felt sure that they had found something. He felt it, and when the women appeared at the table beside them he thought he knew it.

They were strangers, three of them, tall and striking in sundresses, fair-skinned but strange of voice and when Stick and Cullen had asked they said that they were Scots and one who lived in New Zealand now, the brunette whom Wes found himself alongside. He did not know what he asked but she turned to him and said they had been traveling across Central America on holiday and having a lovely time, and you?

He did not hear his own answer but turned from her deep green eyes and found himself looking out again at the streets, the dark people somnambulant there. After they had talked only a few minutes he felt strangely close to her and later he realized that in part at least it was their whiteness. This woman, fair, beautiful, even courtly, beside him, the pair of them gazing down on the natives like conquerors. He felt lordly, exultant, turned to the blue sea with the sun warm on his face and almost shouted with joy at a day so shot through with the goodness of — what? — creation and the sense of his own freedom in it. He had another drink. With the salty taste and the rich ocean breeze and the sweet lilting voices in his ear, he was nostalgic for the moment before it had even passed.

He felt it then, what he had not felt so fully since Venice just before the war began: a closeness to some rich secret that lay beneath the dull surface of life. But something was different. Now it came bound up with the threat of time. Now with the war past and this their final campaign, this his one venture into the extraordinary, there came with the closeness a half-sensed conviction that he must seize the secret, whatever it was, and make himself its master.

The others must have felt it too, some kind of elation, for with Cullen in the lead the drinks kept coming and the talk grew louder, great heaping plates of food spread out on the table and beer now, *cerveza*, its taste with lime and then the spicy beef and the tortillas too, and the smell of the sea. A mariachi band played behind them, somber men in gaudy outfits that made them smile. They talked and laughed. The food and the drink were good and the day was beautiful. Anything was possible.

Then the women left.

They grew quiet even as Stick and Cullen grew louder, began to check their watches. Handbags rustled. Farewells were said, plans made to meet, maybe, later that night. The plans were vague. Then they left.

In the quiet that followed, Cullen was told by a waiter that there would be no bullfights in Ensenada. He thanked the man, gave him some dollars, then turned to his audience with sodden aplomb. "It is no matter, *aficionados*," he said, lifting his drink. "The true bull is to be found within." Some of the beer spilled down his chin as he turned it up to drink.

At that moment, Wes still believed him.

They were waiting for the night, but now the sun was shining down thick like butter and they still had to pass through mid-afternoon. They went to drink by the courtyard pool at their hotel. It was a Best Western and they found themselves talking to not the European women but a pair of divorced hairdressers from Arizona who had arrived on a cruise ship.

They were older, closer in age to his mother than to him, Wes guessed, but they were trim in their Day-Glo bikinis. They said they tried to take care of themselves. Both had light hair, but against the bright cloth their bodies were a splotchy brown and their skins were thick and shiny as if they had been waxed.

"You boys got it made," the taller one was saying as she snapped open a diet drink. She looked at her friend.

"You said it."

"Oh, I don't know." Cullen was springing up and down on the diving board. "Our lives are pretty stressful right now." He leapt into the air and Stick threw him a bottle that he missed just before he hit the water.

"And I'm not just talking about right now," the woman continued.

"Unh-unnh." The friend was digging in a beach bag.

"I mean, look at you. Young. Good-lookin'. Got your whole lives ahead of you."

Wes was in the shallow end, leaning against the wall. At the far side of the pool John floated on his back in the shade.

"Wish I was that young again."

"Just don't rush into anything, that's all I got to say."

"Don't."

"Anything serious, I'm saying."

"That's right."

"We know cause we been there."

"We have." The friend had pulled out some mini-bottles and was pouring them into their drinks. "Anybody want some rum?"

"I'll take a hit," Stick said. He was sitting on a case of Budweiser and pulled one out, then arced it across the pool. It splashed heavy into the water alongside John. "Hey Johnboy! It's time to wake up and join the party!"

"Anyways, that's all behind us now."

"It is."

"And these two girls here know how to have a good time when they set their minds to it."

"That's right."

"And here we are."

The friend had pulled some lotion out and was rubbing it down her chest. She was near Stick, leaning forward in her lounge chair, and he looked at her until she turned to him and smiled. He got up and slid behind her and began to rub the lotion on her back.

"Lord, Tammy, you done got one to yourself. Now," she said, stirring her drink with a straw and leaning back in her chair, "I reckon I'm on my own?" Her sunglasses glinted bright and her face was still so they could not see where her eyes turned.

"There's your man," Stick said, nodding to Cullen.

"Hmmmm," she said, waiting. None of the others moved. Tammy was leaning back into Stick now and Wes could see that her taut stomach abruptly sagged at the bottom and slid into her swimsuit with just the faintest trace of a scar.

Stick was rubbing her shoulders languidly and nodding at the taller one. "Ol' Billy's always ready to help out. Right, Billy C?"

Cullen shook the water from his head and looked at them drowsily.

"And he knows how to have a good time."

"He sure looks sweet. Reminds me of somebody. Who, I can't say."

Later in the hotel room they decided that Cullen must have reminded her of her son because when he finally got up to rub her back she cooed over him like a mother. But then when she leaned up against him afterwards it was not so much like a mother.

"Stick, you bastard. You're gonna have me in trouble before the night's over," Cullen said.

"That's my job, buddy. That's my job. Takin' the bull by the horns."

"Ah, yes. *El toro.* We must not forget the bull." Cullen smiled but his voice was tired. They had taken another nap and the drink had worn off, leaving them in a moment of sobriety incongruous with the long day passing. Wes could see it in their faces, Cullen's and John's, too, where he sat by the window quiet and watchful. Already the light was dimming outside and they might have just kept on sleeping.

But then Stick passed a bottle around and soon they were walking out into the night. There was a big club in the middle of town and they had dates there with two different sets of women.

The bar was full of Americans. The British women never showed and when the hairdressers did they were with a group of men from their cruise ship.

The place was called Señor Goat's and it was crammed with fat older men in tropical shirts, thirty-five year old men in khakis, San Diego fraternity boys in tee-shirts that advertised suntan lotion. The floor was littered with wood chips and the main room stank like a barnyard. All around it males were sidling, shoving, elbowing their way toward whatever women managed to find their way in. A blue haze of cigarette smoke hung overhead. Mexican waiters in white jeans ran around the room carrying trays of tequila shots, whistles dangling from their necks. Stick pulled one aside and slipped him some dollars and a minute later he rushed up behind Cullen, yanked his head back, and dumped the tequila into his gaping mouth. He did it all in one swift motion, trilling on his whistle like a madman.

Stick was leading them in a slow circle from the crowd to the central bar and then back out again. He had a destination in mind and finally Wes saw it. He was leading them back to the women from the pool.

They had already said one quick hello to the pair and their new companions—a group of balding businessmen from Fresno—but Stick wanted more. He had a grin on his face and when it became obvious where they were headed, he looked back and said, "Gentlemen, here's where it gets interesting."

John nodded his head softly and Cullen only laughed. It was all a game to him. But Wes could see Stick's seriousness and it irritated him.

They walked to the edge of Tammy's circle and the tall friend looked at them and said, "Well, hey! Look who's here. You fellas come join us, you might just learn somethin'."

"Is that right?" Stick said. He looked at her and then at the men from the cruise ship, who were eying the newcomers grudgingly. There were four of them in khakis and shirts that almost matched. They all looked soft in the stomach except one who was slim as a bone and two of them wore pinky rings.

"That's right," she said. "They're like Tammy and me. They *been there*."

John was swaying slightly, friendly but watchful, bobbing his head at them, Cullen laughing and boisterous beside him. The men slid apart to make room and spoke to them with voices that were only half-resentful. But their gazes kept drifting back to Stick, who had positioned himself next to Tammy and lit his own face up with a smirk. And Wes himself—standing alongside the tall woman, Wes felt her gaze sweep over him, but his own eyes turned to Stick and he knew that they were angry.

Even as the world and the people around him grew louder and brighter, he sunk into himself and he found there a great store of resentment. All the heaping sensation of the afternoon had turned rotten. To have believed that he had come somewhere new, to have imagined himself discoverer, explorer — *conquistador*! He felt like a fool. And then the women. Here at the end of the long day the night had come and he found there not the one who had appeared as if out of a dream but instead these two and their small broken lives. He looked at the women with contempt and anger, contempt for their trivial histories and anger that they had intruded on his.

And the allure of the country, of the foreign, was gone, lost in a place that might as well have been a block from La Mirage. He was still in his America, he realized, and he saw it more and more clearly now in the petty inconsequentiality of the scene before him: lives half-led and already half over, decaying before they had ever really begun, on display like a vision of his own future. They had had it all, hadn't they, peace and freedom and money enough, and what had it done for them?

Something splashed on his back. It was the fraternity boys behind him, tussling with one another and sloshing beer.

That was it. That was it, he thought. Orders were coming soon. A year in the West and this is what he had made of it. A year out of the Institute and he was back in the life he had gone there to escape. It was too much. He looked around once more, and he felt now that everyone saw through him, that he had been humiliated, made to look foolish before them all. And when he sought to place the blame he knew where to turn.

Stick's head was inclined, Tammy whispering in his ear, but when Wes turned to meet his eyes Stick glared back as though he had been waiting. "What's wrong there, Colonel? Somebody piss in your beer?"

The others kept talking. Across from them the tall woman was leaning on Cullen's shoulder while John and two of the businessmen tried to divert her.

"Or did you piss yourself? Cause you been looking pretty pissy since we got here. You see," he half-turned to Tammy, "this fella takes himself pretty seriously. Thinks he's just a little too good for the rest of us. And you know what? I got *no* idea why."

"What the hell's got into you?" Wes was surprised to hear the words coming out of his mouth. There was a surge of heat in his chest. It felt good.

"And I think the boy's been down on his luck with the ladies, if you know what I mean."

"It ain't on account of his looks," Tammy said, smiling. Was she just trying to calm Stick down? He felt vaguely flattered by her endorsement and then even angrier at himself for noticing it.

"It's on account of his attitude. Ain't got any balls. Wants to sit back and let it come to him, like he thought would happen today."

"What the hell are you saying?"

"Thought Princess Di or whoever was gonna show up here and they were gonna live happily ever after."

"Princess—? One thing for goddamn sure, her staying away from you shows she had some class." It didn't come out quite right but he knew what he meant.

"Is that right, Colonel?" Stick took a step toward him.

"That's right."

"So it's all my fault, is that it?"

He said nothing.

"My, my. You do manage to have a lot of little problems. But it sounds like you can blame them all on me. Or—" he nodded toward the far side of the circle—"on somebody else. But that's old news, right?"

He was already tightening his hand and trying to form words when Stick, smiling, took one more step forward, laid a hand on his shoulder, and gave him a slow hard pinch inside the collarbone.

His fist landed hard in Stick's stomach, just below the ribs. For a moment, with Stick doubled up in front of him and the figures in the circle spreading half a step backwards, he admired his own accuracy. The scene in front of him—mouths open, arms half-flung outwards, drops of liquid suspended in the air—was strangely lucid. He felt that he was seeing things more clearly than he had in years.

Then Stick's shoulder rammed into his gut, long wiry legs pushing behind it, and he felt other bodies at his back, hips and elbows. He saw someone's knee and then his skull bounced off something hard and the world went black. When his eyes opened again Stick was kneeling over him, raising his fist, and they were both wet and the world smelled like beer. He threw his arm up and half-deflected the punch, rolled out from under Stick and across the sodden ground. One of the dozen legs in front of him kicked at his head and he heard a great yell go up all around him. They had landed in the middle of the frat boys.

After the bouncers and waiters had finally hauled them out to the street and the four of them had broken away and sprinted down an alley and across one street and then another while the cops were taking bribes from the fraternity, Cullen stopped and bent down panting into his knees and then threw his head back and said, "Damn! You guys don't let things get dull, do you?" His hair was wet with sweat and beer and his mouth a little bloody where one of the frat boys had cracked him but between gulps of air he was smiling with pink stuff dripping out of his teeth.

Stick was alongside Wes now, bent over too, and after the fighting and the cops and the run they were heaving and spent and could only look at one another. By the time they finally got their breath back Stick seemed to have forgotten the whole thing. He had something else in mind. "Now," he said, "it's time for the real stuff." Then he put an arm around Cullen's neck and led him off down the street.

"Don't you guys think that's getting close to being about enough for one day?"

It was John's voice. It seemed like it had been a long time since he had spoken, so long that Wes almost started. He had been with them all day but also somehow aloof—staying close enough but always at a little distance, not so much a part of the group as a hanger-on, a waiter and a watcher. Later when Wes could think back and put it all together, he would know that John had been like this since San Francisco, would know that and would even suspect that his roommate had a kind of foreknowledge of the night to come, had come down here to help but was not yet strong enough to master even himself and so had half-stepped aside. It was as though things had gone too far already and he had surrendered to their inevitability, become a witness. A mere witness. And suspecting this Wes would suddenly be faced with the question that surprised him most of all: how much had John been like himself, a part at least of his nature passive and detached and waiting, having to struggle to make things happen even if he did sometimes make it look easy back then during all that long lost year?

But suspicion or intuition or knowledge, whatever it was, was still a long way off. Now he and John were watching the other two disappear into the dark Baja night and it was time to move.

"To hell with them," Wes said as he watched them round a corner. "I've had it with Stick for the goddamn last time."

"I know. I know. But Cullen." John took a step forward. "And we've got to walk that way regardless."

He was right. Getting his bearings back, Wes saw that he was right. Señor Goat's was no more than a long walk from their hotel, but Stick had insisted on driving only to end up having to park a long way from the bar. Then their run had taken them farther from the car and the hotel alike. In order to get to either one while avoiding the street where the police were, they would have to walk back in a long circle.

Wes and John were following now. They were about a block behind the other two and they could see Cullen swaying as he walked, tilting his head back from time to time and bellowing up at the dim stars. Still he moved quickly, close beside Stick, who navigated the unlit streets as though he had known them long and well.

The musicians and vendors who had lined the block around Señor Goat's were gone now and the streets grew darker as they walked. Where they had been earlier the smell of the sea had drifted up in the breeze but here the air was still and moist like a handful of wet earth and hung thick with the smell of heavy food and garbage. Figures lingered in the murky windows and doorways, whispering. Soft laughter. A baby screamed in dismay. Dogs barked. And in a sudden moment it all seemed familiar—the rich dankness of the air, the teeming decay, the collapsing homes where women scrubbed the walls in furious and futile protest against the surrounding ruin. Here, hidden away in the dark quarter of this Mexican town, Wes only found what he already knew not from the Western sea or desert but from the deep woods that had once stood behind his home. It was the lost night world of Freddy and Dayzeerae, the country of the dead.

"Damn." John slowed beside him.

Up the street Stick and Cullen had stopped. There were other figures beside them, and Wes heard high Spanish voices ringing in the night. When they all turned and walked into a square of light that opened like a mouth in the darkness, Wes could see that the other two were women.

"Here we go," John said, lowering his head and quickening his pace.

Wes knew it before they even walked through the scant swinging slats that hung across the doorway as if in a saloon from some adolescent Western, knew it before he smelled the thick honeyed perfume and saw the row of women lining up before them. Stick had been talking about it since they left San Agustin, the women and their dark skin and how it could be bought. "The best thing about these wetbacks," he'd said on the drive down and then again walking through a crowded plaza on their way back from lunch, "is that they know who they're dealing with. For a chance at the almighty dollar, they're ready to bow down and do whatever you want. Hear that, young Billy? What-eh-ver-you-want." Out of respect for the native culture, he said, he favored the word *bordello*. He had been looking for one all day and now he had found it.

There was a tall dark woman slanting her hips at Wes while he stood by the door. When he did nothing she walked over and took him by the arm. The place was small, a long rectangular room with a bar on one side wall and low booths on the other, a curtained doorway in the back. She led him to a booth. It was nondescript, like a booth in a diner, and she slid into the seat next to him. A man appeared with a tray of bottles.

"You want a drink?" she asked.

"Sure."

"You want to buy me a drink?"

"Sure."

"You want to fuck?" Her voice had dropped and she was leaning into his shoulder so that he could smell her. She had a heavy accent and when she said *fuck* it sounded like a new word.

"No, thank you. That's very kind. No." He got out his wallet and paid for the drinks. The woman lifted her bottle to her mouth and turned it up for a second, then gave him a long bored look. She put her hand on his leg and when he still did nothing she muttered something in Spanish and slid out of the booth.

He stared straight ahead and took a drink of his beer. There had been another couple in the adjoining booth but he could not see them anymore. Then he heard noises and looked at the end of the booth and saw two pairs of feet hanging out of it and kicking the air rhythmically as if they were swimming.

He saw John sitting on a stool by the bar and got up to join him.

The place was doing a good business. All the men seemed to be Americans, mostly military but a few who looked like they had wandered over from Señor Goat's. There were even two boys in Panama Jack tee-shirts that they might have been fighting with earlier, they couldn't tell for sure. They could see the back of the man who had been in the booth next to Wes. He was black and after he had moved up and down on the other pair of legs for a while he stood with his pants around his knees. Then he looked at one of the men lurking in the corners and said, "I want my money back."

Someone started making a noise that sounded like laughing or crying or maybe both. It was Cullen. He was sitting in one of the middle booths with his head resting on one hand and a beer in the other. There was a woman with him.

"What a scene." Wes was looking around the room. "Pathetic. I mean, pathetic."

"Yep. "

"A farce. That's the word—a goddamn farce." He took a drink from his beer. "What's it about history repeating itself, as farce?"

John shook his head. "The second time."

"What?"

"The first time it's tragedy."

"What tragedy?"

"What history?"

"That's what I want to know."

"What are you talking about, anyway?" John scowled like a man who was being distracted from serious concerns. Then he slid off his stool and walked over to Cullen.

"I thought for sure it was the other way," Wes said, and got up to follow.

When they slid into the booth across from Cullen, he did not notice them at first. With Stick and the tequila and the long afternoon he had drank a little more than the rest of them, and after the fight it seemed to have descended upon him all at once. He was a wreck.

"*Aficionados,*" he said, seeing them and reaching across the table and nearly knocking his drink over, "*amigos.* My very good *amigo* friends. Allow me to introduce Miss Rosa, a very good woman. We have been discussing the tragedy of the bulls. There not being any."

The woman sank back into her seat and gave them something like a smile. She was shorter than the one Wes had talked to and smaller and maybe darker. In the dim light he could not place her features. At one moment the shadow would curl beneath her cheekbones and she looked Indian, but then she would turn and he wondered if she had African blood. And once when she looked almost straight at him he saw what surprised him most of all: her eyes were soft and open.

"Miss Rosa here's got a family." Cullen looked at her reverently. *"Dos bambinos."*

"He is good man," the woman said. "Your friend." She turned toward them and into the light and one of her cheeks looked darker than the other. Wes thought maybe it was bruised, a purple mark long and speckled, but then she sank back again and he was not sure.

"We have talked long and well." Cullen put an arm on her shoulder and slumped backwards.

"Well, how are things proceeding, gentlemen?"

Stick stood beside them. He had initially been in one of the booths but then had slipped out of sight.

"Ah, *amigo numero* tray. Where have you been, *muchacho*?" Cullen asked.

"Just checking out the management. Want to make sure you're in a reputable joint here. They're a little concerned," he said, leaning into Cullen, "that your friend here isn't earning her keep."

"What?"

"She's a working girl, you know. She needs to be making some cash."

"Money, money. I pay her. We have good talk, I pay her."

"Not talk."

"Donation, then. Rosa is mother, her family need money."

"A mother?"

"Sí."

He gave her a long look. "Mother my ass."

"Muchacho, *es* true."

"You're getting your leg pulled, my friend. She reads you for a softie, and you know what? I think she's right." He turned back to her. "Come with me, now."

The woman looked at him and then at Cullen.

"Come on."

174

"*Amigo*, what's this? Rosa is fine."

"Oh, no. Any 'donations' around here are gonna be earned."

"Come on now, Stick," John said.

"Is OK," the woman said. Her eyes had gone flinty and she was pushing her way past Cullen. "Me and your friend talk, hey?"

"That's right," Stick said. "We're just going to have a little talk."

He took her by the arm and motioned to someone and they walked through the curtained doorway in the back.

"This is bullshit," John said. "I've had enough."

"The shit of the bulls, not the bulls themselves," Cullen said.

Wes was silent. He did not like the turn things were taking. At first the place had almost made him laugh, its sordidness so straight-forward as to be almost ingenuous and in any case too much to take seriously, the whole place not so much real as just another of the boy-hood daydreams they had lived out with Cullen. It was a farce, alright, but one that brought back some comic glimmer of the hope he had had earlier in the day—a farce but a harmless one, the last welcome diversion from the whole question of orders and the larger questions that had been hanging over him for so long now.

This last woman had changed all that. Cullen getting choked up about her kids. Wes felt somehow disgusted by it, not by her likely deceit but by the petty sentimentality of it, even if it were true. Especially if it were true. A mother. Her winning Cullen over made it all the worse, somehow broke the spell, rendered even the farce less significant than it had seemed. Wes suddenly felt himself not hero in some burlesque epic but trivial bystander to some domestic melodrama. It was the final step in a long day of degradations. The last disappointment. For a moment he saw himself clear in all his floundering mediocrity, and somehow she was to blame.

"Alright," John was saying, "let's get out of here." He had slid over to Cullen's side and was trying to get him out of the booth.

A loud shout erupted from the back of the room. Wes turned and saw the curtain over the doorway shiver, then flutter and part. Stick was backing out of it, one long arm stretched forward and pointing, his voice hurling profanity across the room. Three men followed him out, short but thick, dark taciturn faces set like stone. One of them carried a baseball bat.

Wes and John stood instinctively and the men saw them and Cullen now, drew up short and stared. One of them yelled into the back.

"Come on," Stick said, hardly looking at them as he turned. "Let's get the fuck out of here."

Chests taut, arms swinging rote and narrow, they walked out two abreast and turned up the street fronting the alleyway where Stick and Cullen had met the first women. Two more emerged from it now clicking their heels and singing in low sibilant voices until they recognized the faces passing by. Then they grew silent and sank back into the gaping shadows behind.

They were still a few blocks from the car and the whole walk there Stick would say nothing except, "Shoulda known these people don't know how to negotiate." He said it three times with his hands waving in the dark but it was only when he had started the engine and reached for his back pocket that he said, "Son of a bitch. That cunt got my wallet."

The voice was not angry. Stick's eyes lit up and the tires shrieked when he turned the Blazer back the way they had come, but his voice was not angry. It was steady, almost calm, the voice of a ready violence so cool and so deep that it sounded almost perfunctory. It was strangely familiar to Wes. It had been building all night and he recognized it now. The tone, the phrasing. It was the voice of the warrant.

"What the hell are you talking about?" John was leaning forward now. "Slow down."

"The hell I will. I'm getting that thing back." He was swinging the Blazer onto the street they had come from. "Slipped it out when she had her hand on my ass. Shoulda known better. And you know which one it was, Cullen. Your mama friend there wasn't waiting for handouts."

"You're not going in there," John said. "You're already in trouble there and you're going to blow up."

"I will see to Miss Rosa," Cullen said. His voice trailed off at the end and in the glare of a passing streetlight his face looked sad and confused.

"I can take care of my own business," Stick said.

"If we're gonna try this stupidness we need somebody with the car running, anyway." John pointed. "That's you."

They were in front of the place now and before Stick had even pulled to a stop Cullen opened the door and began lurching toward the entrance.

"Dammit," John said. "Alright, it's me and him, I guess. But Wes— you check if we're not out soon." He got out and followed.

"Five minutes I'm coming in." Stick revved the engine.

Through the flapping door Wes could see Cullen wandering into the main room. The bartender was suddenly there too, flustered then calmer when John appeared beside him, hands spread wide, and began to talk.

In the back seat of the car Wes could hear nothing but the silent street and the whisper of Stick's breath.

The absurdity of the brothel had distracted him but alone in the Blazer now he could feel it again, the adrenaline, like something that had come upon him from outside. Swelling under his skin. It had been there, ready, ever since the fight, and it felt good. The pulsing rush of it. He realized that he had liked the fight itself. When Stick had touched him, it was clear what had to be done; the offense had been given and there the offender stood, right in front of him, almost like he was waiting. The clarity of it. Almost as much as the satisfaction of landing the punch itself, Wes savored the clear imperative he had been given to throw it.

Now it could happen again. The four of them, these alien men—it could happen again.

Thinking this he felt no anger toward Stick. What he felt was a vague gratitude. He was wide awake now; things were happening. Watching and listening in the darkness of the street he felt expectant. Leaning up into the front and peering out at the bar door, his knee bouncing up and down beneath him, he spoke without care, joking to fill the time.

"Hope Cullen isn't getting too carried away talking to his lady friend in there. Man in his condition—no telling what he might try to do. Or how long it would take."

"You'd like that, wouldn't you?"

"What's that?"

"Him and the whore. Closing the deal."

"Huh. Just kidding."

"I'd think you'd like it."

Wes looked at the back of Stick's head. He had a hand on the wheel and was gazing steadfastly across the street, chewing listlessly on a toothpick he had pulled from the glove compartment.

"Why's that?"

"Then you could help Cynthia find out about it. After all, she deserves better, right?"

For just a second he was stunned and then his face went hot so that he could not speak. He only made a sound like spitting.

So he had been happily expectant and even grateful but in the quiet moment now everything changed. Wes felt his body warming, blood surging hard in his temples, fingers curling together against the back of the vinyl seat. Stick had not even turned as he said it, left his back open so that he could have popped him unseen right then, but the unmanliness of it stopped him so he had just a moment to linger and taste how good the insult was. It had been thrown at him not face to face but over the shoulder, the offhand delivery only heightening its clear intent. That he could savor. But in the moment he also felt something that was less clear, something he had not expected.

He would not be sure until later. At the moment he could only have half-admitted it to himself even if he had had the time to articulate it, but surely then he first sensed it: there was something to what Stick said. But it was different, maybe even more, than what he meant. It was not that Wes would have told her such a thing, it was beneath him, or that he would waste time denying even to himself that he might have imagined her finding out; anybody was capable of imagining and there was little shame in it. No, it was something else. It was his hidden conviction that if she herself was in fact of any importance then Cullen really did not deserve her. For a part of him held a nascent but real disdain toward Cullen. Disdain for his friend's weakness—his fascination with the trivial, the boyish way he had of taking interest in the everyday. It was exactly what had made Cullen's company so appealing at first, and Wes's sudden and half-grasped suspicion that it was what made his friend weak now both surprised and saddened him.

But with his fingers curling and all the heat of the night surging through his veins he let it go and the suspicion became just another grievance he had against the leering figure in the front seat.

One hand was ready to grasp the neck, to force Stick's face backwards, the other balled and cocked to lurch up into it when he saw that there was another figure standing in front of the driver's window. It was the first woman, the one who had led him to his booth. She had a purse in hand and a shawl on now and she was pointing back toward the alley that ran alongside the bar.

"Hey, cowboys." Stick's window was rolled down and she was leaning in and almost touching his face. "You not like inside, hey? Shy. I know." She pointed at Wes. "Shy cowboys. But come back for more. We work out new deal."

"One of your other bitches," Stick said, "took my wallet. I don't get it back, I'm gonna fuck someone up. Bad."

"*Por favor?*"

Stick said something to her in Spanish and she spoke back, leaning in close to his mouth. Wes had stayed where he was, muscles taut, half-leaning into the front seat. He could smell her scent thick like honey filling the car. Through his own window he could see another woman standing alone at the entrance to the alley.

"Come," the woman said, walking away from the window. "We deal."

Stick sat back and the Blazer began to roll forward, slowly turning toward the alley.

"What's going on?" Wes said.

"No car, no car, *por favor!*" the woman said. "Light no good."

"I'm going back there, I'm driving," Stick said out the window, easing the wheel around with one hand. "That's the deal."

The woman shrugged, yelled to her partner. The two of them were walking back into the alley.

"What the hell's going on?" Wes said.

"Just remain calm, Colonel. Your friend there says she can get us the wallet back. Don't believe her but what the hell?"

"That's crazy. What about Cullen and John?"

"They'll be fine. We ain't going far. And we can't let them have all the fun, now, can we?"

The Blazer's headlights were swinging across the walls of the alleyway now, illuminating shoddy brick and fading stucco and piles of junk and litter mounting up beneath. Then they pierced the narrow darkness of the alley itself. It ran like a cave between the bar and the silent building across from it. In the light Wes saw a couch and some mattresses on the ground nearby. There were doors in the walls alongside, then more doorways and heaps and shapes growing steadily more obscure until they were lost at the far end where the walls squatted still and black beneath the dim sky. A distant yellow streetlamp faintly marked the road beyond.

The woman was standing by a doorway and signaled for Stick to stop. Then she leaned in his window and said, "Okay. We have privacy. You come out, we talk."

The other woman seated herself on the couch.

Stick did not move.

"Okay. We busy. You waste time."

"Get in the car."

The woman scowled. "What?"

"In the car. We deal in the car, or that's it."

She looked back into the darkness and paused for a second.

"Okay." She yelled to her friend, then walked over to the front passenger door and slid in next to Stick.

Stick kept the lights on and the engine running.

Her friend stayed on the couch. "She no come in car," the woman said.

"That's fine." Wes was sitting still in the back now. He did not like what was happening but he felt alert and ready and he liked that. He felt ready for anything.

The woman moved closer to Stick. She was right up against him in the front seat.

"What about the wallet?" he said. He did not sound interested. He had one hand on the wheel and started to move the other along the front of her shirt.

"We talk wallet soon. Money is no problem." She was leaning into him now.

Wes saw a light out of the corner of his eye.

One of the doors alongside them had opened and two figures were moving there. It was Cullen and the woman he called Rosa.

He had his arm around her and she was leading him out into the alley.

"Hey, Cullen," Wes said. Before he knew what he was doing he had opened his door and was standing beside them.

"Wes!" Cullen looked at him as though he were just waking up. "Hey, what's up man? Miss Rosa here's showing us where the stuff is. She's making everything okay."

"Yes. Okay." The woman was half-looking up at him from under Cullen's arm. "Very drunk." Her voice sounded strange and when Wes helped take Cullen from her he could see that she was trembling.

"Where's John?"

Cullen stared at him for a second as if he did not recognize the name. Then he blinked his eyes and said, "Inside. Speaking with the management."

"Get him," Wes said. "We need to get out of here."

Watching Cullen lurch back through the door Wes thought that maybe he should go too. But somehow he felt that something was to be done here. Rosa was still standing alongside him. He looked at her and knew what to do. "Get the wallet," he barked. She moved toward the couch.

Things were happening quickly now but he felt good. Things were in motion and he was moving too, making decisions. He should tell Stick. He opened the back door to the Blazer again and looked in.

In the moment that he did it something happened. All at once he could see what was going on in the front seat—the woman's breasts, Stick leaning into them—and the thing that was happening now. The woman's hand was sliding down the ignition and grabbing the keys. Then the engine went silent and the headlights died and the woman yelled something into the darkness.

"Goddamnit," Stick whispered, "you're gonna pay." There was a scuffling sound and the woman let out a quick cry. Then there was shouting and the jangling of keys and with one hand fumbling she had her door open.

Through the front window Wes could just make out the dark figures moving toward them out of the shadows.

"Bitch!" Stick yelled, shoving the woman so that she lost her balance and fell headlong in her rush out the door. He had the keys back in his left hand now and struggled upright clattering them toward the ignition. "The doors! Shut the fucking doors!"

Wes had lurched into his seat and with his stomach gone tight now he yanked his door closed and leaned into the front to grab the other. It was then that the engine came up and the car surged forward so that the door slammed back and shut itself, nearly crushing his hand. The lights had come up too and he could see the men scattering before them dropping boards and bats and something that shimmered like silver as they went, flinging themselves back behind the piles and the doorways where they had lain in wait.

In the thick glare of the headlights the alley opened up as they shot through it and toward the streetlamp beyond. Then they were there, in the street, spinning right as Stick locked the brakes and turned hard so that the back wheels drifted beneath them and the Blazer was pointed almost back toward the alley again.

Down the street other lights glimmered, cross streets, cutting back around the block to the front of the bar where they had been waiting before.

Wes saw that and Stick did too, sitting up front and hanging onto the wheel, the two of them panting harder than they had been throwing punches at one another a few hours ago. And they saw the dim figures back down the alley, eight or ten together now, scurrying out of the dark and clustering in a hazy circle at the end of their headlights.

Stick looked down the alley and turned to Wes. Then he looked down the alley again and turned back to him and waited.

"Do it," Wes said.

The engine was roaring and the darkness yielding to their light, the brick walls and heaps of broken furniture and twisted metal rushing toward them and then past while the figures grew larger, the men moving quick and low like cats and the women low already, kneeling when the light first hit them, struggling to rise but stumbling so that for a moment they were not three but just one mass of grasping arms and wide eyes glowing yellow in the headlights. Still they were moving but not fast enough and just before it happened Wes looked away and his eye caught something alongside the car, just one of the hundred pieces of trash that littered the earth here.

It was a small chest of drawers, a child's, with all the drawers missing and the sides bashed in and just a sliver of bright mirror on the ground next to it. It was only a glimpse and he could not have seen for more than half a second but he would not forget because when he looked up again he saw it, saw her, the shorter one Cullen had called Rosa, shadowed face turning away from them and mouth open but speaking no sound that he could hear, the back side of leg and hip and torso rushing beneath the front of the Blazer and then rolling upright alongside him, spinning so that the face and one clutching hand came toward them again, hung up for a second on the mirror, sliding into the darkness now but brushing one last time against the window where he sat.

That was how Wes remembered it, anyway, a year or two or five later. By then it was almost a dream, the dream that never went away, the dream that maybe came less frequently but only grew more vivid every time he thought he had woken from it. The dream told him more than the happening because when it happened he didn't quite know what they had done. When it happened he saw the woman and heard a thump at the front of the car and another along his side and then they were spinning again out into the street. John and Cullen were there and Stick was yelling and suddenly they were all three in the back seat together, the car rushing forward again and all the things they left behind them disappearing like spirits into the night.

He let Stick do all the talking. He suddenly felt exhausted, and he decided to let Stick do all the talking.

"What in the hell was that?" John was asking. Wes had not seen him like this before and he could tell that John was angry.

Stick had been leaning forward in his seat and gripping the wheel like a man hanging onto the side of a cliff, but now he sat back and stretched his left hand and then his right. "Goddamn beaneaters," he said. "Told us they had my wallet back there. Told 'em I wasn't going in without the car and it's a good thing. Soon as we got back there a bunch of knife-toting dudes jumped us and if we hadn't had the wheels we'd of been toast." He reached into the glove compartment. "Those motherfuckers." He settled back with a toothpick in his mouth and breathed deep and almost smiled. Wes could see his eyes searching the rear view mirror.

John turned to Wes and looked like he was about to speak when Stick turned back to them. "Gentlemen, I'd say we'd just as soon get out of this town. We ain't made too many friends around here."

"What—now? It's after midnight," John said.

"Well I'm feeling cold sober. I can drive it. And I don't think Billy C has any objections." Cullen had passed out in his seat. "Wes?"

Wes turned away from them and looked out his window. "I'm ready," he said. He had not known his voice would sound so shaky.

"Alright," John said, confused, looking back and forth between the two of them.

They went back by the hotel to get their things and while John was loading the bags into the car Stick went to the lobby to check out. When Wes walked up as he was about to finish he heard him tell the clerk that they had to leave early because his friend was sick.

They were turning onto the coast road that would take them back north when John looked at Stick and said, "What happened back there, anyway?"

"I told you."

"I mean, all that talking with the 'management.' What were you trying to pull?"

"Hey, I just wanted to set my buddy up."

"Cullen?"

"You got it."

"Did he want to be 'set up'?"

"Man's taking life a little too serious lately. Got to make sure he's got some good times left, you know." He glanced back at Wes in the mirror. "And sometimes a man don't know what's best for him. His buddies have to look out for him."

Wes was silent.

John was sitting across from him now in the back seat, behind where Cullen was passed out in the front. He was giving their driver a long appraising look, a look that registered not surprise but a deep and curious understanding.

"How'd you pay for the hotel, anyway?"

"Credit card."

"It wasn't in your wallet?"

"Huh." Stick paused and fiddled with the radio. "No."

"Did your wallet get stolen?"

"Fuck, yes!" He threw an angry glance at the back seat. "I had my cash and cards in my front pocket. Knew I couldn't trust those bitches."

There was a long silence.

"It was a really nice wallet."

They were midway back to Tijuana when it came out, the truth or at least a version of it.

"I just nicked her. *Clipped* her, you might say." Stick was shrugging, gave a little laugh. "No serious harm done."

John threw his head back into his seat. Wes waited for a long time for him to turn and stare but he never did. .

So he sat in the great enveloping darkness and rolled down his window and listened to the night. It had grown cloudy after twilight and there was not much of a moon. Once in a while he could make out a glimmer of light on the waves. Otherwise sky and sea were one vast Pacific blackness but for the occasional dim lights that marked the lonely fragile homes scattered up along the hills. There were those and then at last, as they grew closer to Tijuana along the rim where the hills touched the sky, there rose the sure mark of flames. The bonfires they had seen earlier were ablaze now, lighting their path home. They shimmered strange and brilliant against the night and surely he thought they must mark something beyond themselves. Later he would learn that this late night was already Palm Sunday morn but when he saw those fires burning bright up on the hills he thought not of the man-God of whom his own people sometimes spoke but instead of prouder deities once regnant here. Surely it was those gods who were being celebrated tonight, gods of strength who demanded in sacrifice not themselves but their subjects. The defeated, the enslaved. Those who had been vanquished.

◁ 10 ▷

When he woke the next afternoon things were already in motion. He
did not know it yet, did not even know all that was happening around
him that day. But everything was changing. When he looked back later
it all seemed so strange: how for so long nothing seemed really to have
happened, and then this one night came as if it had been looking for
them and suddenly their lives here were at an end.

The end came very quickly. After almost a year of waiting, only one
more day until it was over. Orders were coming—distant authorities
marking their names at last—but with them at least one final choice
had to be made.

It was on the day when the unnamed history of that long expectant year finally came to an end that he saw Cullen begin to turn.

Noontime sun flooding in his window, he woke with a start and
knew that he was alone.

Even before his body moved his mind was racing. It was all there,
waiting for him: the night before and the long drive home, the hazy
half-dreamt hours lost beneath silent passing streetlamps along the
border, the still darkness north of Mount Soledad, the first dim glow
of dawn seeping through the eastern canyons as they left the highway.

By then he had felt near dead and how he had made it to his room he could not tell.

Now he was alone.

In half-dreams too he had heard John stirring across the hall, turned to the window and saw the pearl-gray luster of morning, lost himself to darkness again as the front door drifted shut outside.

He was alone and he had to fill up the day. He made himself get up and eat and with hands still shaky turned on the shower. He was in a long time but finally when he did not yet feel any better he got out and dried his wilting skin. Then wearing his towel he lay on the floor and he dozed and it felt good until again he woke.

He sat in his apartment until the stillness became too much and then he went outside.

The early gloom was gone now. It was a clear day, beautiful, sun not too warm and a light breeze coming off the ocean. It was like most of the three hundred and three score days that had come before it.

There were voices from somewhere and he looked into the court-yard and saw women by the pool. Elizabeth in a robe and Terri and Louise and Julie sunbathing. They were laughing.

He began walking around the edge of the courtyard and when they saw him Julie and Terri laughed louder and then they all bent over and held their stomachs and tried to stay quiet. Only Elizabeth did not laugh. She sat up straight and beamed at him and yelled, "Hey, cowboy!"

He stopped.

"Looks like you're walking kinda funny there. Saddlesore?"

The others had snickered when she called him and now they were sputtering. Julie rubbed her face along the edge of her chair.

Elizabeth kept beaming and when he looked again it was not the smile he was used to from her. There was something else. Her posture—sparrow chest thrust out, sitting so rigid that her back almost bowed. She held his gaze two beats too long and he saw it: she was smirking at him. Triumphant.

Without asking he knew who they had been talking to and knew it was not worth finding out what story they had been told. Looking at them he could guess that it was both less violent and more lewd than what had actually happened and that he had been given one of its lead roles. A comedy. He felt an impulse to protest but his gut was sour and his head still dull from broken sleep so instead he tossed a hand at them and kept walking.

A door slammed. It was across the courtyard and a floor up but still loud enough to make him look, and even before he turned he knew. Cynthia was there, turning sharp on her heel, long hair fitful in the still air behind her; then walking fast, almost trotting, to the stairs that led down to her car.

He stood waiting for Cullen to follow but the door did not open again.

In the rich warmth of the afternoon he felt lost now, sick. There was what had happened last night and he had not told it to himself but it was all there, clear enough, in his head. It was not going to go away until he told it to himself or somebody else and maybe not even then but he did not know this yet and so he kept moving.

That was how he found Stick.

His feet took him into the open glare of the day, sandals shuffling on warm asphalt, hand trailing loosely along the smooth shining surfaces of cars. He knew Cullen would not be out, but still he turned toward the far corner where the sailboat sat in the cool whispering grove.

Stick was there with a hose and a bucket. He was washing his car.

When he saw Wes he squeezed his sponge and only half-turned toward him.

"Well, well. Up a little late now, are we?"

Wes stood silent and when he found his voice it was soft. "Feel like crap. Seems like sleep's about the best thing to do. I'd think you'd need some yourself."

"Oh, no sir. There's work to be done, work to be done." He was scrubbing a fender hard now so that his hand shone back at them in the wet silver gleam.

"You've been talking to the girls."

"Hell, you only got to tell one. Then she'll take care of the rest. Can count on that." With a grin and a nod he looked at Wes over his shoulder.

"What exactly have you been telling them?"

"What they need to hear."

"What's that?"

He shrugged. "They got to hear *something*. I'm just satisfying their curiosity before it gets out of hand."

Wes paused and looked at his foot and looked back up again. "What do you mean?"

"Nothing any red-blooded American boy should be worried about. I mean, you know, I think they've got the idea that one or two of us might have had a little too much to drink down there and spent a little time with some *señoritas de noches.* But hey, a little spice is good sometimes, keep them interested. "

"That's ridiculous. Goddamn ridiculous." He was looking at his foot again and then he looked up and saw Stick's back but his own voice was still soft when he spoke. "What do you think you're doing?"

Stick dropped his sponge in the bucket. "Well, listen up. I know you and if not you then definitely John, right, you're gonna be moping around for a week like something big happened, when all it was was fucking self-defense and it happening down there with somebody who ain't worth much to anyone anyway, we got nothing to worry about." He was slowly and deliberately wiping his hands on a rag. "But these girls here—they notice things, give 'em credit for that, they'll know something somebody's a little queasy about went on down there and I'm just beating them to the punch with a little spin."

Wes stood and stared and was about to say something when he saw that Stick was moving toward him. His steps were careful, as if each one were planned, and he inched closer until Wes could see the veins in his eyes and the dead-gray flesh beneath them. "And you know, what the fuck do you care about what they think? It ain't like you've got a woman to get pissy with you. Only one of us got to worry about that." He lowered his voice and arched his brows, tilted his head toward Wes. "Right?"

Wes stood silent. He realized that he had stopped breathing.

Stick broke into a long smile. "You know, that poor fucker, I don't think he even knows what really happened yet."

Wes stared back at him and his face must have had hate or weakness in it because when Stick saw it he smiled and moved closer like a stalking dog that had reached the end of its chain. He was leaning in tight now so that all Wes could see were the dark eyes and raised hand, could smell the hot breath and hear the sharp confidence of the voice: "And yes, you've had a part to play in all this, Colonel. No thanks to you. If it weren't for me you wouldn't even have that. Had to hold your hand the whole way. I mean, you finally said it. 'Do it,' you said, and I'm glad you did because you wanted it and now you know you're fucking involved." He moved a step back and jabbed a finger at him. "But don't give yourself too much credit. Don't think *I* needed you to *tell* me to do it. See, *I* don't need to be *told* what to do, Colonel. I just wanted to see if you had the balls to tell your*self*."

He paused and the only sound was the two of them breathing. Stick was close again, like a lover, almost touching his chest.

"Why? You want to know why? Well, it's real simple. You got all kinds of complicated reasons for taking yourself seriously. But me? I just get a kick out of seeing you fuck up." He put his hands on Wes's ribs, shoved himself off and walked back toward the Blazer. Without breaking stride he tipped the bucket backwards with one foot and then walked off into the sun.

Wes stood alone again and he was surprised.

In the first rush of words there had been something, enough to make him hold his breath, but now he felt almost nothing. Not any of the anger that had welled up in him the day before, and lacking even that he could only feel a kind of curiosity about all that had happened. Part of him wanted to feel guilty but even that seemed false pride because when he looked at himself he saw neither good nor evil but only someone unimportant, someone who merely stood by.

He tried to move out of himself and back into the world. But when he looked up all he saw was the stream of dirty water snaking its way across the asphalt and into the weeds.

He walked down to the ocean, sunk himself for a while in the sea, lay on the sand watching the great ships drift into the horizon.

But it was a Sunday and he found himself surrounded by voices. Whole families come for a day at the beach. Among the busy parents and yelping children—how often did he see children?—he felt even worse than before.

A gull circled overhead.

Under an umbrella beside him a young father held an infant in his lap, pointed at things and gave them names, *sand* and *shell* and *water*. The child bobbed its head, gurgling, fell back into his arms.

Wes got up and left.

Back at the apartment he almost told himself that he should talk to someone. Not any of the women, who mocked him now and who were too inane anyway except the one and that was all done with long ago. Not Stick. And remembering the night before he now knew not even Cullen, doubtlessly bound this long Sunday in trying to make sense of himself to Cynthia.

There was only one possibility and that was the other witness. He had felt it before but felt it most surely now. He should have grabbed hold of John and made him talk a long time ago.

But today was too late. The clock turned as it had all the long drowsy afternoons he had known there and still John did not come back. He was gone and Wes had his suspicions about it but it would be at least another day before he could know.

For now, he only knew that he was alone.

In the still of the evening he picked up some books and then put them down. He needed noise. He had to turn away from the things that were in his head and knowing what he might find there he wandered down to the bars.

Standing on the broad deck of the Shellback with a drink in his hand, watching the fat bright sun sink into the Pacific, he heard the news. It was the one day he almost did not care and he would not believe it until tomorrow, but he first heard it then.

Sunday happy hour — "The Seventh Day," a drooping sign over the bar proclaimed. There was a big group of ensigns on the deck drinking and making noise, Hooper and some of his crew. Even Donkers and Smith were there. Donkers was in uniform and the others had formed a circle around him.

"No fucking lie, I'm telling you." Donkers did not usually swear and maybe he thought it made him sound important. "This is the real shit."

"Don't believe it," Hooper said. He still stood with a pronounced list even though his leg had finally healed. The injury slowed him down with the ladies at first — he had confided this to Wes at the TPU once — but eventually it won sympathy points. Sometimes he still used the crutches.

"You'll see tomorrow. Ten more days, and that's it. We're out of here."

"Don't believe it." Hooper had only half his attention on Donkers. He was scanning the deck for women, though Wes could not tell if he were still trying to compensate for lost time or if he secretly feared the news might be true and wanted to make the most of his last days of liberty.

He himself could not believe what was being said. But talk itself was all he had hoped for from this place. He wanted to hear more and soon he did, Donkers himself leaning over his drink, cursing with cocky sobriety and trying to speak like a man who had authority.

The news was not what Wes had expected. If it had been a few months ago, if it had been any day other than the day it was, he would have been enraged. As it was he was numb and grateful for the distraction, and when he first asked questions he had to work hard to sound like a man who cared. So it started as an act, but still his mind worked at the story, played with it like a puzzle, and almost despite himself he began to be interested. When he had heard it all and Donkers sworn up and down it was what he had seen on Ragis's desk, he began to see the peculiar and disappointing logic of it.

His mind was working now and he told it to stop. There was no use speculating because tomorrow he would know. He was standing there fighting back a vision of the future when he heard the voice he had been hoping not to hear.

"Hey look! Cowboy's back out on the range!"

Elizabeth was suddenly strutting in front of him, Terri and the hippy chicks trailing behind. They all surrounded him smiling and he was about to leave when Hooper and the other ensigns pounced on them and gave him a respite.

With the four of them together Wes knew Stick could not be far behind and then there he was, easing coolly into the midst of them. For a long time he ignored Wes until suddenly he turned and said something small, as if nothing had happened between them, with no trace of the past day's events but a murky ripple that passed once or twice across the surface of his eyes. And soon enough they had drifted into a circle again, the six of them, talking languidly about the others who were in hiding somewhere, Cullen and Cynthia fighting and John (saying it, Stick bit into his gum and looked at Wes darkly) doing who knew what. Then everything went empty and silent and Wes was about to leave after all, but that was when the other news, the news he had never expected, came up. That was when the conversation turned to Cullen and Cynthia and what lay ahead and Wes knew that he had to stay.

When he remembered it later he was at the center of a circle of female voices which he could not tell one from the other.

"She's had it," one of them said.

"She's wound a little tighter than the rest of us."

"What's his deal anyway? He's been acting like he's got a lot on his shoulders."

"Ha."

"Months and months waiting for him to settle down, and she sits with him through all that with his brother."

"And now this."

"Hookers."

"*Consorting* with prostitutes."

"She won't put up with it."

"Why should she?"

"Well. It's just guys, you know, they're like that."

"And it's not like they're married or even dated that long."

"Yeah."

"It wouldn't bother me so much."

"So long as he used protection."

"Gross." This was Elizabeth. He was reasonably sure of that.

"Hey, cowboy's here, let's not get him upset."

"Live and let live, I say."

"You're only free once."

"She'd give him one more chance."

"Maybe."

"Better be quick."

"Not this week." It was Stick now. He had stepped into the circle and was swirling a cocktail in one hand while he grabbed Julie with the other. "Not gonna happen."

"What's up?" Elizabeth asked.

"Cullen's with us." He turned to Wes and winked. "Been working on him for weeks."

"Guys," Elizabeth said, "Y'all are gonna have such a great time. I've gotta come."

Wes was not in on this trip, despite the wink, but he knew what they were talking about.

The hippy chicks were spending Easter in Maui. They both had frequent flyer tickets and were going because one of them had a friend in a band there and it was "fucking Hawaii," they said, and it was going to be great. They were going to drive up the side of a volcano and camp. There was going to be another band there and a hundred people and Ecstasy and it was going to be a big party. Wes had heard it all over the past couple of months, that and the two of them trying to talk everyone else into going. Within a few weeks they had won Terri over and Elizabeth had been thinking about it too.

She kept saying no because her parents were coming that weekend and she hadn't seen them in almost a year and she couldn't get out of it. She loved her parents but they drove her crazy after two days. That was what she had told Wes. But listening to John he knew something else: that her parents had not seen how thin she was and when they did, she knew, they were going to get upset and insist she do something, go to counseling or see a doctor or move home, and she did not want that. That was what he knew from hearing John talk about it with Cynthia, Cynthia worried too and wanting to make sure the parents did see her because she thought Elizabeth was destroying herself. The two of them had tried to talk to her and she ignored them, but still, Wes knew, they were trying to keep an eye on her.

And as for the Hawaii trip — Stick was in on it from the beginning. For months now he had been pitching Maui to the others as the logical conclusion of the spring travel season, the ultimate road trip (*except there's no road*, Cynthia said). He had been at it again just last week. It was going to be a beautiful thing, he said, one arm around Cullen and the other waving at the sky. The clincher was that it was going to be free. There were P-3s flying between SoCal and Pearl every day and he had been working with the warrant to schedule a hop over for any motivated ensigns who were interested in furthering their professional development. There were at least two slots guaranteed that week. When he said it he squeezed Cullen tight like a brother.

Now Stick and the four women were making plans and Wes saw that Elizabeth would go unless John and Cynthia talked her out of it. For John was not going. He had made that clear long ago. On Easter he was eating at his father's house and he had invited Elizabeth and her parents and anyone else who was free.

Wes had thought that he might go there, to the desert, but walking home that night in the descending darkness he found he did not care. He was tired of them all. He would not go anywhere and would just as soon be alone.

The apartment was dark. He ate a bad microwave dinner and then tried to go to sleep but could not. There was too much going on. There was what had happened the night before and now, too, the news about orders, which he had known or at least hoped would come one day, but also there was the news he had not foreseen at all. Cullen and Cynthia and what was coming for them. It was this last he tried to think about because he found it came without pain, even with a kind of cool pleasure.

He saw it all together now, what was happening to those two, and it started to look like something larger than the parts that had gone into its making. It was going to be interesting to watch. It was not clear then but later he could see it, how that night he had already been given the conditions of the choice that would be played out tomorrow, as if the script had been glimpsed first not by actor or actors but by an audience of one.

And so for a time he lost himself in the detached pleasure of the voyeur, felt better, forgot himself. But still he did not sleep well. He did not sleep well at the end of this long weekend, this long empty Sunday, knowing that tomorrow they would all step back into ordinary time. Tomorrow, orders would finally arrive, and history begin again.

He was awake before the sun first came through his window. He had not heard John come in during the night but still he was quiet and as he showered and began to dress he left the room dim. His window was open and looking out at the cool gray of the morning and the still dark hump of the hillside — it had been a long time since he had been up this early — his mind went back to the Institute. He dressed slowly now, careful as his first week in training, tucking his shirt tight and wiping his shoes to a dull shine.

He drove to a diner and bought a paper and breakfast. He had time, plenty of time. He would be the first one there.

The roads were empty and a thin fog hung over the harbor as he turned into the base. Lights moved on the water. Tugs. A pilot boat gliding toward the hulking ship at the end of the lone pier.

There were two cars in the lot and one of them was Stick's.

Dew clung to the door handle. He wiped his hands together as he stepped in, saw down the hall the back of the yeoman standing over his desk and shuffling stacks of paper. As he turned around Wes nodded at him and went into the conference room. He was cold, restless, bracing himself for the bad coffee.

The room was dark but Wes saw Cullen sitting across from the door with his head on the table, framed against the great single window in the wall behind him. He looked almost asleep and Wes was about to say something when he heard a voice on his left. Stick was there, at the far end of the table beneath the clock.

"Well, well. Looks like we're not the only ones up early."

"Nope." Wes kept his eye on Cullen. "You'd think we'd all need some more sleep."

"Where's your roommate?" Stick had been leaning back in his chair but sat up now, pushing a cup aside.

"Haven't seen him."

"Hope he's not causing any trouble."

"What do you mean?"

"Just don't want him causing any trouble, that's all." Stick sank back again. "I'd think you'd feel the same way."

Wes still looked at Cullen. "What's his deal?"

"Just taking a little nap. We been up talking."

"All night?"

"Half. He was with his lady friend until about three. But she didn't get the last word." He was pouring himself some coffee now, smiling. "That went to me."

And that was how they stood, the three of them, Cullen just beginning to stir and Stick encamped at his side and Wes paused rigid at the doorway. That was how they stood when John entered behind him and moved to his right and told them for the first time the things that he would tell Wes again later that day and yet again much later, in the time to come.

It could never be complete but afterwards, free of Stick's shouts and protests, he would hear it in full, all there was to know: how John had risen alone in the early dawn and driven back south all the long road they had passed the night before, windows down and raw wind rushing in and stopping once to jump into the sea, all so that he might stay awake and go on. In Ensenada again he found the street, alien and empty in the daylight, the city bright and restless and the places of the night fallen silent now. So he went haggard to the hospitals and found nothing and passed the police station and wondered and doubted and then drove his car beneath the shade of a tree and slept in the back seat through the heat of the afternoon. And waking he found the street again and there one of the barmen, the one he had spoken to the night before and who took pity on him now; who said the woman was badly hurt, somehow, and is gone and will not be back; who said that was all he knew; who warned John that if he lingered and returned when the men responsible for her had come back, there would only be more violence. So lost and defeated he walked the streets and into the churches nearby, at first because he had some hope that there might be news of her but finally, walking into a Mass, stopping and kneeling because he had admitted to himself that she was now, to them, lost, a ghost. One of the dead.

The whole time John told it Stick muttered and cursed and finally yelled, but when it was done he sat back and opened his lips so that they could see his teeth. "So," he said, looking at Wes, "that's it. Just like I said. We're free." Then he turned to Cullen as if he were waiting for some reply.

Even under the spell of what he had just heard Wes felt it then, a shift in the room, not only of attention but of voice or energy or something more. They stood crosswise now, Stick and John at far ends of the table while he and Cullen faced one another across it, all the weight of the day and the hour now placed onto their axis and rolling down upon the figure who sat at the window with his head in his hands, sinking, while standing before the door Wes felt somehow that he was rising higher and higher until it almost seemed that he was not there at all but only looking down and watching.

"I saw Cynthia this morning." John looked at Cullen as he spoke. "What are you going to do?"

Cullen was silent.

"This weekend," John said. "I want you to come with me."

"Oh no. He's got his mind made up, I believe. Heading west. Flight leaves tonight — tomorrow morning — at O-dark thirty. Already talked to the warrant." Stick was still sitting like a man at ease, eyes glittering and lanky arm stretched on the table. "Billy boy knows who's good to him."

There was no voice but only a laugh or a groan when Cullen dropped his head, wrested the chair from beneath him, slowly spun it toward the window. "Guys," he muttered, sinking down again with his back to them. "Guys. Sleep. Right now I just need some sleep."

"Resting up for the big flight," Stick said. "Smart move."

"Cullen," John said, "I want you to come with me."

In the long silence that followed Wes watched and waited and he was interested. It occurred to him that they had been free for a year now, free to make decisions and free not to, and maybe John had done one or two things and finally even Stick too but for the most part they had just drifted. He had done that and he saw that Cullen had too; even the whole thing with Cynthia, even that was the kind of thing — at least the beginning of it — that Cullen drifted into easy and unthinking.

But this was different. He saw that something was about to happen.

Outside two sailors stood in dress whites beneath a flagpole, one clutching the limp dangling line, the other a tightly bundled flag. Morning colors. Cullen, feet shuffling beneath his chair, leaned into the window as if he were studying them. Somewhere in the distance a long horn sounded. A ship was getting underway.

The door moved behind Wes, lights flickered. The dry voice of the lieutenant filled the room and over his shoulder came the warrant's yellow smile, calling their names. "It's time, boys." Papers were placed on the table. The door closed.

Orders.

After all the wait they were here, only a page and a half each and even then most of the characters meaningless, endless routing codes and jargon in mismatched print, but the substance itself simple and plain, no more than a short paragraph. And when he had read his a fifth time and then a tenth and had been to the meeting that Ragis called later that morning, Wes understood them no better than he did the first time he read them. As he stood there reading still too numb even to be disappointed, the future was suddenly even less clear than it had been before. There were decisions to be made. And he, all of them now, could be sure of only one thing: that Donkers had been right, that their time here was at an end, that in ten days they would be scattered and not a one of them in San Agustin.

It was knowing this and standing as he had before that John spoke for the last time.

"Cullen. This is it. And I'm telling you to come with me on Sunday." He paused and sighed and put his hands on the table. "I know she'll come. Because she's worried about Elizabeth and knows that if she's there then Elizabeth will stay and come too and see her parents. She won't be coming for you but she'll be there and she'll listen."

"Jesus Christ," Stick said, "What is this crap?" He sat up straight, red now at his end of the table, but then he sank into a deep silence.

"Come with me," John said again. His voice was moving toward something like certainty. He had come like a newsbearer with no sure news but now found what it was he had to say.

Then he watched.

Wes watched too, Cullen's shoulders tensing and loosening as though he were a swimmer about to plunge into a pool.

The flag was aloft now, falling and rising again, fitful in the breeze.

The distant horn sounded a final blast, the great ship now clearing the harbor and casting off its pilot.

Wes looked at Cullen and he felt that something was happening.

After a time Cullen leaned back in the chair. He settled his feet beneath him and then he began to turn.

Part Four
November, 1999

Wes was waiting for John. It had been a long time now, and he was waiting for John.

The room was mostly empty now but beginning to fill, parties of two and three pulling up stools alongside the ones who had been sitting alone with their drinks and cigarettes and flooding the bar with their slow blue smoke while they could in the early hours before other people showed up and began to complain.

It was a strange place to meet a priest, he thought. But it was what John had suggested and it was the kind of place they had spent a lot of time in all those years ago, after all, even though they were on the other side of the country now. He was trying not to spend so much time at these places, but still — John was a stranger here, it was a place he knew, and he supposed it was as good as any.

He had found a small table at the back where he could see both doors. There was someone he was hoping not to run into, and this way he could see John when he came in. Then they would talk and eat.

While he waited he ordered a drink. He did not especially like remembering but with the drink and the waiting and watching the ones at the bar look at the clock memory came and he was lost to it.

By the end he had liked John more than any of the others — he could say that, for what it was worth — and he still heard from him from time to time. They had not kept in close touch. More so at the beginning, but even then it was strange because the end had come so quickly. They had been scattered and then, within a year, they were all civilians.

Looking back on it now he had to admit that the orders made a kind of sense. He could be almost objective, could understand that with the budget cuts and the base closures it was the reasonable thing to do. And even then he had been given a choice, could have hung on. But they had to get rid of people somehow and they had started by driving out those who were not willing to give up everything for a shot at flight school and after that long year he knew that he was one of them.

Still, they had given him something. They had at least given him something that he could call experience and the knowledge that he would have to look for work and then the time to do it.

How it all started he never knew. Someone in Washington must have looked at the TPU at last and knew that it was a joke. And so the orders came, split the ensigns up, gave them temporary but real assignments during which they could briefly ponder the choice that had finally been presented to them: they could wait another year or more to begin flight school, or they could resign their commissions and be awarded honorable discharges.

The temporary orders sent Wes to an air station in northern Nevada that had been slated for closing within the year. He was assigned to help monitor the decommissioning of a squadron of aging bombers. It was there, in the desolate highlands east of the Sierra Nevada, watching the weeds sprout up beneath the broken runway, that he knew he had had enough. He was going to quit.

He almost changed his mind one Sunday when he took a long hike up into the deep evergreens near Tahoe, stood atop a rocky ledge, and saw a great taloned bird wheel by. When it had passed he looked down at the dry desolate world beneath him and felt a great sadness welling up, a sadness so deep and heavy that he almost sank to his knees.

The bird wheeled again before him and was gone.

Though he was not inclined to hope for such things, he thought for a moment that it might be a sign. But then driving back through one dying town and another and another he asked himself why the Navy had a station in Nevada in the first place and when he had his answer he knew that he had to get out.

In war a man could do something, but the peacetime military was too absurd for him.

He did not immediately tell Cullen or John or Stick because they were no longer with him. That was fine. He had been tired of them all, told himself he was glad to see them go. The only ensign from the TPU who had ended up at his station was Smith, the stock market man, and in their new circumstances Wes took a liking to him. He knew about things that counted in the civilian world, and that was where Wes was headed.

It was Smith who set him up with a *headhunter*—he had never heard of such a thing—that specialized in placing ex-military officers. The man had an office in Los Angeles and one morning Wes drove there and sat in a chair while the headhunter shuffled through some files and ran his thumb up and down his tie and asked him about "marketable skills." He took notes, shook Wes's hand, told him they would have something for him soon. "Self-discipline, leadership ability," he said, tugging on the tie. "Gets 'em every time."

It was September before Wes's physics degree and four months overseeing the disassembly of jet engines landed him an interview at the engineering headquarters of a national airline.

He got the job. Two months later, he received his discharge papers, folded his uniform and turned his car east. He was going back home, and that was fine, too, because somehow he had always known that he would end up there.

It had been a strange time in his life, the six months in Nevada. Looking back the days seemed sharp and clear as the desert itself—a time and a place for vision. By then, of course, he had known the waiting would not last long. He felt like a man who had taken control of his destiny, a man waking from a long sleep to a life of promise.

It had been a good time but in the end maybe too good a time, because the years that followed seemed faint and humdrum by comparison. Objectively speaking, he supposed, they had been satisfactory enough. He had done the kinds of things that won praise from acquaintances. But often when he thought about those eight years, it seemed that not much had really happened.

When it all started he had quashed the old dreams and told himself that it was time to grow up. This was his one life, all he had, and he had to do something with it.

His job had started well enough and after a year or so everyone told him he should get an MBA, so he did. He worked days and took night courses and in that way he turned twenty-six. He got a promotion and then took another job. It was a smaller airline, regional, but he was in line for an executive office there and he could take free trips to Memphis and Key West and Louisville and New Orleans. He made dates with flight attendants. He got a raise and then another one, made plenty of money.

Life ain't too bad, coworkers would say to him with a wink, and he found it hard to disagree.

He lived by himself in a small condo in a tall building that rose out of the thick green oaks down near Emory. Most of his time he spent at the office, and when he was not there he worked out at an athletic club and sometimes saw women. Often he did not return to his building until after dark. But in the long summer evenings he would come home in time to stand on the balcony and watch the dying sun sink behind the crystal skyline that drifted glistening over the great sea of pines, blue now to westward, fading to black beneath him. He would lean against the hard cool railing and stare at the horizon and feel his drink sweating cold in his hand. When it had finally grown dark he would turn his eyes to the ground and think what a long way down it was.

Then he would go inside and watch TV.

He had given up on reading for a long time now, ever since he had started the MBA, but after the sitcoms and the hospital dramas were over he still followed the news. When that was done and he could not stomach the talk shows, and lately sometimes even earlier, he found himself flipping channels deep into the night.

He had started watching the History Channel.

There between commercials for guns and Viagra he saw it all spread out before him, the story of mankind. Occasionally it was suffrage or manufacturing or art, but mostly it was war: ancient and modern, New World and Old, Romans and Confederates and Nazis—mostly Nazis, history's most exhaustively filmed villains, waging world war against his grandfather on the small screen.

That summer, especially, the nights had all seemed the same.

Grey amphibious behemoths disgorging troops off Normandy, the Enola Gay rolling heavy down a runway at mid-Pacific, the doomed *Indianapolis* steaming back to America behind it.

The stories framed, the film ticking, black and white, before his eyes.

He watches and is silent and fixes another drink.

He has plenty of money, twice as much as he would have made as a lieutenant, and he has done what people say a man his age should do.

He is free.

Why does he feel that he has missed something, that he has learned to settle for something small?

The others had not fared much better.

That was what he told himself. But sometimes he wondered; maybe they had. He could not decide. In a way each of them had made something happen, or at least had something happen to them. There was the big thing John had done—Wes still could not even begin to understand that, wondered sometimes if it was all a trick, just his way of pulling something off, though he had to admit it was so much that sometimes it seemed like the only thing any of them had done.

There was Cullen, too. But they had all seen that coming, by the end, anyway. And it was not only predictable but small, smaller in its way than what Wes himself had done.

And then there was Stick, who had at least died.

Now that was something. Wes had never let on when he talked to the others, but yes, it had satisfied him, as if Fate or Justice or whatever there was had caught up with the son of a bitch at last.

Of the four of them, Stick had been the only one who chose to stay in. He had landed a choice temporary assignment — probably because he was in good with the warrant, Wes thought — at a base just outside L.A. He had the life there and maybe for the same reason told all the others that he knew he would be in within the year, on his way to earning his wings.

And he was in alright but no amount of luck or connections or whatever it was he had was going to keep him in once he started pushing the limit on discipline the minute he got there and then tried to screw the first female instructor at the flight school, this right after the Tailhook mess, and he was out with not an honorable but a general discharge and lucky to have gotten that. Then he headed back to Florida, talked himself into a job as a pharmaceutical salesman, peddling drugs and traveling all over the place but living mostly in Jacksonville, a sprawling messy city that's not really a city at all but a big redneck town, messing around with a lot of women he met at bars and trailer parks and ending up with a big-haired blonde with even bigger breasts that were two-thirds silicone and getting engaged to her because maybe she was pregnant. But whether she really was or not nobody ever knew because one night two months later Stick was driving home from Valdosta and wrapped his car around a tree, drunk, the coroner said, and that was the end of that.

That was how Wes heard it from Hooper, anyway. Hooper was in pharmaceutical sales himself when they ran into one another at the Dallas airport not long after it had happened. The blonde wasn't in the car, Hooper said, and he supposed she went on to lead her own life and maybe even had the kid, if there was one; but his own interests went only so far as Stick's end of it, and so that was another story, a story not one of them knew.

Stick's story was a messy one. Lots of loose ends. But that was the way things went sometimes, Wes knew by now, and in a strange way hearing it made him almost jealous, not because of what had happened but because of the way Hooper told it. A life that sordid at least sounded interesting, even if Hooper—just a dumb horny boy from south Alabama who still drank too much and walked with a slight limp—couldn't help but make it sound ridiculous too.

How would his own life sound? he wondered afterwards. Who would tell it?

For all that he had first heard the news about Stick not from Hooper but from John. Somehow John knew the day after it had happened, called and told Wes about it and where the funeral was and that he would be there. It was not too far and Wes could have made arrangements to go but when he said he had a big meeting scheduled that day he was not lying. He was just glad to have the excuse.

So he did not see them then, neither John, whom he heard was even part of the ceremony, wearing a robe or something and following behind the priest, nor Cullen, who whatever he had finally thought of Stick had come down after all and stood watching while they put him in the ground.

Cynthia had not come, though whether it was because she was less forgiving or because of her own pregnancy Wes never knew. How could he have known her reasons or her plans in the first place? Not that his knowing would have changed anything—if she had been coming with Cullen he could have borne that. After all, he had been at the wedding.

It had taken them a while. Even after Cullen went to her in that last week it had taken a year or more. She had listened to him and screamed at him and thrown him out and taken him back, all in forty-eight hours, and then a few days later he was shipped off to some weapons testing range in New Mexico.

It must have been hard for Cullen, Wes knew, harder than it had been on him, because of them all Cullen was the one least suited to solitude. They had talked on the phone a few times back then and Wes heard how bad it was, Cullen's base almost empty now and a hundred miles from nowhere. He could catch MAC flights back to see Cynthia every other weekend but the rest of the time he was like a man in exile. The year waiting had not been as hard on him, he said on the phone. But now being yanked around the country like this and knowing it could happen again, this and what had happened with his brother—he knew he had to get out. "Only got one life to live," he told Wes when he had made his decision. He was not going to let the Navy run it.

"You've got to make every day count." That was the other thing he had said, and of course everyone said it, the kind of thing you really couldn't disagree with except maybe when it came to what made a day count. Cullen had his own ideas about that. Mostly what he had talked about, ever since the business with his brother started and maybe even before that, was his family. But then after he had resigned his commission he went home for only a week before he drove back west again, to her.

Wes heard all about it later. Cullen had enough money to live for a while and so it went on for a few months, he staying in her apartment while she worked and he trying to figure out what to do with his life and she coming home and they trying to figure out what to do with theirs. But it was already in motion and probably they already knew. By the time he went back home again to look for work he had asked her and she had said yes.

When they found a place to live it was in Maryland, but she was a Kentucky girl after all and so they had the wedding up in the soft blue hills north of Lexington and south of the Ohio. This time Wes had no excuse, said he was going to have a good time and did, with people like Hooper there and Elizabeth, too, looking healthier now but still living in California and still eyeing him so that a couple of times at the reception he had to dodge her, ducking into the bathroom or behind the buffet or outside to smoke a cigar. He finally met Cullen's brother there, too, healed and doing fine now and about to become a civilian himself. They talked about his letters and the war, but after a drink or two they looked at one another and realized they did not have much else to say.

So it was a good enough time and he had not thought any of it was going to bother him until during the ceremony he found that he did not want to look at the bride and groom. Instead he looked at the bridesmaids— yes, Elizabeth was looking good, but he knew better—and at John.

He was up there in the robes, not a priest yet but assisting or something, holding things. Cloth, glasses, water, wine. Looking on, smiling, a witness.

It was one of the first weddings Wes had been to where the people up there were his own age, where he felt like he knew them. Later there were married people from work but he mostly only saw one of them, usually the husband, and going to their houses once or twice he felt like a stranger and never stayed long.

It had been different when he had seen them again in the middle of this last summer. The Cullens.

He was in D.C. for a meeting and stuck there over a weekend. The company had set up some tours, Arlington Cemetery and the museums and the Mall, but he had done all that before and the thought of doing it again — Lee's mansion lonely up on the hill, Jefferson and Lincoln looming above the sweaty crowds, all that open space — depressed him. It was less than an hour to where Cullen lived and he had a standing invitation, so he made a phone call, rented a car, drove west into the long blue hills that rolled down from the Appalachians.

It was early July, a Saturday afternoon. He found them in a white wooden house, two simple stories and black shutters and a stone chimney, that he wanted to call Colonial or Federal but he wasn't sure which. Cullen and Cynthia and the three-year old they had named Joe and another just now on the way.

They were far enough west that it wasn't a suburb yet, but it wasn't just the quaint little town it looked like, either, Cullen told him, pointing at brick buildings and historical markers and construction sites while they drove to the ballpark. The occasional young lawyers and lobbyists had begun to find their way out here and were steadily infiltrating the town, settling amongst the old Marylanders, the ones who had been here forever or at least since the Revolution or whenever it was they got here, Cullen said. He talked like he knew them all, or at least their kids.

He was a teacher now and Wes could see that he was probably a good one. He had been surprised to find that he liked it. He had been unsure when he started, was more interested in the coaching, but enjoyed the classroom well enough after all and had good students and good subjects: econ, civics, American government. He had been a government major at the Academy and he found that he liked keeping up with politics, at least from a distance, flipping from the editorial columns to the sports page and back again in the mornings. And the coaching—well, here it was summer and his job at the high school done, and he was helping out with Little League on his own.

Cullen was himself. He was well again, the way Wes had first seen him, and behind his excitement and pointing and talking Cynthia had been mostly silent. She rode in the back seat with the boy, hands crossed over her belly where the sun shone in, an easy smile playing on her lips.

When they got to the park Cullen carried little Joe down to the bullpen and Wes found himself alone with her.

She liked it here, she said, stooping to pick up an empty Coke cup that rolled beneath their feet in the stands, the wind blowing her hair across her face. It was a good place. She had work, part-time for the Frederick paper and sometimes freelance for magazines, and for now it was just enough. She was busy with Joe while Billy was at school and they liked it and soon there would be another. One day they would need more work or more money and then there was law school—she could get interested in it, she had decided, there were so many things she could do with it—but for now it was just enough.

"And Bill seems pretty happy with the job," Wes said.

"Yeah."

There was some noise down on the diamond. Cullen was standing outside the bullpen, pointing, shouting at a boy as he rounded first base.

"He's got some friends who say he should take more courses, be a principal or something, but he's not sure. Administration, you know," Cynthia said. "Then some of the parents around here—they're trying to get him to run for county office." She grimaced slightly.

"Politics."

"Yeah. I've got my doubts, too. But small-town, local—somebody's got to do it." She shrugged, squinted, lifted a hand to shield her eyes against the sun. " Maybe it could be good."

"Something different."

"Something different."

"Like that with everything, I guess," Wes says. "I mean, sometimes I feel the same way. Like my job's not quite right." He paused. "Something else I should be doing."

"Something more challenging?"

"I guess. 'Challenging' isn't it, exactly, though."

"Well. You're not dumb," she said. "That's never been your problem."

She said it offhand, carelessly. Compliment or insult? He turned to Cynthia and saw only her profile, still looking off into the distance.

"But overall things look pretty peaceful here." He was speaking to fill the silence. "Married life and all."

She leaned back in her seat. "Oh, yeah. There's more to it than they tell you, of course." She grinned. "We were having a little fight just before you called this morning. But," she shook her head — "now I can't even remember what it was about. Money, probably." She wrapped her hands around her knees, tucked her legs up close against her chest, shrugged. "Part of the deal."

Her voice was easy, and listening to it Wes felt somehow privileged. He had not been able to talk to her like this since the month when they had first met.

Their eyes were back on the game now. "And you've become a baseball fan."

She laughed, turned to him, smiling. "Well, now. I don't really have much choice, do I? And around here you get your entertainment where you can." She looked back down to the bullpen. "But yes, I like it fine. Sitting up here in the stands. Watching."

"Well," Wes said, leaning back himself now, looking out at the park and the town behind it. "It's kind of relaxing. Seems so low-key here, you know. Simple." He paused. "In the best way, I mean."

"Simple." She was looking down to where her husband stood, her son now beside him. "Well, it is and it isn't." Then she broke into a new smile, a smile that lingered and grew deeper.

After dinner that night they put the boy to bed and stayed up late talking, the three of them and then just Wes and Cullen, drinking beer and remembering California, the good stories. It was after two when they went to bed.

In the morning Wes heard the others stirring. They had asked him but he slept in instead and got up alone and drank coffee and read the paper.

When they came back Cullen watched Joe and got out the plates and glasses and ice while Cynthia finished cooking. They were still dressed up, as dressed up as they got, anyhow, and he imagined them walking into the church together and the old people smiling and nod-

ding to one another and calling them "A nice family." It had surprised
him a little because Cullen had never seemed too serious about these
things and because he had always assumed Cynthia was a journalist
and a skeptic and not the type. But she had been with them too and
seemed happy now overseeing her meal and when the table had been
set and the food laid out she sat down smiling.

Dinner was good. "I'm not too much the cook, you know," she
said, "Billy does it half the time"—while Cullen protested dutifully
and leaned over to cut the steaming beef on the boy's plate. It was
good food and a sunny afternoon with the light pouring in the windows and playing off the crystal and sitting there with the three of
them Wes felt both out of place and strangely at home. When it was
over and they had all cleared the table they sat together for a while
and then he felt it was time to say goodbye.

Driving back to Washington, he was full, relaxed, almost drowsy.
He rolled down the windows and took his time.

He hadn't noticed before, but looking out into the wooded hills,
the stands of oak and pine, he could see that it was a plain but beautiful country. It was a strange kind of a place when you looked for it
on the map, wedged tight between Pennsylvania and Virginia, so thin
and unexpected you could almost pass through it without knowing
or forget that it was there.

He remembered coming this way only once before. He had been
with his father. They had some obscure relatives up this way but that
was not why they had come. He was very young and they were on
their way to Gettysburg, where, his father was telling him, something
important had happened once.

John stood before him. Sitting alone at the table and lost to memory
now, Wes looked up and saw him there.

"Well, sir," he said, smiling. "May I join you?"

Wes had been waiting to see what he would wear. He was not
a priest yet—that was coming soon—only a "deacon," he called it.
But still Wes had been hoping for the whole thing, the black suit and
the little collar. It would have been something. A little embarrass-

ing, maybe, but something. Then John had reminded him he was not actually a priest and most of the time they just wore regular clothes these days anyway.

So he was not too disappointed to see that John seemed to have come down somewhere in the middle. Ratty black overcoat, dark pants, snug ash-gray sweater. The whole outfit could have come from a military surplus store. He looked as much like an artsy type or even some kind of disheveled commando as he did a priest. But still Wes could see what he had been looking for. Just a hint of the cleric. "Halloween's over, you know. Not gonna be meeting too many ladies in that getup," he said.

"One of the benefits of my new profession. No need to spend too much time worrying about wardrobe."

"Where did you get that stuff?"

"The shelter. I didn't bring my winter clothes, and it's colder down here than I would have thought. So I'm just borrowing this for a while. The director doesn't mind."

"I don't believe it. I don't frickin' believe it. I'm having dinner with a homeless person." Wes laughed. "Well, the drinks are on me."

"All donations gratefully accepted."

Then they settled down and began to talk.

It was good, joking, laughing, telling the old stories. John seemed his old best self and with the drink and the people moving around them Wes soon felt at ease. He had been a little uncertain. Even when they had lived together John had his moods, kept to himself a lot of the time. Then, too, there was the whole religious business. Wes did not even feel comfortable with the terminology. What did you even call this thing that John was doing? So he was going to be a priest, but wasn't yet. But he was already a "seminarian" and now a deacon, too. What else was he or would he be? Minister? Preacher? *Father?*

Wes rarely gave religion much thought and on the few occasions when he did he had not known what to make of it.

His family had not helped. His father's mother's parents had been Catholic, he knew, but her husband had been something else and whatever it was had not counted for much because it was the Army that told him how to live. So Wes's own father had grown up passing in and out of base chapels all over the country, mostly on major holidays like Thanksgiving and the Fourth of July. The girl he ended up marrying, though, was a Southern Baptist. He had few strong opinions about religion one way or another but he knew he was not going to stand for any of that. Still she had insisted they go somewhere, so they tried the church where most of his law partners and the women in her garden club went. It was an old building with plain windows and stately architecture and a sonorous black-robed pastor whom Wes's father approvingly described as "moderate," as though this were the highest praise that could be bestowed upon a member of the clergy. When he later discovered that Colonel Byrd had attended the same church, their membership was sealed.

In that way the church had served the family well enough until Wes went to college. Then his father's attendance slackened and finally ceased altogether. By that time, though, his mother had joined an elite lady's group that was well represented in the congregation and had enough friends of her own there that she decided to stay on. Sometimes Wes still went with her at Christmas or Easter. The three of them were never together anymore. But that was true all the time, not just on Sundays. It was something Wes tried not to think about.

But now John was asking.

"How're your parents?"

"OK." He took a drink. "Not so good. But each of them, you know, they're OK."

"Yeah?"

"Yeah. They're kind of, separated. Nothing formal, I mean."

John nodded.

"Just not getting along. I mean, for a while now. He was doing his thing, more and more history—now it's Jacob Byrd Jr. and Admiral Dewey, the Spanish-American War, for God's sake—and she wanted him to go to all these social functions she's into now. Charity auctions. Debutante balls. The goddamn Junior League." He flinched. "Sorry," he said. Then he felt sorry for apologizing.

"How long?" John's expression had not changed.

"Going on a year."

"But they both seem OK?"

"She is. Definitely. She's more busy than ever, clubs and stuff. And working part time at a little store—a boutique, for God's sake—one of her friends owns. Him? I don't know. I guess so. He goes to work, but then he just sits at home alone. Reads, writes." Drinks. He was drinking more now. "But that's what he likes."

John nodded. "What about you?" He paused, tilted his glass. "You like the job? Being back here?"

He had a perfunctory answer to the job question and he gave it. Describing his work depressed him.

The place—that was something else, especially coming from John. They had talked about it occasionally in California. It wasn't until he was in the West that Wes had felt like he came from a place that was old, that had a history. He had missed it sometimes. Now he was back and driving around the city from time to time he would see tarnished bronze markers and read that Hood's cavalry had rallied here or this was where McPherson was shot or Sherman made camp here once. But mostly these were forgotten now, lost, hidden or indistinct in the traffic and the billboards and the bright signs that led the way to the gas stations and convenience stores.

A few people fought it. His own father had joined his newly suburban county's historical commission and was writing letters to the newspapers to stop development on the old Byrd plantation. There was a movement afoot to build a new regional airport out there. Wes's own company was about to sign onto the project and he didn't care so much himself, but he hadn't admitted it to his dad yet—hadn't found the words to tell him that he, too, had somehow become a part of it, whatever it was that was making this new world.

It was a different place than he remembered, different than it had looked while he was sitting long miles away reading the old books. Now there were Seattle coffee shops and Malay restaurants in the shadow of Stone Mountain, strip malls lining the interstate, and even when he drove out to where his father still lived there was the Wal-Mart where Freddy's woods had once stood. Even the stark old border of black and white was gone, not only the Vietnamese and Cambodians come east from the Pacific but the swarthy children of parents born in Calcutta and Cairo thriving too, moving easy among the richer whites of the suburbs. And then walking slow in the hot fields outside the city and paving the roads inside it, cutting grass and blowing leaves for the others, were the ones who had come to take the place of the blacks. They spoke a tongue that went back to Rome but looking at them short and dark and broad-cheeked Wes knew they had been in this land longer than Spain had, knew they were closer to Cherokee and Creek and the thousand other tribes who had been here longest than to any people come cross the Atlantic. Arriving from the south they bore the name of the country that brooded there now, but sometimes dreaming or half-awake Wes saw them less new than old, not the last in a wave of invaders but instead the original inhabitants of the land come to take back what was their own.

Sitting with John now he did not tell all this but he told some of it. When he was done he felt glad of his listener because he had not laughed or mocked but nodded, as if it made a kind of sense. He listened soberly and then he did the right thing. Changed the subject.

"Any women?"

"Ha." Wes smiled, shook his head. "Well, here we go." It was the kind of question any friend was going to ask, though coming from John now it was so ordinary that it seemed different. "There've been a couple, I guess."

Once he was a civilian again he had discovered that it was not so hard to find a woman. It was hard to find one worth having around, one whom you could put up with or who could put up with you, but it was not so hard to find one. Since he had come back he had been with a dozen of them briefly, women whom after a few weeks he began to look down on but kept up with because he had to do something with time. Then after a while he got tired of them or they got tired of him or both, and that was fine. There had only been two who were worth talking about.

The first he had met while he was getting the MBA. She sat next to him in finance class and was serious about her career and when they went on dates at first they mostly talked about their jobs and then later about salaries. Before they graduated she got a good offer from a medical supply company, the same company Wes had almost interned with after his one year at the university back when he was nineteen. They put her in charge of marketing for enemas and laxatives and other products designed to maximize the performance of the human gastrointestinal tract. She took the work very seriously and then she told Wes she had begun to take him seriously too. After a couple of months of writing him into her daybook and blocking off occasional weekends for them to spend together, she showed up at his apartment one night and told him she thought it would be more efficient for them to move in together.

He did not resist. He had begun to like her, her quirky smile and the way she knit her brow and looked so serious when she was talking about suppositories. He thought it was cute even if it was a little pathetic, too. She was not a dumb girl and she had a discipline that he admired. She seemed like she knew what she wanted.

So she moved in and they lived in his condo looking out over the trees and she bought a little dog that they would take for long walks on Saturday and Sunday mornings. In the evenings they would stay at home and watch movies or sometimes go out to a little wine bar where some of her friends from work met. They were all just like her. They drove BMWs or SUVs and came from Ohio or New Jersey but had moved here for the jobs and weather. The women sat around and talked about work and makeup while the men talked about work and sports and eventually snuck into the pub next door to watch a game.

This had been going on for a year or so and she had begun to ask him about long term career goals and 401(k) plans and where he wanted to retire when one morning he woke up and found he had nothing to say to her.

They were sitting at the little breakfast nook—this was her word, *nook*—that she had set up in the corner by the balcony. It was a beautiful day, and they had decided to sleep in and then cook a big brunch. The sliding doors were open and the warmth of the morning sun fell upon them. The little dog slept on the floor by her feet.

Wes was holding his fork over his eggs when she looked at him and said, "Why are you being so quiet?"

He felt the morning breeze on his cheek; her robe moved gently, thin as gauze, shimmering in the sunlight. A neighbor's wind chime tinkled in the distance.

"Why are you being so quiet?"

He put his fork down, looked at the table, shrugged. "This," he said.

"What?"

The little dog yawned.

"What we do."

She looked at him.

"What?"

"What we do. Our life."

"Yes?" She looked puzzled, truly and deeply puzzled.

"It's so small."

The dog rolled over, whined, rubbed against her feet.

She stared at Wes open-mouthed while he began to eat. Suddenly he realized that he was starving, and within five minutes he had cleaned his plate.

That was the end of that one. It took a few weeks, of course, she denying and recriminating and finally yelling but still stalling, waiting for him to come to his senses, until at last she showed up one Saturday with a moving van. He helped her load her things and she never said a word except to ask him to split the bill and then she was gone.

The second one. Now, that was different.

She was a nurse and studying to be a nurse practitioner and he never saw how she was making it through the classes because at least a part of her was crazy, completely undisciplined. They had met at a party and she was a little drunk and asking him big questions in a corner just a few minutes after they met, but still she kept enough distance between them until a month or two later. They went on a hike up in the mountains and were standing by a waterfall when she turned to him and said "You," closed her eyes, leaned away from him. He had never actually seen a woman swoon before but he thought this might be it, so he grabbed her by the hip and elbow and then she held onto him and did not let go. They spent the night in her tent and in the morning when they got up she asked him to read to her.

She loved music and the arts and she told him that she was deeply concerned about the environment. She had been an English major in college but then did a volunteer service program for a few years and got interested in public health, took some night courses, moved on to medicine. She gave him long searching looks and talked a lot about his soul touching hers, but then she wasn't really sure that they had souls; she was forever trying to reconcile the harsh claims of science with her fervent hope that somewhere in the vast cold universe there was a soulmate who had been ordained just for her. She was a passionate woman with a turbulent romantic history and heartfelt political opinions that Wes found mildly annoying, and more and more he had begun to wonder what the two of them saw in one another unless it was the old thing about opposites. Still he liked her because she was smart and she was beautiful and she asked big questions. She was a troubled girl trying to be a good woman and sometimes she turned to Wes in the middle of the night and asked questions like, "What's the worst thing you've ever done?"

In the end she had proved too much for him, her and her soul-plumbing inquiries. There was the side of her that was practical and got things done—he liked that, seeing her come out of the emergency room when he went over there sometimes to pick her up, blood on her scrubs and she telling him how she just spent an hour stitching up a knife wound or something. That was good. It was the other side — the side that got quiet and probing and hungry in the dark of the night — that he could not handle.

"So that's over now. Just a couple of months." Wes looked out across the room now, scanning the doors. "Tell you the truth—I'm a little worried we might see her tonight. Used to hang out here some."

"Things end on bad terms?"

"Not so bad. But not the best. It's always kind of weird, you know." John did know, he assumed. At least remembered. He wasn't supposed to be thinking about that kind of thing now, of course. Celibacy! As if the rest of it weren't strange enough.

Looking at John, Wes figured he still knew. Even now, in the middle of this crowd with the women dressed to look good and passing around their table, wasn't he looking at some of them a little wistfully, just a beat too long?

Something, though, was different. Wes could tell. Behind the banter and the smile there were moments when John's gaze lingered longer than it once had—probing, somehow questioning and knowledgeable at once—but in most respects he seemed the person he used to be. Hell, Wes had just admitted to him that he had lived with a woman out of wedlock. Neither of them had seemed to notice.

John lit up a cigarette.

They had smoked together in San Agustin when they were drunk
and bored, holding their cigarettes awkwardly, self-consciously, huff-
ing smoke between their lips and now and then breaking into slow
muffled coughs. But now John took a long deep drag and the cigarette
hung from his hand like an extra finger.

"Stuff'll kill you," Wes said.

"Something's gonna," John shrugged. "The Doctor always said."

His father—John had called him that sometimes, the Doctor, and
Wes regretted what he had just said. John's father was dead.

It had started about the time they left the TPU. John had been
stationed at a Marine base north of Palm Springs and when his dad
didn't show up at the volunteer clinic one morning he got the call,
drove down there and found his father, unmoving, at the edge of the
little garden he had planted in the desert.

The stroke had shaken up John and his whole family. For all
Wes knew he had been thinking about the priest thing for a long
time—looking back on it now it seemed likely enough, hanging
out with the chaplain and reading what he read, doing charity work
and that kind of thing—but what happened later that year must
have helped make it stick. It was John's father who brought him
back east, where the old man could be taken care of by one of his
sisters up in Maryland, and surely it was what had happened with
his father that finally drove John to the seminary there. When Wes
tried to think about what could make someone do such a thing
he thought of trauma and guilt. John knew something about both.

That was how he saw it, and it was part of what had made him
feel strange about meeting John here alone. But now looking at him
and thinking about what had just been said, he only felt awkward because he had been the one who brought it up. He had been the first
one to talk about death.

On the brink of all that he felt the need to make a joke or say
something comforting and what he heard coming out of his mouth
was, "Guess all that isn't a problem for a man in your position." He
paused. "A man of the cloth, I mean."

John looked at him, took the cigarette from his lips. "All what?"

"What?"

"All what isn't a problem?"

"Death. Immortality of the soul and all that. Heaven, hell."

He smiled, knocked some ashes into the tray between them. "Yes."

There was a silence and Wes felt that he had to fill it. What was he talking about? He didn't want to go back to cigarettes or John's dad, so he just kept going.

"Heaven, I can see. I mean, it's the kind of idea that makes people feel good. But hell?"

John was silent.

"I guess it scares some people, kids at least. Tell them bad people end up there. The worst, anyway. Hitler. Stalin." Something in his stomach twisted. "Stick, I guess you'd say?" He smiled, looked at John, waited.

"I'm not in charge of hell."

"You don't believe in it?"

"I'm not in charge of it. Who goes there."

"But you believe in it?"

"I have to."

"Why?"

"Because I believe people are free."

John put the cigarette out now and sat up in his chair.

Wes thought for a moment. "That follows?"

"Free to choose."

"Free to choose?"

"Good or evil. God, or—not."

"Good or evil." What were they talking about? John had been asking normal questions, asking about his life. It was his own fault that they were talking about religion or whatever it was they were talking about now. He regretted it. But there they were. And the simple words seemed new in a way: he tended to think of things as important or unimportant. *Good or evil.*

John moved his shoulders, nodded.

"Pretty simple."

"Well." John's hand lifted slightly off the table.

Wes waited.

"Yes and no. Simpler for some than others, maybe."

"Yeah?" The room seemed to have closed around them. Wes was vaguely aware of figures moving in the dim light around their table, but his eyes were on John.

"Well, Stick. I'm not excusing him—anything he did, I mean. But there's more to things than we can know. And something was happening."

"Something?"

"At the end. With the woman down there, the one he was going to marry."

"The one he got pregnant?"

"Yeah."

Wes felt the side of his mouth pulled back hard into his cheek.

"I saw her at the funeral. I mean, I know what we usually think about someone like her, but—you've got to give people credit sometimes, you know? She was lost by the end of the ceremony. Wailing. There's no other word for it. Sad—sad as you can get. She loved him, and it's a strange story, but somehow they had ended up together and who knows what they were doing for each other?"

Wes's expression had not changed.

"It's a possibility. At least a possibility."

Wes shrugged.

"And another thing—it wasn't easy for him."

"Yeah?" He felt his features hardening.

"His father. Gone. From the time he could remember, and his mother alone, stuck with him, not knowing what to do. Stick told me some of it, the way he saw it at least. And then I met her at the funeral—some guy with her, hanging around, touching her shoulder, putting up a show but looking bored underneath it, ready to get back home and have a drink. There was a whole line of them like that from the time he was a boy: a stepfather for a while, then just boyfriends, coming and going, bribing him at first and then fighting him. Fighting him and winning and he just kept fighting back and then fighting her, too, until she'd come home and cry over him for awhile and then go out again to bars and parties and wherever else it was she went."

"Pretty sad," Wes said.

"Well, it is. And I mean he's still a man, still free, and you can't write off everything he did because of how he had to grow up." He was staring hard at Wes now, hands crossed in front of him. "I mean, it seems harder for some than others."

"Yeah?"

"But none of us start with a clean slate."

"Right. OK," Wes said, leaning back in his chair. He felt confused now and he wasn't sure he liked the way John was looking at him. "Heredity, environment. All that stuff."

John shrugged. "Well, it's there."

"Who you are."

"Part."

It was something Wes thought about more now: genes, acculturation, family dynamics. As he got older and history became more and more depressing, he found himself tempted to turn back to science. He watched shows about it on The Learning Channel. Personality, habits, character itself—all those things they had talked about shaping back at the Institute—explained away by men in laboratories. It made a certain kind of sense. He had been a physics major and an engineer, after all, and he preferred clear, linear explanations. Statistics; charts; maps of the medulla oblongata glowing gold and purple on the TV screen. Brain chemistry. Sometimes all of it seemed a consolation, as if meant to absolve him of responsibility for turning out to be as insignificant as he was. But at other times it only made things worse. Sometimes he turned off the TV, looked out his window at the lights of the city, and thought, doomstruck, that he was bound to end up like his father.

He turned up his drink and gave John a weak smile. "They got you taking psychology courses at that seminary?"

John laughed. "No. You don't have to be a psychologist to think people are born and raised with certain tendencies to screw up."

The meal came and they ate in silence. Wes wolfed down his food, but he found it didn't satisfy. He kept looking up in between bites. Across the table John ate slowly, leisurely, as if he were savoring each taste or waiting for something or both.

When they were done they sat and looked at the crowd moving around them—the place was filling up now—and then Wes felt the words coming up out of him. "Most things people do don't count for much, do they?"

John had another cigarette in his hand now and as he spoke he leaned forward to tap it into the tray between them. "What do you mean?"

"I was looking at the TV up there and thinking back." There was a ball game on the screen over the bar. "I mean, we lived in a time when big things happened. The war, all that. Remember how big it was? And people already forget, don't think about it much. Just something that happened on TV. And for us I guess it was. But it was big for some people, you know. But us—you and me—we missed our chance."

John said nothing.

"I mean, the way I see it, you've probably got only a few shots in life to do something important. And somehow we missed ours. Ever since then—everything's been so ordinary. Know what I mean?"

"Well—that's not how I see it, exactly." He paused. "But I think I know what you mean."

Wes barely heard him. There was something coming up out of his throat that he couldn't stop. "You know"—he found himself ducking his head now, smiling even though he didn't think it was funny — "sometimes it seems like the most important thing I've ever done was that one night."

John looked at him.

"That one thing, you know." He was smiling so that his face hurt and then he heard himself starting to laugh. "And you know what's so fucking sad, what's the most pathetic fucking thing of all? I didn't even do that." He was bent over now, his face close to the table, twisted and hurting. "It was just like everything else. I was just along for the ride."

John did not say anything. His eyes were shuttered, half-sunk in shadow, and glancing into them Wes was glad he did not see pity—the one thing he could not abide—but he was not sure what he did see. They might have been turned in on themselves.

"What are you looking so damn glum about?" he said, still leaning down over the table. "You — it's not like you were even involved."

The cigarette was smoldering at the edge of John's fingers now, unused. "We're all involved," he said. He tapped ashes into the center of the table, sat up straight, looked like he was about to say something else. But when he did not Wes felt somehow grateful.

There was silence and the figures moving around them again and at last Wes spoke. "That whole year together and it seems like we've talked more today than then."

"Yeah?"

"You kind of kept to yourself." He didn't say it, but as the words came out he knew: this was one of the things he had actually liked best about John, that he didn't say much.

"I guess."

"You never told me what you were up to."

"You never really asked." He sat up. "Plus, I was figuring it out for myself. I didn't really know."

"Didn't know?"

"That I'd end up here. Doing this."

"It's something." At first Wes thought this sounded lame but on second thought maybe it was true. It was better than nothing. "It's something."

John nodded and reached into his pocket. "Got something for you," he said. "Was gonna mail it, but since I'm here—personal delivery."

He handed over a piece of paper, stiff and ridged like a wedding invitation. *Mass. Sacrament of Holy Orders. December 24th.* It was written in English in the middle. The bottom was in Spanish and the top something else.

"Holy Orders?" Wes said.

"Ordination. Becoming a priest."

"Huh," Wes said. The words made him feel strange. "What's with all the languages?"

"The Latin's traditional. And then some of the other seminarians are from Chile, Colombia—you know."

"Right." John had these classmates from Latin America now, had studied down there himself. He had told Wes in a letter how he and all the Anglos were sent south to get more familiar with the language "and the culture, too." It had all sounded so odd. They made him wait a year or two before they would even let him enter the seminary and then when he finally started they shipped him out of the country for the summers. Wasn't he going to be an American priest?

Wes was thinking about it and looking at John and something happened in his head. It was all in front of him now and his mind was working and before he could stop the words were out: "That isn't why you're doing this, is it?"

John sank back in his seat and looked puzzled.

"To—." Wes was struggling now, but he had started and he might as well finish. There was a word he was looking for. He couldn't find it. "To make amends. For what happened."

John stared at him for a second and then his eyes lightened. "No," he said, looking at him seriously but almost smiling, "no, no. Things just worked out like this."

Wes moved his eyes and felt embarrassed somehow. He nodded.

"Well?"

"Well what?"

"Think you might come?"

"Oh—yeah. I mean, I'm honored." Was this the right thing to say? "Of course. I mean, it sounds interesting."

"Well, thanks. It'd be good to have you there." John started to move, hesitated, turned back toward him. "Look—I've got to go."

"Yeah?" For some reason Wes felt relieved.

"Back to the shelter."

"Big night ahead?" He was trying to say something casual. Did he sound irreverent?

"Actually, it kind of is. Some of the migrant workers passing through—there's a lot of them—it's a big holiday."

"Yeah?"

"Yeah. All Souls' Day. I'm helping with the vigil later. Anyway, it's the end of the Days of the Dead."

Wes looked at him.

"Kind of like Halloween—candy skulls, skeletons—but for them there's more to it. Laying out food for the ancestors. That kind of thing."

"And you go along with that?"

John shrugged. "Well, it's All Souls' Day. Makes a certain amount of sense."

Wes said nothing. It sounded like nonsense—the dead were buried, part of history and meant to stay that way. But he didn't know how far he could go mocking this stuff before he mocked John, too, so he kept his mouth shut.

"Why don't you come with me?" John asked.

Wes had turned away. He was feeling uneasy now and he knew that part of it was the time. He glanced at the bar clock and then scanned the crowd, keeping his eye on the far door where John had come in.

"What're you looking for?"

"Her."

"Is she really just gonna show up? All on her own?"

"Probably not."

"Why don't you call her sometime?"

"Maybe I will."

"Alright then. Call her." John drummed his fingers on the table. "But for now, why don't you come with me?"

Wes looked back toward the TV. He felt annoyed, in part because he was taking romantic advice from a celibate. He grimaced and shrugged.

"What else are you doing?"

The room was full now, throbbing, and John's voice was almost swallowed up in the dull clamor. Wes looked out into the crowd and for a moment the indistinct figures looked familiar, their faces as clear as those of people he had known for years. They swarmed around him like ghosts. Over their shoulders now he saw the doorway, the one he had come in. He felt an urge to walk toward it: he could get up, say goodbye, slip out and be on his way back to the place from which he had come.

John stood up.

"Come with me." It was his friend's voice but timbered with something new, a note of firmness that had been lingering and building there all evening. Something had changed. Suddenly Wes knew: John spoke not like most people, but like a man who had authority.

There was the door and the crowd and the TV and something else, too, something coming up out of his head or the past or the darkness outside and pulling him back. But still he heard the voice ringing in his ear, sensed John present and waiting beside him.

"Come with me."

He felt himself begin to turn.

◁ About the Author ▷

Farrell O'Gorman, a native of South Carolina, earned his B.A. from Notre Dame and served four years aboard U.S. Navy ships before completing graduate study in North Carolina. His book on Flannery O'Connor and Walker Percy, *Peculiar Crossroads*, was published in 2004, and his creative work has appeared or is forthcoming in *Image, Shenandoah, The Gettysburg Review*, and *Best Catholic Writing*. He lives in Mississippi with his wife and children."

Printed in the United Kingdom
by Lightning Source UK Ltd.
119730UK00001B/259

9 781595 970084